the SILVERS

J.A. ROCK

ANGLERFISH
PRESS

Anglerfish Press
PO Box 1537
Burnsville, NC 28714
www.AnglerFishPress.com
Anglerfish Press is an imprint of Riptide Publishing.
www.RiptidePublishing.com

The Silvers

Cover art: Simoné, dreamarian.com
Editor: Delphine Dryden, delphinedryden.com/editing
Layout: L.C. Chase, lcchase.com/design.htm

ISBN: 978-1-62649-432-9

Second edition
July, 2016

Also available in ebook:
ISBN: 978-1-62649-386-5

the SILVERS
J.A. ROCK

For my parents

table of
CONTENTS

part ONE

chapter ONE

hey bleed the same as humans, but they are more satisfying to cut, thinks B. Something about the way the silver skin tears, like cloth, like the fat ribbon his mother used to wind around the Christmas tree back home.

This place is called the Silver Planet because of them, and because the lakes are like soldering metal and colors look accidental, like stains on the land. And they are called Silvers, though they aren't shiny, aren't metallic. The hue of their skin is an all-over bruise that hasn't yet settled into those deep, wounded colors—blacks, purples, yellows.

They are bruised only on the surface, a cold, smoky gray.

They are called Silvers because of that surface bruise and because of their quick, gleaming tongues. Because their eyes look like glass, the irises not round, but thin, jagged fissures around the pupils.

B hates them, can't say why. They are much like humans. They think, reason, laugh. Their language is complex, mathematical. They speak like an equation, factors on both sides. They derive each other's meanings instantly, but the humans who have attempted to learn the Silver language struggle to find x.

B thinks he hates the Silvers in part because they are indistinct. There are no warriors, no politicians, no professionals or criminals. Just efficient regulators of an uneventful society. Males and females are nearly indistinguishable. Females lack prominent breasts, and the male organs descend only when they breed, which one pair is selected to do each month to produce a single offspring. B knows all this. He reads the reports.

Silvers don't get angry. They feel affection, joy, even desire, but they don't have that red spectrum of anger, hatred, jealousy. They don't display it. They don't outwardly grieve when something's lost, but you can see the emptiness fill them, collapse them. They may wander into a lake and never resurface. They have no word for revenge, no concept of it. They want things like food, water, each other, but necessity, never greed, is what drives them to pursuit.

They do not fight. They do not kill. They are faster than humans and can go into the lakes and hold their breaths for a long time. B and his team have tried provoking them, taking things from them, turning them against each other. The Silvers simply run away or hide in the ground. They can do that. They press themselves to the earth and become part of it. B has ordered his team not to harm any more of them until the next project begins, but it happens anyway.

B rubs a hand across his chin. He stares across the pale plain but sees nothing unusual. The sky is always black and starless. The planet's atmosphere is a shroud that blocks the rest of the universe from view. Light here comes from within the ground, and different sections of the planet are illuminated at different times of day. The plain he looks at is all bright earth. It's cold.

He hears a sound, like a clock ticking half seconds, quarter seconds. Grena finds him moments later. He starts to ask her if she knows what's making the sound, if she hears it, but she interrupts to tell him the tranq guns are loaded. He asks her if the lab is ready. She says yes. He asks if Gumm has stopped puking. She says mostly. Gumm has trouble with the atmosphere. Grena and Joele can go outside without first dosing themselves with Atmoclere, a drug that helps them all breathe. Vir did all right too, back when she used to go out.

"Then prepare for Project HN," he says, wishing he had the theatricality to imitate one of those barking commanders from old TV shows and movies. His order just comes out sounding tired. B is a captain in title only. He handles paperwork while the others explore.

They've told NRCSE that HN stands for Humanoid Neurogenics. But to the team, it stands for Hard Nipples. It's so cold on the Silver Planet that their chests chafe raw against their shirts; Joele heats stones over the stove and puts them in her bra. Having this private joke lends color to their exile.

They've spent three months observing the Silvers, interacting with them. Cataloging the terrain of the planet, the few and scattered life forms. It's not so much an ecosystem here as it is a barren garden tended by the Silvers. One species of flower is a blue, bulbous thing that looks like dead, swollen lips. The Silvers pollinate the flowers, pinching pollen from the centers and depositing the grains in the carpels of others to produce a flat, gray fruit called quilopea, the only thing Silvers eat. Moon chips, Joele calls it. The rest of the plants are menacing, brittle weeds. The only other creatures look like snakes, but they are blind and harmless.

The team has dug into the cold, gleaming earth and filtered the liquid-star lakes. The Silvers have let Grena and Vir study their clans, but they have fared better learning English than Grena and Vir have trying to master the Silver language.

Now the team wants answers the Silvers can't give. Why the empty space where blazing emotions should be? Why don't they fight? They are certainly intelligent enough to see that if you hit hard enough, you get what you want. Project HN involves tranquilizing three Silvers and bringing them into the ship's lab. The team will study three things: the ability to rouse Silvers' emotions through physical stimuli, solidarity among the captives, and the Silver brain itself. They are targeting three Silvers Vir and Grena don't know. Vir's request.

Grena boards the *Byzantine* to collect materials. After a moment—still that damned ticking noise—B follows her. He goes to the kitchen for a soda. Joele is there, and she's got blood on her suit.

B nods at the spatters. "What happened?"

"Nosebleed."

He knows she's lying. He pops open a soda. Hal's AstroFizz in Lunar Lemon-Lime. Joele started calling it AstroGlide, and now B always feels a little funny drinking it. "We'll collect them tonight."

"You still say 'tonight.'"

"Force of habit." B tells his team "good morning" too. The sky never changes. Sometimes B could swear time isn't passing at all. Yet he wears a watch. He lives his life by the hours of his old existence.

"You seen my flashlight?" he asks. "I wanna check something out."

"What are you, ninety? You asked me last week if I'd seen your reading glasses, and you were wearing them. You sure it's not tucked down your pants?"

"A lot on my mind."

"Worried about Hard Nipples?"

I want to go home. I'm worried about the things I left. I'm worried about what this place is taking from me.

Aloud, he says, "You ought to be too."

"Yeah, yeah. This fails, it's back to Earth for Team Fuckup. Think we'll spend the rest of our lives behind desks."

"That doesn't bother you?"

She shrugs, stands. She towers over him. She towers over everybody on the team. "I'd like to make a name for myself, sure. But I wouldn't say no to getting the hell off this planet." She unclips her flashlight, hands it to him. "Don't lose it." She leaves.

B finishes his soda and crumples the can. They've tried to bring Silvers on board the ship before, but the creatures died within the first hour. B assumed they were unable to tolerate the ship's circulating supply of Atmoclere. Now Gumm has found a way to shut off the flow of Atmoclere to the lab. They've picked and stored enough quilopea to feed three Silvers for a week. They have drilled holes in the steel table, looping belts and rope through.

Three. One will be Joele's. She is going to test her Silver's reactions to physical stimuli. One is Grena's. She will offer her Silver the chance to influence and abate the suffering of the first. The third Silver belongs to Vir. She will perform a vivisection. She will examine the creature's brain and try to learn something about its heart.

A Silver's heart drifts through its body, bumping softly against walls and other organs. Sometimes it's illuminated, and you can see it beneath the bruised skin, floating along like a lantern underwater. In the past, when they've had access to dead Silvers, the team has cut the bodies open and examined the hearts, but they've learned very little. When a Silver dies, the light of the heart dies too, and the heart no longer drifts. It returns to the center left of the body and rests there like a cold stone. What they want to do now is study the heart while the Silver is still alive.

Privately, B worries Vir will have a hard time. She has always hated to kill Silvers or cut them still alive to watch how that delicate skin tears and the blood sneaks out. The Silvers stay away from humans now.

They look like sea creatures, and in a way they are. Now that they know what the crew members are capable of, they flee to the lakes when they hear humans approaching. They can hide in the liquid metal of the water, grabbing a breath every ten minutes or so. B has watched them. They are fast but not terribly graceful. They have lumps on the backs of their ankles, like pasterns on horses.

He leaves the kitchen and goes to the lab to make sure everything's in order. They've dragged the kitchen table down there and fixed restraints to it, so they'll have more than one workspace. The third Silver can be kept in the narrow closet Joele has cleared out. There is no danger of the Silvers becoming violent, but they may try to run.

Vir is in the corner of the lab, writing in a notebook.

"Hey," B says.

She doesn't answer.

"You all right?"

She snaps her pen down, rubs her eyes. The lab is dark, except for a ring of light from the lamp next to her notebook. "I lived with them," she says.

"I know."

"They're smart. Smarter than us, probably."

"All the more reason we should—"

"It's okay to hurt them because they don't fight back? Because they won't get angry? It's like chopping up a fucking manatee."

"Vir, they're not us. They don't think like us. They don't feel betrayal. They may not even feel fear."

"They understand danger."

"They may understand it, but they don't *feel* it."

Vir draws a shaky breath. "You remember the one Joele—"

"Joele was out of line."

"It didn't make a sound."

"Precisely. Can we even be sure they feel pain?"

"Of course they can." Vir rarely raises her voice. It's a horrible sound, Vir amplified. "I've *asked* them."

"We're not going to kill them."

"Mine will die," says Vir. "We'll be lucky to get a few minutes looking at the heart. We don't have the right space, the right equipment. We were supposed to come here for water."

The uncrewed mission sent to the Silver Planet last year picked up only the most basic life forms—the flowers, the fruit, the snakes. The Silvers must have used their ability to become part of the planet's surface when the rover came through. It didn't pick up a single one.

Why hadn't the Silvers hidden from humans when they'd arrived? The creatures had been as dumb and trusting as dodos. They'd approached the *Byzantine*, babbling in that strange tongue. One had tried to put its arms around Joele, and she'd shoved it so hard it fell.

"What we found is much better," B says. "When we're gone, they'll send other teams better equipped to study these creatures. But we're the first. People will remember us."

Vir shakes her head. "I'm doing this. But I want you to know that I have lived with them. They've told me stories. Many of them picked up our language very quickly. They are not robots. They're not insects. They're people."

B feels a little sick. "They're not us," he repeats.

"Grena read to them. I don't know how she can—"

"Vir," he says, "pull it together."

Outside, B listens again for the ticking sound and doesn't hear it at first. He switches on the flashlight and walks to where he stood earlier, about a hundred yards from the main port. Just when he starts to think it was his imagination, he hears it again—a rattle now, like dice. He follows the sound to a pile of low, flat rocks and is startled when one of the rocks moves at his approach. It is not a rock at all. It's a Silver.

Dark hair, slight build. It drags itself on its belly, using its elbows. Its back bleeds from a dozen lacerations. Blood steams on the cold, bruised flesh. Its heart is lit up. B can see the pale gold fist of it ghosting along the creature's spine. The Silver stops and lies perfectly still on the ground, and as B gets closer, he realizes that the noise is the thing's teeth chattering. B looks again at the blood. It's red, like human blood, but this is a race adapted for extreme cold. Their bodies are naked, hairless. *That blood is all that keeps them warm. And losing so much of it . . .*

The creature whispers something.

"What's that?" B asks.

"S-h-h-it," the Silver says. It curls into itself, shaking so hard the ground beneath it seems to move. B can see part of its face. Its lip is split, a clump of dried blood under its nose.

B nudges it with the toe of his boot. The creature goes so still, B could swear it's died. Then it shivers again.

B crouches. "What's your name?"

"Wh-who's askin'?"

He starts at the unexpected response. It must be one of Grena's, if it knows English. "I am."

"I d-don't have to t-tell you a b-blasted thing."

B wonders where the creature learned to talk like this.

He remembers that Grena once read her clan a novel, some awful paperback Western.

"What're you doing here?"

The Silver stares at him. The look in the creature's eyes doesn't match its brazen tone, and the tone doesn't fit with what B knows about Silvers. The Silver's rebellion is stagy, as though the creature is imitating audacity. B knows that Grena is a good storyteller and wonders if the Silver is mimicking her reading of lines from the novel.

"You speak good English," he says.

The Silver closes its eyes. Its heart bumps the bottom of its ribs, drifts down its leg. B watches, fascinated.

"You know Grena?" he asks.

"You b-better h-h-hightail it outta here, m-mister."

"Who did this to you?"

The Silver doesn't answer. It rolls its eyes up to the black sky.

B runs a hand over his mouth. He needs to make a decision. He can leave the creature to die out here, or he can bring it aboard the ship as another test subject for Project HN. It's half-dead anyway. Maybe Vir can put it under and cut it up without feeling too bad. "Look," he says, "we've got some medical supplies on the ship. Let's get you inside. You're not gonna make it out here." He reaches out, and the creature instantly sinks partway into the ground.

It doesn't go any farther. It gasps, slapping the ground with its palm. "Shit," it whispers. "Shit, shit, shit."

"Come on," B says. "I'm trying to help you."

The creature gazes at him for another moment. B can't read those cracked eyes. "Pardners?" it asks finally.

"Yeah, if you want." B reaches out again and just brushes the chilly skin. The Silver draws back and sinks the rest of the way into the ground. B can see it just below the surface, as if it's encased in ice. Blossoms of red adorn the tightly curled body.

B sighs, stands. "All right. Have it your way."

He starts toward the ship. He turns back once and swears he can see the gentle glow of the creature's heart rising from the ground.

B's room on the ship looks nothing like his room back home, for which B is grateful. The floor in his room on the *Byzantine* is hardwood, the rug nailed down, the bed stapled neatly to the wall. Beside it is a standing lamp, painted to look like a flower and stem. As captain, he gets the room with the largest bath, though "large" is relative. B showers every three days in water brought from home. The water will run out soon. Not just on the ship, but on Earth.

That's why they're on the Silver Planet, to determine the silver water's suitability for human use. He sets an extra quilt on the bed. Finds his own flashlight in the desk drawer.

His room back home has thin, soft carpet, something expensive and cream-colored that Matty picked out. Living with the same man for seven years, and B never had the courage to say he didn't like the carpet. He could've replaced it when Matty left, but he and the thin pile were grudging friends by then. He even toasted it, on his first night as a divorced man. He set one open beer on it and raised another. *"Here's to you, you ugly rug."* A year later, he still found himself whispering to it sometimes. *"You ugly rug."*

He tells Grena he won't be going with them to collect the Silvers. Between Joele and Gumm, they'll manage. He asks her what story she read to the clan she'd stayed with. She asks why he's asking, and he says he's just curious. She says the book is called *Tin Star and Thunder Sam.*

B gives Joele her flashlight back. Looks again at the blood on her jacket. He wouldn't be surprised to learn she's responsible for the injured Silver. But why wouldn't she say anything? He told the team to leave all Silvers alone until Project HN starts, but Joele is never shy about flouting rules, especially B's rules. Vir looks composed, inscrutable. Gumm still smells like vomit. He decided last week to find out if a human could survive strictly on quilopea. B sees them off as they drive west in a Planeterrain vehicle, toward a stain of rusty trees near a lake where Grena has observed a small clan feeding by night.

B finds a shovel and a sweatjack. The sweatjacks are uncomfortable, like wearing a rubber shell, but they help. They have little heat pustules inside that burst every few seconds, then fill and burst again. Joele is the only one on the team who can go any significant length of time outside without one.

He goes to where he last saw the Silver. It is still in the ground, but its heart isn't visible and its eyes are closed. It doesn't move. It's not quite the same color as the earth, but its limbs have a liquid way of mimicking the bumps and spills of the terrain. B sticks the shovel into the ground near the creature's side. The Silver doesn't wake. He digs until he exposes a shoulder, then traces the legs with the thin ravine he's making. The Silver is dead, he thinks. No new blood is flowing, just old, dark drool on the gray flesh. But as he continues to dig, the creature wakes. B doesn't realize it is awake at first, but when he stops to wipe cold sweat from his forehead, he sees the creature's eyes flutter. A second later, the Silver seems sucked from the earth by the air. The ground knits together beneath it, and it lies on the surface. It meets B's eyes, and its soft brows lean toward one another.

Then it screams.

The scream doesn't work well. It is ragged and unemotional, unpracticed and ugly. B drops his shovel and claps a hand over the creature's mouth. It lashes out, and B is so startled he lets go. The Silver tries to roll onto its belly, to get its legs underneath it, but it's too weak.

"Stop, just stop," B orders. The creature goes still, sides pumping with each shallow breath. This is like watching a bug die, a spider that still waves its legs no matter how you grind it into the carpet. B unclips the flashlight from his belt and shines it over the thing's body.

The wounds are deep. Dark patches, almost black, mar the Silver's ribs. "You'll die out here," B says. "Will you let me take you inside?"

It doesn't answer. It is not shivering anymore, a bad sign. B extends a hand.

The Silver moans, but it doesn't pull away or go into the ground. B touches its shoulder and the cold pricks his hand. He feels like he's grabbed a cactus. But once his flesh gets used to the cold, transfers some of its own warmth, B is aware that the Silver's skin is smooth as water.

B grabs the creature under its arms. It draws a quick breath and goes limp. Its heart is on again, but the organ's path is shaky. Instead of drifting in straight lines, it shudders in a circle, like a fish missing a fin. Its light is fainter too.

B lifts the creature and carries it toward the ship.

B tells himself the Silver has to be taken to the lab. He can clean it up, strap it to a table, and donate it to Project HN, for however long it has left. But B doesn't go to the lab. He goes to the main deck and hurries down a narrow hall. He takes the Silver into his room, sets it on the floor, and throws a quilt over it. It doesn't stir.

The atmosphere will kill it, B thinks. And that will be a relief—will absolve him of further decision making. Still, he heads to the lower deck. The storage room across from the lab has tents and bedrolls. He grabs a sleeping bag and a first aid kit along with a basin for water collection. He enters the lab and takes a bag of dried quilopea. He pauses for a moment, looking at the tables and restraints. Hurries back upstairs.

The Silver's heart flickers on and off like a dying bulb. B unzips the sleeping bag, spreads it out, and rolls the Silver on top of it. He goes to the bathroom and fills the basin with warm water. The Silver remains unconscious as B cleans the worst of the mess. Its skin seems to shy away involuntarily from B's touch. B tries to be gentle, wondering why he bothers. Most likely the creature won't wake again.

B talks to it, asks it questions, liking the way silence hangs between each one. He changes the water in the basin three times. When he is done, he opens the first aid kit, disinfects the wounds, applies salve. Lifts the creature and winds a bandage around its ribs. It has started to shiver again, and B feels unexpected relief at the movement. He zips the bedroll and repacks the first aid kit. B thinks that he should do something to restrain the Silver in case it wakes. Gag it, at least, in case it screams again. But B decides this is either going to be a disaster or it isn't. Either the Silver will recover, or it will die. And if the others on the team discover what B has done, well, so what? He is the captain.

B places a hand on the side of the Silver's neck. Feeling for what, a pulse? Fever? The flesh is cool but not frozen. A bit of dark hair is stuck in a slick of ointment on its forehead. According to Grena, Silvers' hair never grows past their ears. It's black when they're young, white when they're old. Something about this Silver's body, about the timbre of its voice when it spoke, makes B think it's male, but he'll have to get a second opinion. From whom? How is B going to explain bringing this creature into his quarters?

Helping it?

But B brushes the lock of hair back, his thumb sliding through the ointment. The Silver stirs. B watches as it moves its hand, places it on B's. Something comes to him from one of Grena's reports. Something he's tried not to remember. That Silvers often sleep holding hands.

B pulls away, takes the basin to the bathroom and empties it. When he comes back into the room, he notices a paperback on his desk. It is *Tin Star and Thunder Sam*. Grena must have left it for him. Grena is like that. You ask her a question, and she'll answer it as best she can, then come find you later with additional resources. He picks up the book. He needs to find a way to let the others know that his quarters are off-limits.

He reads silently for the next hour, while the Silver breathes softly on his floor. It is still alive, asleep, when the others return. B goes to meet them. They have captured two Silvers. The third escaped. Both captives are drugged, unconscious. Project HN begins.

chapter TWO

h e opens his eyes, counts four walls, a ceiling, a floor, a door. Thick air. Blood smells, sweat smells, wood smells. Smells he didn't know before humans. He swims against a torrent of pain, gasps in it. Holds his breath. Something squeezes him, he tears at it. A strip of clothes—no, the word is *cloth*. He pulls himself further into the warm cave and tries to go into the ground, to become part of this softness. He can't. Stuck here, warm, alive, nothing to do but wait. The floor is a puzzle with thirty-seven pieces that he can see. No plants. He can crawl out of the cave, but he'll be cold. He's lost what keeps him warm. The large female took his blood.

Nineteen places he feels his skin torn. Three places he's crushed inside. His heart stutters, afraid of the dark spots.

Why would the female damage him? It is counterproductive, a word he loves. Grena was nice. She read them the book. She tried to learn their language. That's why he crawled toward the ship after the large female finally left him. He thought maybe he could find Grena. He could have gone to his clan, but they would not accept him, smelling like humans. They would have gone into the lake, hidden from him as if he were a human himself.

His throat is pebbled from his scream. He doesn't know why he tried it, only that humans in the book did it when they were hurt or when they didn't want somebody near them. Grena had demonstrated the sound when she'd read aloud, and he had been tempted to try it too. But he hadn't wanted to miss any of the story.

He remembers the thick-muscled man who tore him from the ground. The man with 7,618 hairs in his beard. Rough estimate.

He sees four walls, a closed door. This means he is in prison, like Tin Star in the book. This means he should dig with a spoon and spit on the guard when the guard orders him to talk. But if the guard here is like the guard in the book, he won't like the spit and will take more blood. If the guard is the large female, he won't spit, he decides, but if it is the man with the short beard, he will.

What's strange is that he hurts in his mind, too many places to count. He has always known what it is to want, but now he knows what it is to *not* want. He does not want to be hit. He does not want to be trapped. He does not want the man with the beard to come back. The man hasn't taken any blood yet, but his voice scrapes like rocks.

He tries to count threads in the soft cave, but pain batters the numbers. He tries another sound, one he hasn't made before. Sounds that are not words have always seemed pointless. But now he lets this sound rest in his throat, then pushes it slowly out. It is high and wavering. He does not want to make it anymore. Stops.

He is caught somewhere between sleep and waking when the man with the beard comes in. He almost opens his eyes, stops himself. He goes perfectly still and holds his breath. He listens as the man sets four items on the desk, then takes three steps toward the soft cave's entrance and crouches down.

He opens his eyes and spits.

The spit hits the man's beard.

He's done it wrong. In the book, Tin Star spits *after* the guard speaks.

He watches the man comb the spit from the short gold hairs and holds his breath again.

"I thought you guys couldn't get pissed," the rough voice says.

He calls the man an improper pollinator in the Silver language, because that is what humans do in the book when they would like to modify another human's behavior—they announce the other person's deficiencies. They do it very loudly, and a feeling called anger is behind it, which moves humans as strongly as love.

The man splits the cave open, and now he can think about nothing else except the light, sweeping his eyes, and the cold, leaping into the rips in his skin.

"How much English do you speak?" the man asks.

A lot. Grena said I was the fastest learner in the group. She said I speak better than most humans. I'm the only one she taught to read.

He thinks of all he wants—food, water, to leave this place—and is surprised when none of these matter as much as what he does not want. He does not want the man to take more blood.

"Can't believe you're still kicking. I'm gonna call you Roach. Back on Earth we've got these bugs, they'll crawl around with half their guts hanging out. Ugly sons of bitches you can't kill. That's what you remind me of."

Strange, these critical words, when he isn't doing anything wrong.

"Unless you want to tell me your real name," the man says.

A thrashing clarity tells him to keep his real name from the man. Because humans take, and they do not share. Once you let them take something from you, you won't get it back.

"I like Roach," he says. He and the man can share this new name. The man will call him Roach, and he will respond, but he will not have to give the man anything that truly belongs to him.

The man laughs, but he doesn't sound happy. "Roach it is, then. How do you feel?"

Roach hesitates. He has no reason not to tell the truth. Except that the large female asked him this question. When he answered, she hit him, and when he didn't answer, she hit him too.

"Hungry," he says finally.

The man goes to the corner of the room and reaches into a bag.

"What's your name?" Roach asks.

"Call me B." B returns to the cave—not a cave now, razed and torn open. He opens a small package, sets it down beside Roach. "There. Quilopea."

Roach shakes his head. "That's not quilopea."

"Sure it is. It's just dehydrated, so it'll last longer."

"It's not right," Roach says. For just a second, something lunges forward inside of him, a crazy need to make B understand. Then the feeling is gone.

B shrugs. "Eat it or starve. Up to you."

Roach takes one of the dried fruits from the package, sniffs it. B isn't lying; it is quilopea. He takes a tentative bite. It is sour and chewy. Soon it is gone, and he takes another from the package.

"What happened to you?" B asks. He sits at the desk.

Roach doesn't answer. Four dried fruits. He chews two hundred and forty-three times. The package is empty.

"No predators here, I know that," B says. "And Silvers don't fight each other. Which means someone from my team did this to you."

Roach licks the fruit from between his teeth. He wishes he had more.

"Still hungry?"

"I ain't obliged to answer you, Sheriff," Roach says.

B shakes his head. "You hungry or not?"

"Yes."

B gets another package of dried fruit. Holds it just out of Roach's reach. "Who did this?"

"Large female." Roach's eyes are on the food.

B stares for a minute, then snorts. "Dark braid, taller than I am?"

"Yes."

B sits on the floor beside Roach. Still doesn't give him the fruit. "Why?"

Roach is suddenly not that hungry anymore. B's voice is softer now, and Roach remembers that same soft voice from the female, the questions she asked, right next to his ear. What he wants is B farther away. He can smell the outside on B, the cold, the white dust. He is aware of his own heart gliding into his throat, a place it rarely goes. He swallows, and it drifts back into his chest.

"Shit," he whispers. This is his favorite human word. It's the best word to whisper.

"What's shit?" B asks.

"Is she your friend?"

"She works with me."

Roach closes his eyes briefly and tries to remember how Grena's voice sounded when she read the part where Tin Star is brought before the Rough Rider Committee. "You try any funny business, you'll be eatin' fist through a hole in your skull," he informs B.

B throws back his head and laughs. "You're all right."

Roach doesn't feel all right. His whole body is trying to get into the floor without him even thinking about it. The dried quilopea doesn't want to stay inside him. B hands him the second package, but he doesn't take it. He mumbles a question B doesn't hear.

"Say it again?" B says.

"Am I in prison?"

B shakes his head. "You're on my ship. You're in my room. You can stay here until you're better. I won't try any funny business."

Twenty-one words. The voice isn't as rough as it's pretending to be.

"I have to ask you something, though," B says. "As long as you're here, you can't make noise, and you can't leave this room. Understand? The woman who hurt you, she lives here too. She can't know you're here. Got it?"

"Yes."

"Good." B reaches over and pulls the two halves of the cave together, attaching them with a tab that seals together the six hundred and ninety-four teeth Roach counts before darkness covers him. Roach goes still, and B says, "I meant what I said. No funny business. Rest."

He leaves the open package of food on the floor, along with a cup of water. It's not real water. It has no color, no beauty. Just like humans, Roach thinks. They have dark skin or light skin, but no color. Their hearts are hidden. He is surprised then, because the fierceness with which he does not want humans makes him wonder, for just a moment, how it would feel to take blood.

chapter
THREE

b could give Roach painkillers, but he doesn't want to take the chance they'll do more harm than good, so he asks Vir about natural remedies without mentioning why he's interested. Surely the Silvers have something on the planet that heals, something that will be familiar to Roach's system. If they do, Vir doesn't know about it. She is getting harder to talk to. Her mind is always somewhere else.

Project HN is two days in. Joele has recorded the involuntary noises her Silver makes in response to stimuli, has videotaped it writhing and struggling as she hits it, jabs it, pinches, scratches, and kicks it. She has seen no indication, though, of anger or resentment on the creature's part. Now Joele is starving it. Sometimes Joele lets Grena's Silver, a female, stand unrestrained and encourages it to try to stop her from hurting the other. The female Silver runs or tries to disappear into the floor.

Neither creature seems to have any trouble breathing. This is supposed to be a plus, but B almost wishes the creatures would suffocate quickly.

Vir works with the planet's water, filtering, mixing, using it to hydrate seeds brought from home. She used to swim in it occasionally, in the lake closest to the *Byzantine*, where Silvers don't come anymore because of its proximity to the humans. She says that she will vivisect Grena's Silver next week, but B doesn't think she is interested any longer in floating hearts or absent emotions.

When he's not busy, B is in his room, keeping an eye on Roach, who mostly sleeps. B's had to change sleeping bags twice, because the damn creature pisses whenever it feels like it and doesn't seem to notice. B finishes *Tin Star and Thunder Sam*. It's a terrible book, trash from a century ago, but he pauses whenever he gets to lines Roach has used on him and smiles in spite of himself.

The story is about a young wannabe cowpoke called Tin Star who weasels his way into riding with Thunder Sam, the most famed cowpoke in the West. Tin Star is arrested following a false accusation of horse thievin', thrown in prison, then busted out by a gang of outlaws called the Rough Rider Committee, who force him to help rustle cattle, kidnap women, and rob banks. Through it all, little Tin Star displays generic pipsqueak bravery, finding ways to thwart the outlaws' plans while making it look like he's one of them, until finally he's rescued by Thunder Sam. The two of them shoot all the outlaws and ride off into the sunset.

Roach is awake when B enters the room that night. The sleeping bag is zipped up to his neck. His eyes—which B has just started to think aren't so terrible—are glazed, and the cut in his lip has opened again.

"S'up?" B asks. It's a phrase Roach likes. Earth slang.

"I can't sleep."

"Pain?"

"I need water."

"I'll get you some."

"I want to go into the lake."

"You're not in any condition for swimming."

"Look." Roach pulls his arm out of the sleeping bag. His skin has become scaly. "I'm drying out. And I'm not clean."

"I don't know where the others are. I wouldn't feel comfortable taking you through the ship."

Roach says nothing. Tucks his arm back in the sleeping bag.

"You can shower."

"Huh?" Roach says it just like Grena.

"You can go into the bathroom and use my shower to clean up. You know what a shower is? Like rain—" He stops. No rain on the Silver Planet. Water comes from the ground, like the light. "Maybe you don't know."

"Rain is in the book," Roach says. "But I don't want to use human water."

"That's the best I can do right now."

"Okay." Roach unzips the sleeping bag and struggles to his feet. B puts out an arm, and Roach steadies himself on it. His back is scabbed and dark, but it's healing.

B guides him into the bathroom, into the shower stall. "Better not try to stand," B says, easing him down onto the smooth tile. He turns on the shower. Roach gasps as a spray of cold water hits him. "Sorry. It'll warm up in a minute."

Something Matty once said comes back to B. *"If you had kids, you'd end up stepping on them."* He's a good enough captain. He can organize, mobilize, instruct. As long as nobody on his crew needs to be spoon-fed or tucked in.

"I'll give you some privacy." B steps away. He's surprised by how beautiful the silver skin looks as the water hits it. Droplets seem to thicken, harden as they find flesh. They glint like crystal. The creature shines.

"Stay?" Roach hugs his knees as the water runs pink into the drain.

"You want soap?"

Roach shakes his head, but he scrubs his arms absently with his palms, as though to satisfy B. "Can I see it?" he asks.

"See what?"

"Soap."

B shows him the bar.

He's not ugly, B thinks, and the thought swims beside him as he kicks toward something to say. Something lovely and mournful about that face. The sleek planes of the body, long legs smooth and curved. Even the bulbed ankles don't bother B right now.

"It's pretty." Roach hands the bar of soap back to B.

B places it on the shelf. His sister used to love new bars of soap right out of the package, the carved letters of the brand still deep and dry. Once the name on a bar became unreadable, she opened a new one. It drove their mother crazy.

Roach closes his eyes. "Why are you here?" he asks. "On my planet? Grena said you're studying the water."

"We are."

"Why?"

"Our planet is running out."

"Your water's not as good as ours."

B senses no judgment in the statement, no sense of pride or disdain.

"Why not?" B asks.

"It doesn't feel the same. My skin can't hold it. It's flat, and there's no color."

"You almost done?"

"Is Grena here?"

B reaches over and turns off the water. "She's on the ship, yes."

"Why'd she stop living with us?" Roach casts an odd look at the towel B offers. "No, thanks."

"Don't you want to dry off?"

"I got in the shower *because* I was dry."

"Right." B helps Roach to his feet. "Water is supposed to be our main concern. Not studying your . . . people."

They're not people, but it seems rude to say this to Roach.

"And you started killing my people, so we stopped wanting you."

"Yes," B admits.

Roach sits on the sleeping bag but doesn't crawl in.

"How do you feel about that?" B asks. "Us killing your people?"

"They weren't my clan. The ones you killed. But I miss them."

"Do you ever wish you could kill us? To make things fair?"

Roach cocks his head. "You sound like Grena. No. That wouldn't help anything. That would just make more death."

"You should get covered up."

Roach is shivering again. "Your water makes me cold. I don't get cold when I come out of the lakes."

B sighs. "If you're feeling better tomorrow, you can go back to your clan. Family. Whatever."

Roach crawls into the sleeping bag. He says, "They'll run from me. I smell like this place."

Someone knocks on the door. B sits up in the darkness.

"Who's there?"

"The fucking reaper," Joele replies.

"Hold on." B slips out of bed. Roach is sitting up. B puts a hand on his shoulder as he passes, and Roach jumps.

"Get in the bed," B whispers to him. "Don't move."

Roach obeys, hiding himself under the heap of covers. B kicks the sleeping bag under the bed. He opens the door. Joele looks at him with tiger-sharp eyes.

"What the hell?" he mutters.

"One of them died."

"So?"

"So, the other one killed it."

"Can we talk about it in the morning?"

"Maybe you didn't hear me. One Silver killed another. Put my equipment bag over its face and smothered it."

"That's strange."

"Strange? It's unheard of."

"Write up a report. We'll talk in the morning."

She stares at him. "What the fuck is wrong with you?"

"I'm tired. And I don't know that it's any great accomplishment to torture a creature to insanity. Good night." He shuts the door.

"Fuck you too." Her voice is muffled. Her footsteps retreat.

The mound of covers doesn't move. B sits on the edge of the bed. "She's gone."

He hears no answer. B lifts the blankets and catches the faint glow of Roach's heart. The Silver's head is tucked against his chest. He draws a sudden breath.

Because he's wanted to since he saw the blue-gray skin glittering under the shower stream, B touches Roach's shoulder. "It's all right."

When Roach doesn't respond or move, B gets annoyed. "Come on. Back to bed." He shakes the covers.

A low sound starts under the quilts, rising in pitch. "Shhhh," B warns.

The sound gets louder. B drops the quilts, holds them down to muffle the noise. Roach struggles. Finally, B slips under the covers and wraps himself around Roach, pinning him.

"Would you shhh, would you just shhh."

Roach says something in his language. Says it again.

"I don't understand," B snaps.

"Who died?" Roach asks.

"A Silver. We brought two into the lab. We've brought others before, but they couldn't breathe the air. So we fixed the air pressure, and now—"

Roach shakes his head. "They shut off," he says.

"What?"

"Some of us, when we hurt too much, we stop breathing on purpose. It's not the air." He struggles, and B eases off him a little. "Not my clan," Roach continues. "We don't. Even if we hurt. Even if we're almost dead. But we can shut others off, if they want us to."

"You're saying it was a mercy killing?"

"Huh?"

"Like in *Tin Star*, when they shoot the snakebit horse."

Roach's eyes widen. The jagged loops of his irises seem for a moment to go smooth. He nods. "Did she hurt them bad?"

"I don't know. I think she hurt one pretty bad. But the other was well enough to shut it off."

"I miss them," Roach whispers.

"Did you know them?"

"Maybe." He rolls out from under B and settles against the wall.

B adjusts his position on the narrow mattress, trying not to touch Roach. "I'm sorry," he says finally.

"Why?"

"We're hurting you because we know you won't stop us."

"Do you like doing it?" A question, but not an accusation.

"We want to know how you can be so much like us in so many ways, but not feel anger, or jealousy, or hate."

"Why should we?"

"Because that's how we get what we want on Earth. We fight. We decide we need what others have, and we take it. Not just humans, all animals." B is suddenly irritated at having to explain. "There are billions of species on our planet. It's not some scraggly garden we can pollinate ourselves."

Roach laughs.

"Is that funny?"

Roach shakes his head, still laughing.

"What's the matter with you? That might be your family we've got in the lab."

Roach neither cowers from nor flares at the words. He watches B with interest, his heart sailing back and forth across his chest.

"Fucking cowards is what you are, all of you." B turns away, adjusts his pillow, and thrusts his shoulder up like a wall between them. He waits for Roach to move or speak, but the Silver doesn't. It takes B a long time to fall asleep. Sometime in the night, Roach bridges the cold space between them. B rolls over and fits the silver body to his, tucks the dark head under his chin, winds his arms around the slender shoulders.

chapter
FOUR

t hey asked the same questions, B and the female: *What's wrong with you? Why don't you fight back?*

The female asked more questions. She asked, *"Which feels worse?"* And kicked him in the side, then in the head. She asked, *"How many do you think you can take before you die?"* as she hit him with her belt.

But B doesn't hit Roach, just turns away when he's done yelling. He breathes three hundred and forty regular breaths before he moves to sleep breaths. One hundred and twenty-three of those before Roach moves nearer and lets B's warmth become his. They take thirty-four breaths together, then B puts his arms around him, and Roach feels, for the first time in days, a pause in the ache of his wounds, an end to his fear of four walls.

Morning comes and B rolls away. Roach is colder now than when he was losing blood.

"If you're well enough today, I'll get you out of here," B says.

"Why don't you study me?"

B pulls on his—Roach can't think of what it's called—the floppy shell Grena used to wear that blasted her with heat. "What do you mean?"

"In the lab."

"That what you want?"

"No."

"Well, then. That's why."

Humans' lies float through them, glowing like Silvers' hearts.

"The others don't want it either."

Roach can tell B doesn't like this comment by the way B yanks on the zipper of his shell. "You're smarter than them," B says. "That's why

I like you. When I let you go, stay away from the ship. Joele's a loose cannon."

"A what?"

"She's a nutcase. Like one of the Rough Riders."

"I know that."

"So don't let her find you again."

"Doesn't she have to listen to what you say?"

"She ought to. But she doesn't."

"That's like me," Roach says. "I was a king in my clan. Everyone had to listen to me." He tries not to grin as he watches B's face.

"Silvers don't have social hierarchies. You're all equal."

"Not my clan. I'm in charge. Someday, I'll be in charge of the whole planet."

It is very easy to lie to someone who thinks you're stupid.

B only says, "I'm sure the planet will be happy to get its king back." He grabs some papers from his desk. "I'm going to work for a while. Rest, eat, shower, whatever. I'll be back when the coast is clear, and I'll take you outside."

"Can I see Grena?"

"No."

B leaves, and Roach counts his footsteps until he can't hear any more.

He eats a package of dried quilopea, thinks how good it will be to eat it fresh again. He wonders if he should try to find his clan. When humans started harming Silvers, his clan made a decision that any Silver who aided the humans, spoke to them, or touched them would be forgotten by the rest of the clan. Roach has done everything he shouldn't. When he saw the large female, he went to her. He spoke to her. She touched him. She took his blood. Then he allowed himself to be taken onto the human ship. He spoke to B. They touched.

He tries being angry. He looks at the empty package of quilopea. "You're a damned coward," he says to it. "What's wrong with you?"

For a second, he feels his blood jump. Maybe B is right. If you want something enough, you can make others listen to you. He stands. He's still sore when he moves, and he has a sense that important pieces of his body are jangling inside him, like coins in the money bags Tin Star and the Rough Riders take from the bank. But he does not feel weak.

He'd like to go to the lab, find the captured Silver, see if he can help. After all, Thunder Sam rescues Tin Star from the Rough Rider Committee. Rescuing somebody is heroic. Most times, if a Silver swims too far out in a lake and can't get back to shore, or accidentally loses blood, nobody comes to the rescue. That's because death is just something that happens, like the light in the ground, like a flower growing from a seed. But in the human world, people are always being captured, rescued, murdered, and loved.

That's something Roach doesn't understand about humans: It makes sense to love your clan. It makes sense to care about your people. But why choose one person to love more than any other? Roach knows six hundred and seventy-three Silvers. He loves them all. He will miss all of them when they die. He has seen that breeding pairs show each other special attention for a short time. He hopes one day he will be selected to breed, so he can find out if something makes his mate especially wonderful.

Tin Star falls in love with a girl he meets in Arizona named Jenny Feathers. She is called a "girl" in the book, not a "female." The thing Tin Star likes most about her is the way she looks, and also the fact that she is "spunky." He isn't supposed to love her, because she's an Indian, which means her skin is a different color than his. But he likes her anyway. When they breed, he puts his mouth all over hers. She tastes like desert air.

Roach walks to the door. He listens very closely to make sure nobody is behind it. Then he opens it and leaves the room. He is in a long, narrow space and moves very fast because he doesn't like the two walls so close together. This whole ship is a mess of walls and doors and odd smells. He doesn't pay attention to where he's going, and soon he is running in a circle around a wide-open space, with the ceiling far above him. There are stairs, but he doesn't want to use them. There are bars along the floor, so he swings from one and ends up on a lower level—the old floor is now his ceiling. He runs to another place where the walls are too close. He opens a door.

He is in a white room, too bright. He has to close his eyes. It smells like humans—sharp, salty, blood-metal. He sees a sink, like the one in B's bathroom, but bigger. A big tub sits beside the sink, lined in a shiny black material that rustles when Roach touches it. Inside are empty wrappers.

He lifts a couple of the wrappers to his nose, smells them. Their outsides are white, but inside they are silver, and the way they are torn makes Roach think of his own skin. They smell like they've never been outside, like they've been trapped a long time without air.

He opens one of the small doors above him and finds more packages. These are not torn, and they are heavy. He remembers how B ripped open the packages of quilopea. Perhaps quilopea is in these. He is hungry, now that he thinks about it, and he starts to tear open a package, then hesitates. Once he opens it, he will see the ripped silver underside of the package's skin. Grena says humans use many materials that are not alive. He is almost certain that a package is not alive and cannot feel. But what if he's wrong?

He pulls at the edges of the package, the way B did. It opens easily and no blood comes out. No quilopea either. Instead he exposes two hard, dry rectangles the color of B's hair. Roach smooths the torn package and looks at the words. He's not sure how to pronounce all of them, or what exactly they mean, but he reads, Hal's Cosmic Granola Bars, and underneath, Orbitin' Oats 'N Cinnamon.

Roach has never eaten anything but quilopea before. He sniffs Hal's Cosmic Granola Bars. They smell sweet, but not the same way quilopea does. He sticks the end of one in his mouth. It breaks when he bites, and little pieces fall from his mouth, stick to his lips, scatter on the floor. He tries to chew, but the bar is tough and prickly, and he doesn't want it in his mouth anymore. He could spit it out, but that will make a mess. As his mouth gets wetter, the bar grows softer, and finally he is able to swallow. The taste is not bad, but it's different from anything he's known, and he can't get it off his tongue. He fears for a moment that he'll have to taste Hal's Cosmic Granola Bars forever.

He sets the package on the counter and pulls open the door to a big white box in the corner of the room. The top half opens, and a cloud of cold bursts out, startling Roach. Inside are shiny rectangular packages, different from Hal's Cosmic Granola Bars. He takes one and stands for a moment, letting the cold touch his face, before he shuts the door. This food is called Spacedream Sandwich.

He opens it. It's darker and softer than cosmic granola bars. He takes a bite and immediately drops the rest and puts a hand to his mouth. Cold floods the areas around and between his teeth, making his whole head hurt. He spits out the Spacedream Sandwich and sticks his fingers in his mouth, rubbing his gums, trying to erase the sensation.

He hears footsteps and quickly opens one of the small doors under the sink and crawls into the dark space. Someone enters the room. A female. But not Joele. This one is smaller, and she makes the air seem shaky when she comes in. Her footsteps are crooked, her breath juts like ribs. She stands in front of the sink. The shadow of her leg covers the thin strip of light between the small doors. She breaks open and cries. Roach knows about crying from the book and from Grena, who cried a little when she left Roach's clan for good. It's what humans do when they get too dry, instead of going into a lake.

It's more than that. This human is sad, scared, maybe angry. She is collapsing under the weight of all that is piled inside of her. Roach understands now what is special about the kind of person who could rescue someone else. You have to not be afraid of being crushed by the weight of the other person's troubles. This is what stops him from helping her. Her invisible enemy is stronger than both of them. He counts the seconds she cries. He gets to one hundred and forty seven when suddenly his stomach muscles contract. He does not want to think about Cosmic Granola Bars ever again, but the taste still lingers in his mouth. He shuts his eyes, trying to concentrate on something, *anything* other than food. He leans over and opens his mouth and the chewed-up bar slides up his throat and out of him. He feels much better once it's gone.

The female is still crying. If she hears Roach, she gives no indication. She stops suddenly and whispers, "Snap out of it, Vir." She turns on the water, and it trickles in the metal tube near Roach's head. She opens the door above the sink, grabs a package of Hal's Cosmic Granola Bars—he hears it crackle—and leaves.

chapter
FIVE

b ack home, B had a shelf covered in awards: plaques, certificates, two medals, and an engraved pen. It didn't matter what he'd done to get them, only that he could display these shining, empty ideas of who he was. One of NRCSE's luminaries. A pioneer of the future.

The NRCSE—*nurk-see* to everyone—is the National Research Center for Space Exploration. B's employer for the last six years.

He wasn't Shepard or Aldrin famous when his supervisor, Kelly Hatchell, approached him about captaining the first crewed mission to the Silver Planet. He'd signed the occasional autograph, visited schools, and appeared on a panel on a late-night talk show, where he was happy to let a D-list comedian and the famously hard-nosed judge of some reality show play wishbone with the spotlight. He even gave a commencement speech at a private college, his throat so dry he asked a graduate in the front row if he could swig from her water bottle—the only joke to garner laughs, and it hadn't been a joke.

Still, NRCSE encouraged him to stay in the public eye. "God knows you're about as much fun as rush-hour traffic," Kelly Hatchell said. "But there's something about you. Your jawline, maybe. People like a handsome hero."

B wasn't sure what Hatch meant by *hero* until three months before B's team was set to depart. *Time* magazine put B on its cover with the headline: *The Great Wet Hope: How the Silver Planet's Lakes Could Save the Human Race.* The day the issue hit stands, B's mother called to ask if it would have killed him to smile. "They didn't want me to," he told her. Saving the human race was serious business. But then, what wasn't serious business to B? He felt so hopelessly caged wherever he was on Earth—home, college, the air force, NRCSE—that he'd eventually turned to infinity for help.

At the time, six months away from Earth sounded like paradise. Matty had just left, tired of playing second fiddle to B's work. B's mother and sister made it clear their sympathies lay with Matty. Any direction B turned, he met accusation. But he didn't turn often. Mostly, he looked at whatever was directly in front of him.

Now he misses everything from his mother's laugh to the crust on his stove burners. He misses humans who act like people, not scientists. More than anything, he misses a sky that changes color. He misses stars. Most of the "comforts" NRCSE sent with them, Grena and Vir have given to the Silvers. The Silvers have a deck of cards and a little sand Zen garden. They have construction paper and markers. Last week B went walking and found a four of spades on the ground.

NRCSE exhausted its funds sending B's team here, and now its flag is planted in one of the most incredible, and fundable, opportunities in human history. The government has showered NRCSE with money, and NRCSE in turn is assembling expert teams, *prepared* teams of pedigreed *-ologists* to study Silvers. B's team will keep telling bad jokes until they're yanked offstage with a cane. Their research on Silvers is haphazard, inconclusive. They've behaved, by turns, professionally and barbarically. They have fucked up.

"Stay off the lower deck," B tells the others. "I'm turning on the filters."

"Don't need to do that till Sunday," Gumm says.

"Air smells funky down there."

"If you're bored, you can help Vir and me mix anesthetic," Joele says. She has refused to talk to B about the Silver killing last night. Says he can read her report. "Or you can help us brainstorm about fire."

"Fire?" B says.

Joele leans back in her chair. "We want to introduce our Silver friends to fire. But we're not sure how, since we can't sustain a flame outside, and fire in the lab is—"

"Not happening," B says.

"So what about a controlled fire in, say, the kitchen?"

"Not on the ship. We can't risk it."

Joele looks at Gumm. "Where's Grena? She could help us do it safely."

"I'm serious," B says. "If anything happened to the *Byzantine*—"

"We'd have to spend our days group-bathing with Silvers until we were rescued," Joele says. "Believe me, no one hates the idea more than me. But can you imagine? Fire. A chance to vicariously experience the birth of human civilization."

"It'd be pretty fucking cool," Gumm agrees. "Seeing what they'd do with it. They might show their true colors then."

"The answer is no."

"You're just buckets of fun, boss." Joele shares a secret smile with Gumm.

"No one on the lower deck. See you later."

He heads to his room, a war mounting inside him. He hates Joele and black skies. He hates that Gumm puts his feet up on furniture. He hates that he's not strong enough to inspire fear or allegiance or anything other than secret smiles. And he wishes that when he held Roach in his arms last night, he'd traced the Silver's wounds, let the scabs scrape his palms, listened to the catch of breath when he pressed too hard on a bruise. He wishes he had breathed in the scent of Roach's hair and bitten his ear and made him understand how much there is to hate in this world, how many reasons to be angry.

He doesn't want to let his captive go. He wants to take him apart, but not the way his team would take a Silver apart. He wants to flay the layers of impassivity, the innocence, the adoration of a trashy paperback. He wants to reach into that Silver body, grab the floating heart, and hold it in place. He wants to find what's buried. You can't be alive and never heave with rage or loathing, never be stung a thousand places by jealousy. Roach is an impossibility. B wants to make him possible.

He opens his bedroom door and is almost unsurprised to find Roach gone. This is what he's been waiting for: a mission, a reason, a disaster. He searches the room, and when he finds no Silver hiding in it, he tears through the ship, cutting the air like a storm.

chapter
SIX

the ship is not big, but it is blocky and confusing, and Roach can find neither a way outside nor the route back to B's room. He doesn't want to open doors, in case he stumbles onto Joele's territory. He can't stay long in the wide center space, because there is too much light. He crouches in the ship's dark corners, but every time he is still, he's sure he hears footsteps coming toward him. It's an exciting game, but tiring, especially since his body is still healing.

He finally opens a door and enters a small room with a flat black box in one wall. When he presses a button on the box, a picture comes up. Silvers don't make many pictures, just with their fingers in the dust on the ground now and then. But Grena explained that humans make pictures many different ways, including with cameras, which capture moments of real life exactly. This image shows white ground. The sky is blue, and a tall, skinny tree with wide leaves stands next to a very blue lake. The colors are more vivid than any Roach has seen before, even more than the colors in the small pictures Grena brought to show his clan.

He presses the button again, and a flat path cuts the green ground, and he sees machines with wheels. Blocky structures cover most of the sky. In the next picture, the sky is black and speckled with little silver things. The sight of the silver things makes Roach smile. Stars. They are visible from Earth, Grena says, but not from the Silver Planet. The Silver Planet's atmosphere hides them, makes the rest of the universe seem absent.

He thinks that if these pictures are accurate, he would never want to live on Earth. Too many colors, and too many unalive things in the way. Then he thinks maybe this isn't true. Maybe what he fears is the emptiness of his own planet, the gulf between what he knows and what B knows. If he lived among these colors, if he knew the names for the structures, B would think he was smarter. B would like him better, too, if he could make himself angry. If he could want something enough to draw blood to get it. If he went to Earth, he could learn. He'd never have to be alone.

He is suddenly too tired to look at more pictures, and he is cold again. He looks down. For a second he can't find his heart. His eyes are still swimming in those colors, Earth's colors.

In the hall, he fights the urge to sink to the floor. If he wants to sleep, he needs to find B's room. Better yet, he needs to find a way off the ship so he can go into a lake. He arrives at the stairs. He doesn't want to use them, but he is too tired to climb the bars. He starts to circle the open space, and suddenly he does hear footsteps.

Something slams into him and shoves him into the darkness of the hallway. His back hits the wall, startling old pain awake. "What the hell are you doing?" demands B.

"Who's askin'?" Roach says, though B's arm across his throat makes it hard to speak.

"You cut that shit out. What did I tell you? Huh?" B grabs his shoulders and shakes him. "I said as long as you're on the ship, you stay in my room. I said I'd take you outside once I'd made sure it was safe. You deaf *and* stupid?"

This is different from anything Roach has experienced before, even the female's attacks. Her anger was broader, less intimate. Roach understands that B's anger is directed at him specifically. B would not behave the same way if Roach were, say, the Silver from the lab who had escaped.

"I ought to fucking let her find you. Let her cut you up, rip your heart out and photograph it."

Roach can't stop watching B's lips move. They are the edges of a tear in flesh that was meant to be, the outline of a wound that is permanent and necessary. Roach puts his own lips on them to see if he can taste some of B's words, capture the flavor of the feelings behind them.

B is still only for a second. Then his lips move again, but quietly, covering Roach's. B's lips do what his hands do, pull Roach close one second, push him away the next. They cannot figure out how to hold on, so they attack, over and over again. Roach is aware of how many layers there are to B: his rubber shell, his clothes, skin hidden under all this. Roach wears only the rips and bruises Joele put on him. Even his heart can't hide. It glows brighter than the colors in those pictures. B puts his hand over the glow, follows it as it moves through Roach's body, his palm dry and hot.

"Come on." B takes Roach's hand. Together they move to the middle of the ship and up the stairs. Roach has never used stairs before, and every step he's sure his feet will get confused and he'll fall. But he has no choice, because B is pulling him, and if he doesn't think about it, he's fine. The old ceiling becomes their floor. They run down the hall, to the familiar door, the door to B's room.

Grena once asked Roach's clan if Silvers had sex-for-fun. Not to produce children, but simply for the pleasure of contact, of connection. She'd tried to ask the question in the Silver language, but the way she worded it was funny and a few Silvers laughed. Grena waited patiently for an answer. Roach wanted to speak, but he wasn't sure what to say. Only one pair of Silvers is supposed to breed per month, a male and a female, to produce an offspring. Limiting the number of breeding pairs ensures that the population stays low, and that everyone has enough quilopea. Since only a male and a female can produce offspring, sometimes two males or two females breed, knowing they can do so without the risk of offspring.

There is a scene in *Tin Star and Thunder Sam* where Thunder Sam purchases the services of a whore, which is a human female who breeds with lots of males. When Thunder Sam gets the whore in bed with him, he puts his organ inside her. Grena explained Thunder Sam doesn't want to produce offspring with the whore. He is having sex-for-fun. To Roach, it doesn't sound very enjoyable for either party. Thunder Sam sweats a lot, and the whore looks bored, and the bed is dirty and makes their skin itch. Still, Thunder Sam leaves "whistling, with an extra spring in his step."

Humans know awful ways to touch each other, to touch Silvers. Maybe their pleasure-breeding is fun for them because they are used to roughness and pain. But it would not be fun for a Silver.

Roach does not think of this right away, because his body feels like it is still running even when they're in B's room and the door is shut. He accepts B's hands, his lips, lets B push him onto the bed, draws out B's hunger and uses it to create his own.

"You know what we're doing?" B asks him as his lips find Roach's neck, his shoulder. "You know how to do this?"

"Yes." Roach feels a flash of fear at his own lie. It is not a dark fear, but a sharp, blazing thrill that leaves behind a smile he can't explain or stop. He now knows what it is to seek adventure. Even if his adventure is not shooting outlaws or rescuing anyone, it is new, and no other Silver has done it. He thinks of lying next to B in the bed last night, B's arms around him, and how it felt safe even though B is unknown and too strong and a little dangerous.

B moves too fast, presses too hard on his injuries, not leaving Roach room to breathe. But Roach knows that without B's force driving them, he would never make it to this unfamiliar place he's going. He would remain a Silver always, something B cannot desire, because a Silver is too stupid, too quiet, too slow for a human's fevered energy.

B holds himself over Roach, his hands on the bed. "You all right?"

Roach reaches up to touch B through his clothes, where he knows B's organ is. On human males, the organ is out all the time; it is never hidden. He likes the sound B makes when he touches him. B moves to undo his pants, and Roach takes his hand away. The clothes don't just hide B, they protect Roach, and Roach balks at losing this last barrier between them. He closes his eyes and feels B's knuckles graze his skin as B pulls the clothing down.

Roach thinks of Joele. Human hands do what Silvers' would never—grab, yank, twist, strike, and drag. B's hands can do all of these things. Roach's could, too, if he made them. If B hurts him, maybe he can make himself hurt B back. The idea is too much to hold on to. He swallows, but his throat is still thick. He shivers and can't make himself be still.

He has let B touch the outside of him, where he was hurt. Now he'll let B touch him inside, where he is still himself, uninjured and unchanged. He thinks about how B touching him outside helped heal him. B put his skin back together, kept him from falling in the shower, and made it easier to sleep when he held Roach. Maybe his touch inside will heal the divide in Roach between what he is and what he wants to be. He wants to be human. To live on Earth, to know the names of millions of objects and sounds, and to be unable to take a step in any direction without adventure spotting him and bounding over.

"Relax," B says. "This'll feel good."

"I know." Roach is frantic for it to be happening, to be over. Then he will be left with just the knowledge that he's done this, has been as close to B as possible. Then the idea won't be frightening anymore. *Humans* won't be frightening anymore.

"It won't hurt if you breathe. Breathe when I say."

Roach breathes, and B enters. Roach perches on top of the sensation, refusing to merge with it. It is too strange, too much. "Please," he says, not sure if he's asking B to retract the touch or continue.

"Breathe." The air around the word is hot against Roach's hair. Roach breathes with B, the way he did when they were in this bed together last night. B's arms are around him, hands seeking uninjured parts of Roach's body. He moves slowly, drawing Roach with him.

"Don't," Roach says, the first command he's ever given. He squirms out from under B and faces the door, not wanting to run but aware if he stays, B might hurt him. B doesn't touch him again. Roach hears his own breathing, ragged, layered over B's quick, sleek panting.

"God, what am I doing?" B whispers, not to Roach but to the ceiling. He sinks back on the bed. Roach wants to turn and look at him but stays where he is. "Sorry."

Roach wonders what B is sorry for. Grena was sorry when she stepped on a quilopea plant. Tin Star was sorry when he blew Thunder Sam's cover at the Seagrass Saloon. Being sorry wasn't enough then. Thunder Sam was angry and left Tin Star for the outlaws to find.

"I keep thinking you're—"

Roach tries to stop shaking. It might make B feel better. "I'm not human," Roach says. He knows this, no matter what he pretends. No matter how many Cosmic Granola Bars he eats.

"No."

Roach rolls and faces him. "I want to be."

B doesn't answer. Roach reaches out and tentatively places a hand on B's rising chest. B still doesn't speak. The collected energy that propelled him moments ago has disbanded and found places in his body to retreat, into nerves and vessels and fingertips.

"We can try again," Roach says. "I know how to do it, B. Have sex-for-fun."

B sighs.

"We don't have to worry about offspring."

B looks like he might smile, but then he shakes his head. "It's time for you to go."

Roach thinks about what will happen once he's off the ship. His clan will not approach him, will not speak to him. He cannot say he's sorry, because Silvers don't understand the meaning of the word. They won't be angry. They will simply forget him. He will have no one to sleep next to at night. He will be Alone—a word, an idea, that seems almost too large to grasp.

B may move too fast, grip too hard, and remind him, in certain moments, of Joele and pain. But B is not Alone. "I don't want to."

B gets up, dresses. Holds out his hand. Roach reluctantly takes it. B leads him to the door.

"I'm still losing blood," Roach tells him. Three cuts in his skin are still leaking through the bandages.

"You're well enough to run wild on my ship, you're well enough to go back where you came from. Your family's probably wondering where you are."

"They won't take me back."

"You're not staying here." B opens the door cautiously. "Come on." He pulls Roach into the hall. "Quick."

They go around the circular part of the ship to a very small hallway with a big heavy-looking red door that says Emergency Only.

Grena said once that an emergency is "*Something that is dangerous right now.*"

He is an emergency to B.

Beside the door is a box with numbers. Roach notes what numbers B presses. He hears a beep and words appear on the box: Alarm Deact. B types more numbers, then comes a click, and he pushes the door open. "Get as far from the ship as you can. I'll keep an eye out for the others."

Things are happening too fast again. In another second, Roach will step outside and the door will close and he might never see B again. He remembers what B said last night—that if creatures on Earth want something, they fight for it. He gets on his toes and kisses B.

B leans back against the wall. Roach falls against him, and B places his hand uncertainly on the back of Roach's head. Then he sends his fingers through Roach's hair, gripping, but not hurting. This kiss is smoother than their last one, not an attack. A truce. When it ends, Roach pulls away slowly. He says something in his own language, something B won't understand, smiles, and leaves through the Emergency Only door.

He goes back to Alone.

chapter
SEVEN

and now what? B punches the wall. He's finally lost his mind.

Or it's been stolen from him by this place that's not really a place; it's a negative place, a void that sucks life rather than sustains it. No wonder Silvers can't feel anger or hatred, bitterness or envy. If they could, they'd never feel anything else.

A Silver is not human. Even one that quotes paperback Westerns and speaks fluent English and claims to know how to have sex for fun is still a pitiable creature, living without color or imagination, fueled by only the most basic emotions—some cross between infant, dog, and machine.

It's wrong to—it's *sick* to—

He's looking for something else to punch, something more yielding than the wall, when Gumm comes up the stairs. B considers punching Gumm, but Gumm would find this confusing. He and the others would want an explanation. They'd see that their captain has lost his mind, and who knows? Maybe there'd be a vote of confidence, and B would be kicked off the ship, forced to stay here forever with the Silvers. He'd gradually lose whatever was still human in him, whatever the Silver Planet hasn't already stolen. Then it wouldn't matter if he fucked Silvers, because he'd be one. Empty, the color of a wound, pollinating flowers to stay busy the way people knit or put ships in bottles.

The new team would arrive, and they'd find one Silver among the others whose heart doesn't move, whose dick is always hanging out. They'd drag him aboard their ship, which would be swankier than the *Byzantine* for sure, into their sterling laboratory, cut him open, and find that he still has the lightless, trapped heart of a human.

"Cap'n, you okay?" Gumm asks.

"Never better."

"Joele wants to know if you puked in the cabinets."

"What?"

"Someone threw up in the cabinets under the sink in the kitchen. Everyone thinks it was me. But I swear it wasn't."

"Who gives a shit?"

"Joele said I should ask you. I think she was kind of joking. I mean, it's not a big deal. Just a weird place to puke." Gumm shoves his hands in his pockets. Reading social cues has never been Gumm's strong suit. Joele makes fun of him, treats him like an errand boy. Gumm doesn't quite fit in, but he looks out for everybody, and B feels some mix of pity and affection for him. "Also, there's a message for you from Hatch."

The message is that they're going home early. Three weeks from now, instead of a month. B should begin preparing the *Byzantine* for takeoff.

B is stunned. He has wanted to go home for so long. And now he can.

Except . . .

What?

"Best fucking news of my life," Joele says when B gets downstairs.

"It'll be nice to get back," Gumm agrees, as though they've simply taken a day trip to unfamiliar city.

"What about the Silver?" Grena asks. B's insides seize, because he thinks she means Roach. But she's talking about the Silver from Project HN, still strapped to the table in the lab.

"Won't last another day," Joele says. "Vir, if you want to have a look at that heart while it's still beating, hop to it."

Vir doesn't respond. She stares at the wall as if she sees something peaceful and comforting in the faux wood panels. B feels calmer just watching her. He feels like he follows her out to sea for a moment before wading back into the reality of Joele and a dying Silver and the fact that just a few days ago he was okay with the idea of performing a vivisection on a creature capable of admiring the aesthetics of soap.

"No," B says, surprising himself.

Joele's eyes narrow. "Problem, boss?"

"Vir, you said you weren't sure about the dosage for the anesthetic."
Vir nods slowly.

He's not sure where to go from here. "Let's—let's discuss that before you attempt the vivisection."

"You won't need anesthetic," Joele says. "It doesn't move anymore, no matter what I do to it."

"Vir and I will discuss it."

This will buy him some time to decide what to do. He envisions himself freeing the Silver when Joele's not looking, an activist springing animals from research facilities by night. He wonders why he doesn't just give the order now to let it go.

Because they promised NRCSE a study of a living Silver heart.

Joele taunts, "Is someone developing a soft spot for our Silver friends?"

"Enough."

"Cranky, cranky. Are you not getting enough sleep? What do you do then, all those hours you spend in your room with the door shut?"

"I'm serious."

"I'm serious, too. Where the fuck have you been?"

B forces himself to be calm. "If you have a problem, let's talk privately."

"Let's talk right here. I went diving in the lakes, I wrote reports, I hacked up Silvers. I've done my job. Why haven't you? Why the fuck haven't you been our *captain*?"

B looks around. He could be in one of those reality shows where a contestant is eliminated at the end of each episode, and the camera pans the huddle of contenders anticipating the announcement. Gumm looks worried, Vir distant. Joele's mouth is set in a hard, angry line. Grena looks resigned, as though she already knows she won't be back next week.

B looks at Joele. "I'm sorry if that's the way you feel. I've had a lot on my mind, and I didn't mean to be inaccessible, or to neglect my duties." For a second, Joele seems satisfied. Maybe she isn't trying to start trouble. Maybe she really is as confused and alone here as he is. Then her mouth curves, a private smirk, and B feels a rush of anger. "However, I am going to write you up for speaking to me that way."

"Excuse me?"

"I asked you to come to me privately if you had a problem. I won't be spoken to the way you just spoke to me."

"You're telling on me? What is this, fifth grade?"

"I'm going to report on your conduct."

Joele stares at him for a moment. B imagines a gory halo of fury and loathing around her head, decorating and intensifying her but not quite a part of her. Inside, she is hollow, lost, doesn't know what to feel. He has hurt her. And it is stupid, because NRCSE won't give a shit.

She leaves without another word.

chapter EIGHT

a n old Silver named Lons is the only one who's ever come back from the ship. He lives by one of the smaller lakes, forgotten by his clan. Roach visited him once, just after Lons returned. The Silver was thin, starving. A single plant grew by the lake's edge, but Lons didn't eat from it. Roach watched as Lons pinched the pollen grains and put them up his nose, made himself sneeze, and laughed. He did this over and over while Roach questioned him about the ship, about the humans. He never spoke.

Grena once explained to Roach's clan that humans can't learn some things about Silvers just by talking to them or observing them. On the ship, the humans can do tests that help them understand how Silvers' bodies and minds work. She never tried to persuade anyone from Roach's clan to come aboard the *Byzantine*, but Roach heard stories from others who witnessed humans carrying sleeping or wounded Silvers onto the ship. Those Silvers never came back.

When Grena stopped visiting Roach's clan, Roach felt the loss of her sharp inside him, and sometimes while the rest of his clan slept, he lay awake and whispered his favorite parts of *Tin Star and Thunder Sam* to the sky.

Grena told them four other humans were with her on the Silver Planet. Roach had caught glimpses of them when they first arrived. Even with their bodies covered, they looked different from one another. Different sizes, different shapes.

In *Tin Star*, characters have different-colored hair and eyes and skins. They are fat or thin, short or tall. Silvers vary slightly in height, but not in color, and not very much in shape. Roach was surprised to learn about breasts, because female Silvers do not have these. Grena let him touch one of hers once, briefly. It was soft and heavy. Humans' hair can grow very long and be many different colors, and they have hair on their bodies. Silvers have no hair on their bodies, unlike Thunder Sam, whose chest is covered in a coarse thatch women much admire.

Roach knew it must be the other humans, not Grena, who were damaging Silvers, because Grena was always kind. But the rest of Roach's clan made no such distinction. After Lons returned, broken, some clans decided if they were captured by humans, they would shut off. Shutting off takes a while because Silvers can hold their breaths for such a long time. Roach's clan decided not to shut off if captured, but to avoid capture in the first place. Clan members formed the No Human Contact rule. No Silver was to speak with or touch a human, or approach the ship. Even if Grena came back, they would not speak to her. They would simply pretend humans didn't exist.

Roach couldn't forget about Grena or the ship. When he learned about Lons's capture and eventual return, he went to find him. Lons had a mark on his body, a dark trail that went from under his arm to his hip. His skin was dry from being out of water so long. Roach wondered why he didn't just go into the lake, but Lons didn't really seem to see what was around him. All he did was put pollen up his nose and laugh.

Roach returned to his clan. A few days later, he went for a walk and found himself within sight of the *Byzantine*. He approached, careful not to get too close. He went to where he could see it clearly, shiny-dark against the flat black of the sky. He saw a light go on in one of the windows. He wondered what the humans did, since they didn't have a planet to tend. Without thinking, he moved closer. He had never seen an object as large as the ship. For the first time in memory, numbers failed him. He didn't know how many Silvers might fit inside. His whole clan, at least. He walked until the ship loomed over him. He traveled around it, seeing more windows on the opposite side and lights in two of them. He was about to leave when he heard a whistle.

A human female, larger than Grena, approached from the lake. Her body was encased in a sleek, gleaming suit, and she didn't wear one of the puffy shells humans used for heat. Her hair was long and black and hung in a dripping braid over her shoulder. She moved quickly.

"Hello," Roach said.

She looked surprised when he spoke. "What are you doing here?"

"I'm taking a walk."

She wrapped both hands around her braid and squeezed. Water fell onto a patch of bright ground and disappeared. "You must be one of Grena's."

"Is Grena here?"

The large female glanced at the ship. "What do you want with her?"

"I want to talk to her. Please," he added.

"What's wrong with talking to me?"

"It isn't wrong."

"Of course it isn't. You and I could have a nice conversation. You speak good English."

"Thank you." Something was happening with Roach's heart. It was brighter than usual, and slid back and forth across his chest quickly before diving behind his ribs. He was breaking the No Human Contact rule. He thought about the stories of dead Silvers. Silvers losing blood. Silvers going into the ship and never coming out.

"Grena's proud of the ones she taught," the female said. "She says you're really smart. Are you smart?"

"I think so."

"Says you're good with numbers—counting. You can count anything."

"Yes."

"How many hairs in my eyebrows?"

Roach moved closer and looked at her face. For a second, he was distracted by her eyes, which were large and dark. They shivered as they followed his movements. He focused on her eyebrows. He counted the hairs, first in the left eyebrow, then in the right. "One thousand eight hundred and eighty-four," he said.

"I'll have to take your word for it. Next question: What's this called?" She raised one foot and slapped her black, sturdy footwear.

"Shoe," said Roach.

"Close," said the female. "A boot. A kind of shoe. You are smart."

Roach was pleased she thought so.

"Third question: Are you afraid of me?"

Roach shook his head. He didn't think he was, even though his heart wouldn't come out from behind his ribs. This female wasn't so different from Grena. She wanted to ask questions. She was pleased that he spoke good English.

"No."

The female shook her head too and made a noise with her tongue. "Maybe you're not as smart as I thought." She moved quickly, caught Roach's wrist, squeezed. Her face was close to Roach's. "Humans are monsters. You know what I mean by that?"

"No."

She let go of his wrist and struck him across the face. He had never hurt before.

He moved his hand to touch the pain, but couldn't quite find it. It splintered from its source and fragments fell against other nerves until his whole face throbbed.

"That's what I mean."

He didn't want to be near her anymore and turned to run. She hit him on the other side of the face. He fell.

She held up her foot. "What's this?" she asked.

"Boot," Roach replied automatically, because he knew now.

"That's right," she said. The boot crashed into his heart's hiding place, behind his ribs.

When he woke, the female was gone and the ship rose above him, seeming almost friendly, watchful, two of its windows alight, like eyes. He didn't want to stay here. The female might find him again, but it hurt too much to move. If he could get to the pile of nearby rocks, it would be harder for humans to see him.

He used his arms to pull himself toward the rocks, sharp bits of the ground digging into his palms and stomach. He glanced behind him and saw he was leaving a trail of red on the bright ground. His skin was open and cold leaped right in. He reached the rocks and put his head against one of the stones. His head was the only part of him that felt warm. The rest of him shook.

He tried to inspect his damaged places, but seeing made the pain worse. He closed his eyes. Now his clan would know that he'd had contact with humans.

There is no Silver word for "alone." Just words for "one" and "one at a time," because Silvers are never alone. A Silver might be the only one in a particular area, but others are always nearby. Silvers' names are numbers indicating birth order. When a Silver dies, the numbers shift down, and each subsequent Silver's name changes.

This shift happens also now when a Silver is forgotten.

Roach would not have a name anymore. He would not be counted. He felt himself wanting to sleep again and hoped he was hidden. He couldn't sleep. His teeth clattered against each other, and sharp pain poked him every few seconds. He heard footsteps, human voices. One voice was Grena's. He wanted to get to her. But his body wouldn't move. He drifted off, and when he woke the next time, footsteps were closer, approaching.

Roach tears off his bandages and leaves them on the ground as he walks away from the *Byzantine*. He heads for the small lake where Lons lives. *Lons*—one hundred and thirteen. The last name he had before he was forgotten.

Lons is still there.

He lies on his back, unmoving, and his ribs look like the row of coat hangers in B's closet. His skin is cracked in places where it has become too dry. When Roach leans over him, Lons's eyes go right through Roach to find the sky.

"Lons." Roach watches closely until he sees Lons draw a small breath that barely fills his lungs. Roach shakes him. "Lons, get up."

Lons's eyes find Roach's and he grins, holding up a hand. His fingertips are yellow with pollen stains. Roach looks for the quilopea plant, but it is torn and sagging, its two weak blooms staring down in dismay at the scraps of their leaves the way Roach looked at his own torn body after Joele left him.

"Lons, did you kill the plant?"

Lons touches Roach's cheek with one yellow-tipped finger.

"You're dry. You need to go into the lake."

But Lons won't move.

Roach goes to the water and scoops some in his hands.

He brings it back and lets it fall on a cracked spot on Lons's stomach. Lons groans. "I'm going to take care of you," Roach says. "When you're better, we'll live here, just us two. Our own clan."

The water seems to help a little. Dried blood slides away, and the wet skin shines. Roach retrieves more water.

"I was on the ship," he tells Lons as he works. "Like you."

Lons murmurs, and Roach looks at him.

"One of them hurt me, but another helped me get better."

Lons's eyes wander again.

Roach keeps talking, hoping the sound of his voice will help Lons focus. "The two of us, we could live on our own. We'll have to move somewhere with more plants." He realizes that he is speaking in English, and repeats the words in his own language.

Lons sneezes and laughs. Ribs shake. Skin cracks and oozes. Roach looks away.

"You're losing blood." Roach remembers something. "Stay right here."

He retraces his earlier steps and finds his bandages lying on the ground. He stares for a moment at the *Byzantine* in the distance. He picks the bandages up and hurries back to Lons.

"Here. These will help." He pulls a couple of battered leaves from the quilopea plant and puts them over the cracked place on Lons's skin. Then he puts the bandages on top. Lons holds very still. The next time he laughs, it's soft, mostly a smile. "You're all right," Roach says. It's what B said to him, even though Roach didn't feel all right.

Roach hopes that taking care of Lons will help keep him from thinking about B, but it isn't working. B is always in his mind. Roach didn't do what B wanted, and B sent him away. Even if he'd said sorry, B might still have made him go. Sorry only works sometimes. You have to mean it. Maybe B doesn't want him now at all. Maybe Roach had only one chance, and he ruined it.

He thinks he knows now what sorry feels like.

He keeps one hand on Lons's bandages so they don't slide off when Lons laughs, and he tries to think what to do. He could stay here with Lons. Lons needs help. Roach could finally rescue somebody, which he wants very much to do. But Roach also wants to go back to the ship and find B again. This time, he'll be different. He'll be what B wants.

He smiles, remembering B's look of surprise when Roach kissed him. B didn't expect Roach to fight for what he wanted. You can be *like* humans without being human, he thinks. Roach can learn to be all the best things about a human and still be a Silver. He can make B want him without losing himself.

Roach thinks the somebody he would most like to rescue is B. He wonders if B has ever been in danger. B is smart and very strong, but B can't know everything. He can't always know when something is dangerous *right now*. And some things even humans with large muscles can't do.

Maybe B doesn't know how to swim. Humans can't hold their breaths very long. If B fell into a lake, Roach could swim out and get him and pull him back to shore. If B was scared after that, Roach could say, "You're all right." B might want him then, because when B started helping Roach, Roach started wanting B.

"I owe you a great debt," Thunder Sam tells Tin Star, after Tin Star puts a bullet in the greedy saloon owner who's about to stab Thunder Sam in the back. It is the first time Sam hasn't seen danger coming, and if it weren't for Tin Star, Sam would be dead. Later, when Sam rescues Tin Star from the outlaws, he says, *"Now we're square."* They are friends after they're square. They stop bickering, and Thunder Sam no longer tells Tin Star to *"Run on home, kid"* because he doesn't want him around.

B saved Roach from losing too much blood, and now Roach owes him a great debt. The only way for them to be square is for Roach to rescue B.

Lons coughs. His eyes roam, and he doesn't laugh anymore. He struggles against Roach's hand. Lons will not last long without eating or going into the lake. Roach pulls a single, shriveled fruit from the quilopea plant and brings it to Lons. "Eat this," he instructs. Lons pinches it between his thumb and forefinger and keeps squeezing until the juicy center oozes out and falls with a *plat-plat* on the ground. Lons is left with the drooling skin, which he flings aside.

"I'll find you better food," Roach promises. "Stay right here."

He leaves and gathers the best quilopea he can find. As he searches, he forms a plan that, if it works, would help both him and Lons.

He sees a member of his clan by one of the lakes and calls a greeting, but she doesn't answer. He senses nothing like human anger or judgment in the rejection, just that Roach doesn't exist at all. He takes the quilopea back to Lons, who refuses to eat.

"It'll be okay," Roach tells him. "I have a plan. I'll help you get better."

Lons doesn't seem to want to get better. Lons does not seem to want anything, except yellow fingers.

chapter NINE

b finds Grena in the kitchen. He tosses *Tin Star and Thunder Sam* onto the table. Some foolish part of him doesn't want to let it go. "Thanks for letting me borrow that," he says. "I wondered what kind of bedtime story aliens like."

"It was my nephew's." Grena picks up the book. "He's convinced we'll all be time-traveling soon, and he wants to go back to the Old West."

B grunts. "Don't know where I'd go." He nods at the book. "Did they like it?"

"Most of them. Some were bored or hadn't learned enough English to follow along. One really loved it."

"Yeah?"

"Mm-hm. Younger male. Practically memorized it as I was reading. It'd take us an hour to get through a chapter, I spent so much time answering his questions. But he remembered everything I told him."

"That's funny."

"Must be what it's like to have kids. Always asking 'why?'"

Does Grena think about kids? B has never asked.

"What was its name?" B asks, surprising himself with the question. He's already decided it doesn't matter. Roach is gone, so what does it matter what his real name is?

"Imms," Grena says. "When I knew him. Four Hundred and Seventy-Two."

"Huh?"

"Their names are numbers. Their birth order. You remember? It was in one of my early reports."

"I forgot."

"When a Silver dies, the numbers shift down, and the names change. That Silver was called Imms—four hundred and seventy-two. I guess that's changed since I was there." Her voice is steady, but B sees an old pain nudge her. "And there's more to the name. It's longer. He just went by Imms, though."

Imms. That's his name. A number. How depressing.

B clears his throat. "Do you ever miss them?"

Grena looks at him as though his expression might influence how she answers. He wonders if she's remembering his pissing match with Joele, if she thinks less of him or is wary of provoking him. "Sometimes."

"Do they still talk to you?"

She shakes her head. "I haven't been out there much. Mostly working inside."

"Right." The Silver in the lab is still alive. Joele's been withholding water from it, watching its skin parch and crack. B keeps hoping it will die and absolve him of the decision to either let it go or let Vir cut it open while it's still breathing.

He grabs a can of soda and sits at the table. If there's anyone he can talk to about this, it's Grena. She's kind when she can afford to be, brutal when necessary. "Do you ever worry about what we're doing?" He curses himself silently. He sounds weak, uncertain, and not at all like a leader.

She's quiet for a moment. "You've always said, 'They're not us.'"

"They're not."

"No," she agrees. "But I don't think you ever really meant for us to harm them. Did you?"

"How should I know? One day you and Vir are living with them, the next, Joele's got one aboard the ship, saying it's half-dead already so why don't we finish the job." He sounds like he wants absolution, validation. He sounds like the self-styled victim of others' incompetence. He takes a deep breath. He wants to tell Grena the truth.

I hated them. From the moment we saw them. Their eyes gave me nightmares, and they just seemed so stupid to trust us like they did. They don't even understand how empty their lives are, their world is. So yeah,

I'll hit them if there's a chance it'll open their eyes. I'll cut into them and search for what's missing. I'll let one worm its way into my idiot heart until I start to wonder if maybe it has more, feels more, understands more than I do.

Maybe there's nothing missing at all.

"Do you think of them as human?" he asks. The all-important question. One they asked each other during the early days. *What are they? Are they human? Do they have rights? Are they ours—our treasure, our subjects, our friends or enemies . . . Or are they us?*

"I think they're similar to us in many ways. Not just in appearance."

"How do we know if what we're doing hurts or frightens them if they don't protest? If they don't fight back?"

"Do you feel guilty?"

B doesn't let himself hesitate. "No. But it's an interesting ethical dilemma."

Grena nods. "But remember, NRCSE approved Project HN. You're not the only one who thinks it might be worth sacrificing ethics for knowledge."

"Who says that's what I think?"

B sees the hard edge to Grena's kindness. Her words have desire beneath them, longing. Until now, B thought the Silver Planet had brought out the scientist in each of them, the cool, rational, impartial researcher who had no use for desire, doubt, or fantasy. But it is just the opposite. This place brings out what is truly human in each of them: a craving for violence, for the unexpected. A need to trespass inside strange bodies and on new terrain.

Nothing about respecting boundaries is human, even boundaries as elemental as skin. It *is* human to take, to need, and to desire. To form alliances when necessary and to break those unions as soon as they cease to be of use. A word as small and easily blown apart as *don't* shouldn't be a puzzle or a barrier.

"Don't," Roach had said, rolling out from under B. And B hadn't.

Suddenly, B cannot look at Grena.

He stands up, pushes his chair in. "I don't know how you do it. Go from reading to them to watching them writhe on the table without batting an eye. At least I never pretended to like them."

"I follow orders."

B has to go, or he'll shake her until he hears the satisfying clatter of her teeth. But go where? Back to his room, where a sleeping bag is still crammed under his bed and the first aid kit sits beside his desk? Outside, where he can scream and curse and nothing will change?

"The Silver in the lab," he says. "Does it know English?"

"No."

"I want to ask it some questions."

"I can try to translate your questions, if you want. But I don't think it can say much anyway. It's gone."

"I don't want anyone there. Not you. Not Joele. I want everyone to stay out of the lab. I want to see it alone. You hear me?"

"I hear you, Captain," Grena says.

"Except Vir. I want Vir there."

Vir doesn't want to do it. B sees in her eyes, in her hand as she picks up the scalpel how much she hates it, hates him. But she doesn't refuse. She anesthetizes the Silver, then opens the chest cavity.

The heart is off. Blue-gray like the creature's skin, the organ hides behind the liver, its sides moving softly in and out like a frightened animal. B asks if there's a way to make the heart expose itself. Vir touches the creature's skin, just above the liver, flushing the heart from its cover. It drifts down toward the Silver's stomach. As it travels, B sees it attach briefly to a mass of unanchored blood vessels, pumping them full, then releasing them. It slips under the intestines and disappears. He asks Vir to make another cut.

They follow the heart together—Vir dividing the skin in different places, drawing it away from each incision like curtains. The creature dies quickly, and the heart floats up to its final resting spot just left of the sternum. Dead, the organ is black and heavy-looking. As B stares at it, he reminds himself that this is not what loves. Only the mind can assign value to another person, can create the illusion that something besides alone exists. If that illusion is shared, it becomes love.

If a brain is incomplete, if it cannot experience the full spectrum of emotion and desire, then it cannot maintain its share of the illusion. Therefore it is impossible to love something subhuman.

Unless you are subhuman yourself.

He doesn't want to look at that more dangerous organ, the brain. He concentrates on the limp pile of dark blood vessels draped over the stomach. He imagines that when the body is alive, these vessels wave like the tentacles of an anemone, grab the heart as it floats by, and let go once the heart has filled them.

Latching on, holding fast, letting go. This is how the heart moves.

chapter
TEN

Roach can get Lons to eat a little quilopea by mashing it up and putting it in his mouth, though Lons often spits it back up. Roach drags him down to the lake and makes him lie in the shallow water until the splits in his skin smooth out. What Lons really needs to do is go underwater and stay there for a long time. But he won't.

Roach is ready to put his plan in motion. The idea seemed wonderful at first, though Roach worries now that it is not such a good idea. He thought maybe B could heal Lons. B has dried quilopea, medicine that goes on torn skin, and a shower. B knows how to help Silvers. But asking B to help Lons will not make Roach and B square. In fact, it will probably mean Roach owes B another great debt.

If B rescues Lons, maybe Roach can help with that. They'll rescue Lons together. At the very least, he'll be close to B and can watch for danger B doesn't see.

"I have to go for a little while," Roach tells Lons. "But I'll come back. I promise."

No answer.

"I'm going to get you help." He starts to walk away, but Lons grabs his wrist. Lons's eyes no longer wander but focus on Roach's. They are anxious and do more to pull Roach back than the hand around his wrist.

"I'll be back," Roach repeats. Lons shakes his head.

Roach sits beside him. "They have a Silver. In the lab." Lons looks at him, waits.

"They had another one, too, but she shut off. You're the only one they ever let go. Besides me."

Lons nods.

"Tell me why," Roach says. Lons doesn't.

"I'm going to find the one who helped me. He'll help you."

Lons's eyes are so different from B's, almost colorless, just a thin wire of dark creating a fragmented band around the pupils. B's eyes have circles of color around black centers—greenish-blue, like quilopea leaves. Lons gives no indication that he disapproves of Roach's plan. But then, Lons is a Silver, and Silvers don't disapprove. Only humans do that. But Lons is waiting for something. Roach thinks he knows what it is.

"I'll try to—I will—get the other off the ship. I'll rescue him."

Lons still waits. Roach thinks maybe he'll always be waiting. Maybe he doesn't really understand anything at all. But then Lons reaches up and points to Roach with one finger. Touches his nose. Roach shakes his head, and Lons's hand falls to the ground.

"I'm not afraid," Roach says. "Of humans, or their ship, or anything. They're just scared. More scared than us. So if you're worried for me, don't be. I know what I'm doing."

A thin smile opens on Lons's face, like a crack in too-dry skin.

Roach hides behind the rocks where B found him and watches the ship for a long time. No humans go in or come out. Finally he takes a deep breath and runs until he's under the smooth curve of the *Byzantine*. He finds the Emergency Only door. He sees a box with numbers on this side of the door, just like the one on the inside. Roach remembers the numbers B pushed—B's fingers were fast, but Roach's eyes are faster. The box reads *Alarm Act*, which Roach thinks is what it read before B opened the door. He presses the numbers, and there is a *click*. He pulls the heavy door open.

The ship screams. One blaring, horrible sound repeated over and over. Roach claps his hands over his ears and steps inside. The door shuts behind him, and between the ship's wails he hears footsteps coming up the stairs. He runs down the hall to B's room, which is empty and dark. He enters and sits on the floor where he used to sleep. The noise stops, but he can still feel it in his body. He hears voices,

B's and another man's, but he can't tell what they're saying. Eventually the voices get farther away.

He doesn't know how long he sits in the dark before footsteps approach and stop outside the door. He wonders if he should hide, in case it's not B. He climbs into the bed and buries himself under the blankets. The door opens, and B enters. Roach knows it's him by his boots against the floor, by his smell. B turns on the light and tosses something onto the bed. It's not heavy, but it hits Roach's shoulder and Roach has to hold back a sound of surprise.

B sits at his desk, and for a while the only the sound is his breathing. He opens one of the desk drawers. Roach carefully moves a section of blanket so he can watch. B pulls out a bottle of brownish liquid and a small glass, pours some of the liquid into the glass, and drinks it in two gulps. He leans back in his chair, stares at the ceiling.

Now might be a good time to let B know he's here, but Roach can't move. B has taken the floppy shell off—perhaps that's what he threw on the bed—and his arms are bare. They're pale, furrowed, thick, and Roach remembers them around him. He isn't afraid. He wishes this quiet moment would last longer than moments are meant to.

B refills his glass and drinks. Roach lifts the blankets off his head. B is facing away and doesn't see him. "B," he whispers. B doesn't hear and sets the glass on the desk, hard. "B," he says, louder.

B is on his feet in an instant.

Roach sits up. "It's me."

"You." B says it so loudly, Roach jumps. For just a second B doesn't seem to know who Roach is, or knows but can't believe it. "What the fuck are you doing here?"

"I came—"

"That was you? The emergency door?"

"I wanted—I need to ask you—"

"You can't be here!" B's voice is too loud.

"Joele might hear you," Roach warns.

"You think I give a fuck what she hears, what she does?" B stops at the edge of the bed, leans forward. "You're the one who's fucked if she hears."

Roach winces at the strange, sweet smell on B's breath. He thinks it might be the Devil's brew, which Thunder Sam used to hit pretty hard before Tin Star emptied his bottles onto the dusty earth. "I need your help."

B says nothing, so Roach clears his throat and continues. "My friend is hurt. Like I was."

"So?"

"I thought maybe you could help him."

"You thought wrong, pardner. I'm not running a fucking free clinic. I did you a favor. Now I've moved on. I do not want to see you again. Got it?"

Roach has a feeling that is almost like being hit, except the pain is not in his body. He doesn't want to tell B he's "got it," because that would be giving up. And something in B doesn't mean what he's saying. Roach feels hesitation in the way B holds his body, an uncertainty that roughens his voice.

"You don't hate me," Roach says. He wants B to know he knows this.

"Who said anything about hating you? I said I don't want to see you again."

"If you don't hate me, then why won't you help me?"

"Not hating you and jonesing to stitch up your friend aren't the same thing."

"He won't be any trouble."

"Yeah? He won't piss in my sleeping bags or wander through my ship when I've told him to stay put? Or quote that *abominable* book?"

The worse B is, the less Roach feels the sting of it. B is all show, like Roach was when he spat at B that first night. Roach sits up straight and looks right at him. "No. And he won't stay with you when you don't want to be alone, or tell you about how Silvers shut off. And he won't kiss you or have sex-for-fun. 'He ain't me—and a good thing too, 'cause if there was more than one of me, you couldn't rightly call me all you got.' That's a quote from that *abdominal* book."

B leans forward. "First, it's *abominable*. Second, stop calling it sex-for-fun. It's called fucking. Third, no, he's not you. And that's why I don't want him here."

"Just me?" Roach's lips are close to B's.

"We can try this again, as long as you understand that you're not 'all I got,' not by a long shot. You're not going to stay on the ship, and we're not riding off into the sunset together. Okay?"

"Okay," Roach says.

B squeezes Roach's face between his hands. "Is this what you *want*? Tell me the truth."

"Yes," Roach says.

"You afraid?"

"No."

B tightens his grip. "Liar. Are you afraid?"

"A little."

"Good." B leans forward and kisses Roach, more gently than Roach expects. "Me too."

Roach was never sure if B was afraid of anything. But when B kisses him again, he feels uncertainty, even in those hard muscles. Fear that—what? That what they do will change them? Or that they'll still be the same at the end of it?

Their fear meets in the scuffling of bones and gets shuffled with other feelings, surfacing only occasionally. Roach tastes unfamiliar feelings on B, and welcomes them inside himself, but they never truly become part of him. B takes them back when their bodies separate, and lies with them curled in his arms, falls asleep with them tucked under his chin. Roach is left to look at the ceiling and feel a channel of coldness between himself and B. He puts his hand in the channel. B's heat is so close. He catches it on his fingertips. He is awake all night, catching it and letting it go.

"What about your friend?" B asks the next morning as he pulls on his sweatjack.

"Hm?"

"The one who's hurt. Or did you make that up?"

"Lons."

"Shouldn't you go help him?"

"I can't," Roach says. It's true. He can do nothing for Lons if Lons won't eat, won't go into the water. Roach cannot rescue him.

"But you thought I could?"

"I put bandages on him."

B finishes lacing his boot and lets his foot drop to the floor. "You're breaking my heart."

"Why?" Roach is alarmed. He's heard this phrase before. Grena explained it doesn't really mean that the heart isn't whole. But Roach still doesn't want that image.

"I don't know." B shakes his head. "You're something different, that's for sure." He ties his other boot. "Did he seem any better with the bandages?"

"I don't think so. I don't think he can get better."

"So you're just going to let him die?"

B is not angry. But not happy either. He sounds almost like he's making a joke, but his voice is too rough for joking. "He might die," Roach says, wondering why the thought makes him uncomfortable. All Silvers die. No need to want them not to, no need to try to stop them.

"Then what? You bury him?"

"Put him in the water."

B stands. "I'll give you some medicine and some clean bandages. See if it helps. But I don't want any Silvers on the ship."

"What about me? Can I come back?"

"No."

Roach feels emptiness rushing toward him. "But—"

"I'll meet you outside by those rocks where I found you." B grabs the white box from under the desk, opens it, and pulls out a roll of clean bandages and a tube of the greasy stuff that made Roach's torn places hurt less. "Flush out any open wounds with water. Apply the ointment. Then bandage. All right?"

Roach takes the tube and the bandages.

"How'd he get hurt?" B asks.

"He did it to himself, mostly." The words stick for a second, then tumble out. "He was on your ship. He came back, but now he won't talk or eat, and he's drying out."

B looks for a moment as though something has left him, as though his mind has gone somewhere without his body. "I'll make sure the coast is clear." At the door, he turns suddenly. "*Don't* go anywhere."

"I won't."

"I mean it, pardner."

"I'll stay right here."

B doesn't leave. He stands with his back to the door. "Your name's Imms. Or it was when you met Grena. Right?"

"A long time ago."

"What is it now?"

"I don't have a name. I'm not counted anymore."

B hesitates. "May I call you Imms?"

Roach isn't sure what to say. It's not his name, was not even his most recent name. But he thinks of Lons, and how Lons will always be Lons to Roach, even though Lons is no longer counted by the other Silvers. Imms is who Roach was when he was happiest, when humans weren't dangerous, when Grena read to them, when the idea of Earth was so wonderful he couldn't sleep night after night, thinking about it. What is the harm in using the name now?

"Yes," he says finally. "But I like Roach."

"Roach sometimes. As a nickname."

B is taking this name, Imms, and deciding it is what he wants Roach to be. He has no real understanding of how important the counting is. You cannot alter numbers the way you can words, or opinions. If you are zero, you cannot make yourself count again.

Imms nods slowly. "Roach is ours," he says. "But Imms is mine."

"Huh?"

He repeats what he's said in the Silver language, a surefire way to lose B's interest.

Sure enough, B shakes his head. "Whatever you say." He opens the door.

chapter
ELEVEN

Imms spends days with Lons, using the supplies B gave him to try to heal the old Silver. Lons holds still as Imms fills the cracks in his skin with ointment, lets Imms wind bandages around him. A bit of a smile is always on his face, and Imms wonders if Lons has secrets, which is impossible. Secrets are only for humans.

But this isn't true. Imms has secrets. He has the secret of what he did with B, and he has a secret he's been keeping since before the humans arrived. Something he wants to show B soon.

He meets B each night by the rocks where B first discovered him. The rocks are good cover. Some nights B is distracted and starts at every sound. He touches Imms quickly, frantically, or hardly at all. Other nights B is flooded with feeling Imms can't access. He seems like he wants to draw blood, and Imms goes quiet and still under the weight of that urge. On the best nights, B is relaxed, gentle. His strength is sheltering, not violent. He laughs. Talks to Imms, holds him afterward.

"I saw the pictures," Imms says one night. "In the black box, on the ship."

B props himself on one elbow. "Yeah?"

"Too many colors."

"You'd like Earth."

"Why?"

"Well, it's bigger than the Silver Planet, for one thing."

"I know."

"And there's lots of variety to the land. So if you like sand, you can live where there's sand. If you like mud, there's mud. If you like to be warm, you can live where the sun shines all the time. If you like cold—"

"I like cold."

Imms is lying. He doesn't like cold, not anymore. He used to not even know that he was cold. Then he lost blood. Now, being with B each night, it's worse. He's so warm when he's lying beside B that when B is gone, the cold grows sharp teeth. This sort of contrast has led him to begin to understand anger, simply by lying next to B and feeling the difference between B angry and B not.

"There's a lot to do, too. More stuff than you can imagine. You'd never get bored."

"You don't like it here."

B looks at the sky. "I don't mind it."

"You're lying."

"I wanted to get away from Earth."

"Why?"

"I wasn't having much fun there."

"You said it's never boring."

"That doesn't mean it's always fun."

Imms shifts, turning his face closer to B. "There's lots to do here too. Grena says on Earth everything takes care of itself. But here, we help the plants fuck."

B laughs so hard he coughs. "Plants don't fuck."

"You said to stop calling it sex-for-fun. And breeding."

"Let's get this straight. Breeding is what animals do. With humans, it's just called sex, not sex for fun. Or it's fucking. Or making love."

"Making love?"

"Yeah. That's the nice thing to call it."

"Why don't you call it the nice thing?"

"I'm not much of a romantic."

"Not like George Michael."

"Beg your pardon?"

"Grena sang us the song 'Careless Whisper.' She says it's very romantic."

B snorts. "With all due respect to Grena, she wouldn't know romance if it smacked her upside the head with a box of chocolates and shoved a dozen roses up her ass."

Imms can't imagine why either of these things would ever happen. "Why not?"

"Grena's relationship is with her work. I don't think she leaves herself a lot of time for romance."

"What about Joele?"

"Joele, believe it or not, has been engaged for something like eight years. Gumm was married, but he's divorced. I don't know about Vir."

"Were you in love with someone back home?"

"For a long time. But not anymore."

"Why did you stop?"

"I didn't stop. I mean, not just me. We stopped."

"Why?"

"I don't know. There's not just one reason."

"Oh." Imms tries to count heartbeats for a while, but he can't concentrate. "When do you go home?"

"Soon."

"Will you ever come back?"

"Nope." B is trying to sound like he doesn't feel anything, but his muscles get stiff the way they do when he's angry.

"Will Joele come back?"

"I don't know. More humans'll come, that's for sure."

"Nice humans?"

"They'll probably be a little nice, and a little mean."

"Like you?"

B moves his arm and looks down at Imms, as though Imms is something he's just stumbled upon. "You think I'm both?"

"Uh-huh."

B sits up and rests his back against a tall rock. He's silent for a long while. Imms thinks he'll leave. It's past the time he usually goes back to the ship. "You ever afraid of me?"

"No."

"I don't want you to be afraid of me." B slings an arm around Imms's shoulders, like Thunder Sam sometimes does with Tin Star. Pals, pardners.

Imms leans into him. "I'm not."

"I've done some shitty things to your people."

Imms doesn't answer. It's true.

"But I'm not ever going to hurt you," B says. "Okay?"

"Okay."

"I'm not gonna let anyone else hurt you, either."

"Not Joele?"

B looks at him. Gives his neck a brief squeeze. "Tell me exactly what she did to you."

"It doesn't matter." Imms is suddenly uneasy. He wants that look out of B's eyes.

"It does. She's under my command. I told my team they weren't to harm any more Silvers. She didn't listen."

"I didn't listen either. To my clan. I came too close to the ship. I saw her, and she asked what I was doing. I said walking. She thought it was funny that I spoke English. She said I must be one of Grena's. I asked if she knew Grena. She said yes, and she grabbed my wrist. She asked if I was afraid. I said no."

B nods.

"She said I should be. She said humans were monsters. I asked her what that meant. Then she hit me here." He touches his cheek. "I tried to run away, but she was holding me. She hit me again, and I fell. She used her shoe, until I stopped trying to get up. She asked if I hated her because she was hurting me. I couldn't talk. She hit me with her belt until I—slept?" That doesn't seem right. Sleep is a good thing.

"Passed out," B says.

"I didn't care, though," Imms says, trying to sound like Tin Star after his horse gets snakebit and they have to shoot it. When he tells Thunder Sam it was just a dumb old horse, anyway. "I didn't cry, not like humans do when they get hurt. She kept saying, 'Why don't you yell?' But I didn't yell."

B still doesn't speak.

"B? Could I come in with you tonight? I'll sleep on the floor. I thought I wouldn't miss the ship, but I do."

B shakes his head, stands up. "No. You've got your world, I've got mine. A big metal hunk of it, anyway. You sleep well."

Imms knows he won't. Isn't sure why.

"Can I show you something?" he asks, desperate to delay B.

"What sort of something?"

"I can't tell. You have to see."

B looks automatically at the hulking shadow of the *Byzantine*, checking to make sure none of his team is outside. "How far away is it?"

"Not far."

Twenty minutes later, B is grumbling. "What the hell could I want to see all the way out here?" he demands. "What if they need me for something on the ship? It'll take us another goddamn half hour to get back."

Imms is slightly anxious, but decides B doesn't *really* sound angry. "It's a good surprise. I think."

"You *think*."

They come to a shallow basin, and Imms leads B down into it, toward a cluster of rocks along one wall. Part of the basin is filled with water, stagnant and tarnished-looking. When they reach the rock cluster, Imms goes to work, moving one, then another. B steps in to help. As they move the fourth stone, a slab of dirty steel is exposed, the letters *hroug* visible through the grime.

"Jesus," B says.

"It's yours, isn't it?" Imms can barely contain his excitement. "Grena said you sent something here a long time ago, like your ship, but much smaller. She asked if any of us saw it."

"And you said?"

Imms looks at B, wishing B were happier to see his small ship. He's not sure why he kept it a secret from the humans, from the other Silvers. When he found it, he wanted to keep it safe. Once it was safe, he wanted to visit it. And once he started visiting it, he didn't want anyone else to visit it. "I didn't say anything. I wanted to, but I couldn't."

"What do you mean, you couldn't?"

"I like it." Imms touches the metal.

"Do you know what it is?"

Imms turns back to him. "It takes pictures."

"Did." B uncovers more of the mangled machine.

"I didn't mean to shut it off. It was following me, and it fell off the rocks. It seemed hurt, so I thought it might help to put it in the water."

B shakes his head. "The worst thing you could have done." But he's almost smiling. "So you touched this thing, without knowing what it was, without knowing what it might—" He stops, looks at Imms. "Of course you did." He brushes some of the dust from the metal.

"What is that word?"

"*Breakthrough*. That's this machine's name."

"It's not alive," Imms says. It's almost a question, but he knows the answer.

B shakes his head. "No."

"It moves."

"We made it do that."

Imms doesn't want to know how. It is a strange idea that humans can make something move that isn't alive.

"Do you have any idea how many millions of dollars went into this?"

"How many?" Imms asks.

"I don't know. A lot. This thing was supposed to take pictures of everything on the planet, so we would know what to expect before we got here."

"Do you want it back?"

B stares at the glittering of white dust on rusted metal.

"You keep it. Something to remember me by."

"I didn't show any of the others."

"Quite the rogue, aren't you?"

"The what?"

B looks around at the basin. "You go it alone now, huh?"

"I have Lons."

"Who?"

"He's sick."

"Right, the one you told me about. That's it?"

Imms nods.

B scratches his head. "Your clan won't take you back because—because you've had contact with me?"

"And Joele."

"I don't get it. You guys can't get angry. So why do they—I mean, why wouldn't they let you back in, unless they're pissed at you?"

"They're not mad. This is just the way it has to be."

"Well, I don't see why." B looks at the shallow pond again. "You don't drink from there, do you? It looks filthy."

"No."

B stands. "Good thing there's no predators around. I'd have to worry about you getting eaten."

Imms tilts his head. Why would B worry about him? "Predators. Like wildcats?"

"Mm-hm. Or grizzlies. Wolves."

"I don't know grizzlies."

"Bears."

"I'd go into the ground," Imms says. "I'd be safe."

"What if the grizzly dug you out, like I did?"

"I'd go deeper." Imms has something else he can show B. "I can do that. The others can only go into the beginning of the ground. But I keep going."

"What do you mean?"

"Watch." Imms lies on the ground. He sinks into the surface after a moment, and the bright ground covers him like frost. Imms knows B will have to concentrate to keep track of Imms's outline. Slowly the contours of Imms's body will disappear, sucking down a small funnel of pebbles and dust. Imms lets this happen, imagining B can hear the scrape and crackle of Imms inside the ground. Imms holds perfectly still. He hears the muffled sound of B's voice and wonders what B is saying. He goes deeper, so deep he can't hear B. This part of the ground is soft, cool. Dark. It's harder to fit himself to it, the way he fits with the surface. But he manages. He closes his eyes.

And goes deeper.

He's not afraid, but he knows it's time to stop. It's too dark here, too easy to lose direction. So he works his way up and emerges, dusty and grinning. B's expression is one Imms has seen before—one he wants to learn. It is hard, still, furrowed, and afraid.

B is afraid. This half registers with Imms before his excitement takes over. "That's as deep as I've ever gone," he announces.

"Didn't think you were coming back up."

An idea occurs to Imms. "Want to try?"

"Me?" B takes a step back, as though the question itself might be dangerous. "I can't do that."

"If I'm holding on to you, it might work. I can take things into the ground with me—quilopea, and a snake, once."

"Thanks but no thanks, pardner. I've got to get back."

"Please." Imms suddenly can't think of anything he'd like better than to show B what being inside the ground is like.

"It won't work. And what the hell would I want to do it for? I'd get a lungful of dust."

"You can hold your breath. We'll just be there a few seconds."

B stares at the ground. When he finally looks at Imms, Imms tries to make his face show how much he wants this.

B sighs, sinks to his knees, and lies down beside Imms. For a second, Imms is afraid to touch B. What if this does hurt him? It won't. Imms is sure of this. B will be a part of Imms under the ground, and this will protect him.

They put their arms around each other the way they do each night; pebbles dig into their sides as they shift, trying to get comfortable.

"Ready?" Imms says the numbers three, two, and one in his own language. He starts to sink. B remains on the surface. Imms stops.

"I told you it wouldn't work." B twists to get away.

"You don't want to go under, so you're not going under."

"You're right, I don't want to."

"You have to want to. Think about what you'll look like. You'll look like the ground."

B takes a deep breath. Imms hopes he is imagining himself vanishing. B lets out a sound of surprise when his body sinks an inch or so into the earth. He immediately resists, wrests free of Imms's grip, and gets to his feet.

"Shit."

"You almost did it," Imms says, not wanting B to give up now.

B is breathing hard. "I've had enough. Let's get back."

Imms makes himself frown. "I don't remember how to get back to the ship from here."

"You're not fucking serious."

"I'm really sorry."

Imms tries to look frightened. B's eyes are so wide, so furious. But then Imms's face contorts, his shoulders shake, and suddenly he snorts so hard he falls forward onto the ground, laughing. "I'm kidding!" he shouts gleefully.

B kicks some dust onto him. "You're a shit, you know." He kicks more dust, and through it, Imms sees he's grinning.

Imms spits, and while he's trying to get the dust off his tongue, B tackles him and pins him to the ground. "How do you like that?"

B asks. Imms, still laughing, tries to catch his breath. "Wipe that smile off your face, or I'll wipe it off for you." Imms starts to sink into the ground. "Oh no you don't." B grabs his wrists. "No more of that." He stands, hauling Imms with him. Imms falls forward, their heads bump, and their mouths find one another. Imms tastes the dust, feels the grit in B's mouth. He has the same grit in his own mouth.

B stops kissing him and stares at him. "What?" Imms asks.

"I just—" B kisses him. "I don't know *why*."

Imms does. He knows why B is here, why B touches him, why they both have secrets. It's because Imms has shed the ordinary like a harmful but comforting habit, and now he matches B in strength and in wanting and in restlessness.

He keeps going deeper.

chapter TWELVE

a week before the team is scheduled to leave the Silver Planet, B decides he'd best stop seeing Imms. Part of him wants to be a coward about it: *Just don't go to the rocks tonight. It'll be too awkward, saying good-bye.* And what's the point? He has no obligation to Imms. It's nice to lie beside someone, that's all. He has felt so little for so long. Now his bones have grown fierce, his muscles have a job. Imms is new and alive, in a way that Gumm, Grena, Vir, and Joele can't be. How do you say good-bye to someone who isn't really someone? Who is an idea, a catalyst, an unanchored heart? He wants to let what's between them go, the same way he picked it up—without thinking, without trying.

He doesn't go to the rocks that night, and he lies in bed wondering how long Imms waits for him. He wonders what Imms feels when he doesn't show up. Sadness—*can* Imms feel sadness? Confusion? Nothing at all? The idea that Imms might accept his absence and move on while he's here sleepless is too much. He pictures Imms lying cold and shivering on the ground. He remembers digging the still body out of the pale dust of the planet. The dark blood, the foundering heart.

Someone taps on his door. He thinks for a wild moment that Imms has found his way on board the ship, has found him, but then Gumm's voice says, "Cap'n?"

B gets up and opens the door.

Gumm looks sheepish, uncertain. "You might want to—maybe come to the kitchen. Vir's acting funny."

B goes to the kitchen. Vir is sitting at the table, gripping its edges. Her eyes are glassy as a Silver's. She is silent as B takes a seat across from her.

"Vir?" B says.

"I'm dreaming," she says.

"What about?"

"Home."

"It's been on my mind too."

"Who did you love there?"

B scratches his head. "My family. My mother and my sister. And a man. We were together a long time, but it didn't work out. You met him once. Matty?"

Vir nods.

"Let's get you back to bed. Okay?"

"Grena read them stories. And I taught them the days of the week." She laughs.

B stands. "Come on. We'll be home soon. Get some sleep."

"It talks to me," Vir says. "On the table. In its language."

"It's gone, Vir," B reminds her. "We got rid of it."

"Oh," Vir says. Then, again, "Oh." She shifts. "But now its family won't touch it. Like baby birds."

"It's dead." He waits for her reproach. For her to tell him that he killed the creature or that he forced her to kill it.

"It's still there."

"The body, you mean?"

"Still on the table."

"I'll have Joele dispose of the body in the morning."

"I'd like to go to bed," Vir tells him. "Let me just do one more check on the lab."

He takes her arm, and when they leave the kitchen, she lets him steer her, not to the lab, but to her room. She asks if she can sing him a lullaby. He says yes, even though he's not the one going to sleep. It helps, though. Her dreaming voice is in his mind when at last he goes to his own room and lies down.

They'll go home in a week, all of them, and he can forget the pale planet under a black sky, and bruised people with drifting hearts.

B goes for a walk two days later, desperate to be off the ship. He goes without a sweatjack and walks until he's numb with cold.

As he returns to the *Byzantine*, he imagines seeing Imms, and is so surprised when he does that he stops dead. Imms is wandering near the belly of the ship. He has found the lab's exterior hatch. B feels a surge of relief and irritation. He tries not to run to him.

"Don't you dare," B says, sweeping Imms into the shadow of the ship with one arm. "You have a death wish?"

Imms's eyes widen, then he smiles. "I wanted to make sure you're all right."

"Look—"

"I haven't seen you."

"We're not going to see each other anymore."

"Because you're leaving?"

"Exactly."

"Not for days."

"What's it matter? We ought to get used to it."

"That ain't square."

B whacks his shoulder. "Quit quoting that stupid book."

"Quit being an asshole."

B raises an eyebrow. The tone is pretty good. The right combination of brazen and indignant. "We're not meeting anymore. And you're not coming within sight of this ship. Do you understand?"

"You can't tell me what to do." The defiance in Imms's expression doesn't look feigned.

"I can, and I will. Now you get the hell out of here before I drop-kick you across the planet."

"I hate you," Imms says. And the fact that he can't doesn't make it sting any less.

Imms looks for a moment like he might touch B. Like he might *need* to touch B. But he goes without another word, and B spends the rest of the day feeling like shit. He pummels himself for the promise he made Imms. That he'd protect him. Wouldn't let anyone hurt him. Shit, once his team leaves, others will come. They'll find Imms. Study him, speak to him. Maybe kill him. And B will never know.

He'll never know what happens to his unexpected pardner.

After two nights without B, Imms returns to the lake. It will just be him and Lons now, and that should be enough. He has company, he has food, he has water. Silvers don't need any more than that.

"Wake up."

Lons is sleeping, eyes closed, no smile. His secrets are gone.

"Wake *up*," Imms says, louder.

Imms shakes him, gently. Lons's chest is still. His heart is off.

"Lons."

Lons's eyes open for a moment. They travel back and forth and go still on Imms. His smile returns, but the movement of it across his face is weak. Lons is shutting off.

"Lons, take a breath," Imms orders. Lons shuts his eyes.

"Lons!" Imms doesn't know why he's afraid. Lons is shutting off because he hurts, and he is ready.

"Lons, *wake up*."

Imms carefully removes the bandages, looking for Lons's heart somewhere beneath the cracked skin. He finally sees the shadow of it, slumped at one side of Lons's belly.

"If you go, I'll be Alone," Imms says.

Lons sleeps without breathing. After a while, the dark stone of his heart wanders slowly up to his chest and rests there. Imms turns away and lies down beside Lons. He bumps Lons's quiet body as he tries to get comfortable. He reaches back and tugs one of Lons's arms free and drapes it over his own head, so that it helps block the light from the ground. He sleeps.

chapter
THIRTEEN

the humans have dumped the dead Silver out of the door in the underbelly of the ship. The body lies in the ship's shadow, broken. The Silver's chest is cut. So is his thigh. Imms sees how the humans have chased his heart.

Imms climbs up the belly of the ship. It's difficult. The Silver Planet has little to climb, and he is not particularly strong or practiced. The hatch has a combination lock, like the safe the Rough Riders force Tin Star to rob. This is the door that leads to the lab. He's sure of it.

He tries the same numbers that opened the Emergency Only door and is pleased to hear the lock's quiet concession. The door opens into an angled chute with a set of rungs along one side. Weak light spills through a grate at the top. The air bubbles with unnatural smells. He hears footsteps. This is what he wants. He wants to see the place where Silvers are hurt. Where humans let their anger turn them dangerous. He climbs up the rungs to the grate. He can see the floor of the lab, dark, shiny blue. Joele's large feet go by. Imms hears her say, "What about more of the yellow shit? Would that help preserve it?"

"I don't want to preserve it," says a soft voice. The female who cried in the kitchen—Vir. "I've taken all the pictures I need."

"People will want to see the real thing." Joele's feet pass by the grate again. Imms shrinks against the chute wall.

"How much did you use? It's making my nose burn."

"Sorry. Am I creating a toxic work environment?"

Imms hears a small splash, then Joele's voice moves closer to Vir's. "Double, double, toil and trouble, heart of Silver, preserved in bubbles."

"Get that out of here."

"I thought you wanted to study it."

"You ought to do something about the body." Vir sounds hollow. That hollowness is more frightening than the violence that snaps in Joele's footsteps.

"Why?"

"B will see."

"So what?" Joele stops moving.

"He said to get rid of it. He doesn't want to see it."

"He killed it," Joele says.

"To stop it suffering."

"He *likes* killing them."

In the silence that follows, Imms can feel the rage run off Joele like sweat and trickle down to where he hides. She is not just angry at B, not just angry at Silvers. Her anger is at everything. She is, in her way, as scarred as he is. She has invisible scabs on her back. Flesh-colored bruises on her ribs.

"What, you're not talking?" Her words rattle. Joele is uncertain. She is desperate. Another second, and anger puffs her up again. She stalks to the chute, saying, "I'll throw it in the fucking lake." She yanks up the grate.

Imms knows he could drop. Down the chute, onto the ground. She's not fast enough to catch him if he runs. But he lingers for a moment on the bars and watches as Joele's expression lunges from startled to confused to hungry. She grabs him by the hair. He doesn't make a sound as she pulls him through the floor and into the lab.

"What's going on?" Vir asks.

Joele looks Imms over slowly. "I remember you. Didn't get enough the last time we met?"

He wishes he could say something, something brave and clever, but his tongue is dry.

She steps toward him, arm out, and he kicks her shin, hard. She gasps. "Little fucker." He tries to crawl under the table, but she hauls him up and shoves him again. He falls against the table, knocking his head on the steel corner. The room shrinks in his vision until there's only black.

When he opens his eyes again, he is on his side on the table, his hands tied behind his back. Something clatters onto the surface behind him, and he twists, trying to see what it is. Joele has placed a small pile of wood and paper near his shoulder. She smiles at him. Not a nice smile. "You ever hear of natural selection?" she asks.

"Who's askin'?" he whispers.

"It's Mother Nature's way of getting rid of morons."

Vir is in the corner, writing in a book. She doesn't look up.

"Can you believe this?" Joele asks her. "One actually came to us."

Imms tries to kick again, but one of his ankles is strapped to the table.

"There's something I want to try," Joele is holding a very small box. She opens it and takes out a thin stick. "You know what fire is?"

Tin Star and Thunder Sam make fires every evening when they stop to rest. The Rough Riders use fire to burn a saloon. Fire is pure heat, and fire consumes. He nods.

"You've never seen it, though, have you?" She swipes the tiny stick against the edge of the box, and a yellow drop sprouts from its tip. It hurts Imms's eyes to stare at it. "Fire changed everything on Earth," Joele says. "Think what it could do for your people."

She touches the burning stick to the small pile on the table. The flame catches the paper, flows along the strips. With a soft snap, it grabs the scraps of wood. It grows. Imms feels the heat next to his skin.

"I'm sure you'd learn to appreciate it," Joele says. "It's so cold here. Fire would keep you warm." She watches him intently. The heat, dangerously near, makes something rise in him. His muscles jump with the flame.

Joele steps aside and rummages in a drawer. She returns with a thin glass rod. She sticks the end of it in the fire, and two sparks shoot into the air and vanish. Imms hears a strange noise, a sort of humming, and realizes it's coming from his own throat. Joele withdraws the rod. Its end glows red for an instant. She presses it against his chest.

At first he feels nothing. Then, a rupture of his senses. He rolls over, thrashes. Joele follows him, holding the rod against his skin. Even when she removes it, the flesh still burns, and he tries to curl up. With one hand, she rolls him back to face her. She grabs the rope around his wrists and yanks it until he gasps. "Don't move," she says.

She heats the rod again. This time when she puts it to his chest, he bites down on his tongue. He bites until he tastes his own blood.

"Do you hate me?" she asks.

The fire beside him is dying, but then it catches one last scrap of wood. The flame launches into the dark air around it, and Imms feels the heat inside him, so fast and roaring that he can't think. He thrashes again, knocking the fire to the floor. The leather band holding his ankle snaps. He throws himself at Joele, wanting her gone. His body and hers crack as they meet, and she falls, Imms on top of her. Imms watches the flames, unable not to. They grab Joele's clothes. They flutter up her arm. She wails.

Imms rolls off her and twists his arms until one wrist slides free of the ropes. He gets to his feet, his whole body still throbbing with the burn. They need to get outside. Vir remains in the corner, writing. She looks up, briefly, as the flames catch the legs of the table. Then she turns back to her notebook.

The fire leaps onto the counters. Glass tubes break and spew liquid. Joele grabs Imms's ankle, but she doesn't attack, only tugs gently as she grinds her burning shoulder against the floor.

Imms picks up a nearby sweatjack and tries to cover the flame on Joele's shoulder, to put it out. But the jacket explodes, curling and squealing, and Imms tosses it aside.

Joele screams. Blood runs from her forehead into her eyes.

"Help!" Imms yells. He yells it again and again. He grabs Joele's ankles and drags her to where he thinks the hatch is. Smoke pours into Vir's corner. She coughs but doesn't try to get away.

Joele struggles. Imms doesn't let go. "Come on," he tries to call to Vir.

He can't find the grate, and Joele won't stop fighting.

She's strong. The flames wind around her neck and climb the braid of her hair. In the corner, Vir slumps. Her face rests on her open notebook. Imms lets go of Joele and puts his cheek against the floor. It's the only way to get air. The smoke burrows into him, curls up in his lungs. He closes his eyes, then opens them again, drawing long, distorted shadows.

A familiar voice shouts from outside the lab. The main door swings open with a *thud*. Imms watches through a fence of flames as

B enters and grabs Vir, pulls her from her chair. B notices Joele on the floor and yells something Imms doesn't understand. Then he sees Imms.

Behind Imms, the table buckles, sinks. The lab cracks like bones. He closes his eyes.

He is by the lake. B is beside him. This is different from the first time he woke up and saw B. He won't spit in B's beard this time, but he doesn't want B to know he's awake yet, because B might take his hand away. Right now, that hand is rubbing slow circles on Imms's stomach. It drifts up, across his collarbone. It finds his hair.

Imms can't help opening his eyes to watch the lake. B says his name, and it's all over, this peace. Flames grow around Imms's mind, keeping the memory of the burning lab trapped there forever. He didn't rescue anybody. The fire was his fault. If B doesn't know that already, Imms will have to tell him.

B doesn't take his hand away. He circles the burns on Imms's chest. Imms doesn't say anything. Maybe B will let him be quiet. That's what he would like, to be quiet forever. To never say a word about fire or death. He draws a breath and coughs.

"It's all right," B says quietly. It's not. Imms knows that.

He tests his throat to see if he can use it if he needs to.

It feels clotted, bruised.

B dips his hand into the lake. He scoops the glittering water, and lets it fall from his hand onto Imms's chest. Imms sighs. B does it again.

"Go back to sleep," B says. "I'm right here."

But Imms can't sleep, not with B right there. "Are the others—"

"Shh," B says. "Sleep."

chapter
FOURTEEN

Imms wakes and B isn't in bed, so he moves his head to B's side of the pillow and breathes in. The fabric smells like humans' invented sweetness—cologne, soap, breath mints—and also like the ground and traces of old warmth gone stale and the air outside.

He gets up and leaves the room, moving slowly. His chest aches.

Now that Joele isn't here, he's allowed to walk around the ship as long as he doesn't disturb anything and eliminates only into the toilets. He goes to the kitchen. B and Grena keep fresh quilopea for him, not dried. He thinks of Lons. Is Lons eating? Then he remembers Lons is dead. So are Joele and Vir and even the man named Gumm, who joined B's rescue effort but breathed in too much smoke. Now it is just Imms, B, and Grena.

Grena seemed happy to see Imms again. She has been rereading him *Tin Star and Thunder Sam* a little bit each night. She gave him a book of cryptowords—alphanumeric puzzles B says give him headaches. Imms loves them. Certain letters and numbers in the puzzles are circled, and when you're finished, you unscramble the circled characters to form a message, usually the answer to a joke Imms doesn't understand. Imms sits up at night solving cryptowords, sometimes falling asleep on the floor instead of joining B in the bed.

Imms finds B sitting on the floor near the main port. This happens often now, that they find each other without searching and sit beside each other without speaking. B stands as though he's been expecting Imms.

"Come on," he says.

B and Imms spend as much time as they can outside, near the water. The lake is the only place where the burns on Imms's chest don't bother him. When they are on the ship, Imms can't stop touching the two welts, picking at them. They ooze clear fluid and won't heal.

B puts his palm on the bright earth and watches the light get sucked into his skin. Imms sits beside him, but B doesn't touch him. B's different tonight—hard angles and brows hurled down, tension in his muscles. Yet an unfamiliar ease tunnels out of him like something buried alive.

"You couldn't sleep?" Imms asks.

B is silent for so long, Imms gives up on hearing his voice. "I had to talk to Grena."

"About the fire?"

"Mm."

"Are the people you work for mad?" Imms knows B doesn't like talking to the humans he works for back on Earth. B thinks they're self-interested gluttons who wouldn't know a golden opportunity if it kicked them in the nuts.

B shakes his head. "They're pretending not to be. They have to be nice to the survivors of a tragedy."

If ever there was a time to be sorry, Imms thinks this is probably it. The feeling is real. He is sorry. He regrets causing the fire. It makes him feel dull, empty, to think of Joele and Vir and Gumm dead. "I'm—"

"They have to be nice because the fire was their fault," B says.

"What?" The fire was Imms's fault. How could it be anyone else's?

"Faulty wiring on the ship. The insulation on an exposed wire in the lab wore away. It sparked."

Imms doesn't understand, and he can tell B doesn't expect or want him to. The fire started because of Joele, and the tiny wooden stick that grew a flame. Because Imms moved to get away from the glass rod.

B continues, "The last thing NRCSE needs right now is to be the face of another fucked-up mission. Luckily, no one on Earth will be paying much attention to tragedy or to me once they meet the real man of the hour."

"Who?"

"You."

Imms is more confused than ever. "I'm not—"

"You're a hero," B says. "You pulled me out of the burning lab. You saved my life."

Imms worries B might be sick, or that his mind is gone, like Lons's. "But—"

"That's what I told NRCSE."

"Why?"

He turns and stares at Imms. "Because I want you to come to Earth with me."

The words land in front of Imms. They stare up at him, alive and pleading.

"Why?" Imms asks.

"You want to see Earth. Don't you?"

Imms has imagined being human, living on Earth, since Grena read them *Tin Star and Thunder Sam*. But the fire swept those thoughts from his mind. He does not feel like much of anything now—Silver or human. He feels like the two bisecting wounds that cross on the left side of his chest and that come alive every time he moves his body. Like he is healing around damage, becoming something new.

"But why do you want me to come?"

"Because I don't want to be without you." B's words barely avoid being trampled by his next ones. "If I brought you to Earth, people would be so interested in learning about you, they'd forget to treat you like a human. But if they think you're a hero, if they think you saved me, we have leverage."

"Leverage?"

"Something to remind people of if they start getting funny ideas."

"I didn't save you," Imms says. "I didn't save anyone."

"That doesn't matter."

Humans lie. Imms knows this. The story of Tin Star is a lie. Tin Star is not even a real human. He's a character. But Grena has explained the difference between lying and creating. Telling a story is an act of creation. Refusing to tell the truth to someone who wants to know it is lying. Maybe all B is doing is creating a story about Imms for the humans back home.

"What's wrong?" B asks.

"Would we live somewhere warm, on Earth?"

"Where I live it's hot during the summer. Cold in winter. Best of both worlds."

Imms stares at the water. The burns shriek inside his skin. That's Joele shrieking. And the unmoving water is Vir slumped in her chair. Flames crack and hiss, and they are B, pushing him away, telling him he's a coward. Then B scoops cool water onto the wound, and the flames recede. The memories vanish.

"What would I do on Earth?" Imms asks.

"Do?"

"Humans have jobs."

"I'll take care of you." B closes his eyes and tips his head back. He looks like he's in pain or very tired.

"You want me," Imms says softly. "You don't like Silvers."

"You're different from the others. You feel things they don't."

Imms nods. He wants this to be the truth. He thinks it must be, because of the way it's filling him and almost hurting him. Silvers don't lie, but Imms imagines lies are thin, easily torn, while truth is so strong, it can't be contained.

"That's why I can't just leave here and never see you again," B tells him.

"Okay."

"Okay?"

"Yes." It is the only answer that makes sense. B wants to be with him. B, who hates Silvers, wants Imms.

B pulls him closer, without even checking to see if Grena is near. "It'll be hard at first. But I'll help you."

"Okay," Imms says. "Okay, okay."

B takes Imms's lip gently in his teeth, stopping any more *okays*.

Imms laughs. "Stop," he tries to say around B's mouth.

B releases him. "Why should I?"

"Because I'll fix it so you're eating fist through a hole in your skull."

"When we get home," B says, "we're gonna get you some new books." And then he has Imms pinned to the ground, pebbles in both their palms, and they create a long kiss, better than the fierce, hungry kind they've shared before. Imms forgets about the fire, about death, because there is a future waiting for him in a place no Silver has been before, a place Alone can't find.

Imms imagines Alone is like the head of the Rough Rider Committee, Caldwell Six, who has a coat he opens to potential customers. On the coat's lining are pinned Indian scalps, jewelry, and dead plucked chickens. He makes people buy his wares or win them in a game of cards, and once a child steals a chicken from Caldwell Six. Alone has a similar coat, full of moments that two people can spend together, breathing at the same time, touching, speaking, fucking. On Earth, those moments with B will be free.

Imms will not have to buy, win, or steal them off Alone.

B asks, "Want to hear how you saved me?"

Grena and B take Imms to the lab. It's an even worse place now than it was before. So many things are black, broken, and bent.

"The floors and countertops have a flame-retardant seal," Grena explains. "Trouble was the chemicals that were out on the counters. Joele was working on preserving the—" she stops, then continues quickly "—the Silver's heart from Project HN."

The body they'd dumped out the hatch. Cuts where they'd chased the heart.

"The sweatjack too," Grena says. "That shouldn't have been down here."

Imms hears a crack, sees a wall of flame rise from the black mound Grena's pointing to. He backs into B, who takes his shoulders, steadies him.

"Did you get everything?" B asks. "The wood scraps? The matches?"

Grena nods. "So we just have to work on the story. I think I'll use a wire from the lighting fixture—it's right above the table. Close to the actual source."

"Hard to fake an electrical fire."

Grena shrugs. "The source area's the trickiest. I'll have to create a scorch pattern that makes sense based on the fire's path."

"How will you do that?"

"Rub the insulation off the wire. Then light it."

"You're going to set another fire to cover up the first one?" B frowns.

Imms cringes at the idea of another fire. He doesn't want to be anywhere near the ship when they make this one.

"Do you have a better idea?" Grena asks.

"I don't have any ideas. You're the expert on this stuff."

"It'll be very small, highly controlled. The table we brought from the kitchen isn't flame retardant, which is why it caught when the fire was knocked to the floor." Imms goes rigid, expecting B and Grena to be angry at him, since he was the one who knocked the fire to the floor. Grena doesn't even look at him. "So you have to figure, if a spark—"

"Let's not keep Imms in here any longer than we have to," B says.

Grena turns to Imms. "What we need is for you to remember as best you can what the fire looked like. Where did it start? Where did it go? What burned? Can you do that?"

Imms swallows. "I think . . ."

B jostles him in a way that makes Imms feel better. He looks around, wondering where Joele, Vir, and Gumm's bodies are.

Grena says, "It's important, Imms, that we make this fire look like an accident. So we can protect you when we get to Earth."

Imms walks to what's left of the table and tells the story. Grena stops him occasionally so she can ask questions. It reminds him of doing interviews with her when she used to visit his clan. At first he didn't know the English words for many of the things he wanted to tell her, so he acted out what he was trying to say, and she did the same for him. That was fun, but it was even more fun later, when he was better at English.

Now he doesn't encounter a single gap as he tells his story. He knows all the words for what happened and wishes he didn't.

"This is going to be easier than we thought," Grena says when Imms finishes.

"How?" B asks.

"If the first thing to catch fire was Joele, we might not have to worry about staging a source area. We could say the spark leaped from the wire overhead and caught Joele's clothes. When she dropped to the ground, she landed too near the sweatjack, which exploded. Flames hit the counter where the preservative chemicals are still out—boom."

"All right," B says.

Grena turns to Imms. "You're the witness. You were in the lab doing an interview with Vir. Joele was working with chemicals. You saw the spark shoot from the wire and onto Joele. You tried to help her, just like you said, but you couldn't get to the hatch in time. B arrived and tried to drag Vir and Gumm out of the lab. But he breathed too much smoke and collapsed."

Imms's stomach feels like he's just eaten a Cosmic Granola Bar. He wants to get out of here. The lab smells terrible, and he doesn't want to listen to Grena talk about Joele on fire, or Vir and Gumm. Or B collapsing.

Grena and B show him how he saved B. They place him where he would have stood and tell him how he had to move. B lies on the floor while Imms practices pulling him to the hatch. Imms doesn't want B pretending to be passed out, and this not-wanting makes him stronger than he usually is. He pulls B quickly, even though B is heavy.

When they are done practicing the rescue, B offers Imms a Spacedream Sandwich, which Imms takes outside and tosses into the lake. He has had enough of being human for one day.

A group of Silvers watches the *Byzantine* take off. B sees them through the window on the main deck. Imms is with Grena in the control room. He isn't interested in looking out windows. The Silvers stand in a line. They'd look manufactured—tall, thin, steel-colored—except for the way their glowing hearts glide through their bodies.

One waves.

B leaves the window and goes to the control room. Imms is curled in one corner. Grena watches the screen that charts their progress.

"You can sit in a chair, you know," B says.

Imms uncurls a little, and B feels something more delicate than passion and subtler than love. Whatever B has done on this mission, and whatever he's failed to do or protect or learn—he will make up for it by having Imms. He has done what they couldn't do in Project HN. He has captured a Silver's heart and studied it alive.

"Want to learn a game?" Grena asks Imms.

"Sure."

She teaches him Twenty Questions.

B sits beside Imms on the floor. He doesn't touch him, not with Grena here. But as they move into space, they are side by side. They are bound somewhere.

part TWO

chapter
FIFTEEN

Imms picks at his suit pants. The material is slick and thin and brushes him every time he moves. He tries to be still, to concentrate on his audiobook. He is listening to *Northanger Abbey*, which is good, though the humans in it cause themselves a lot of pain for no reason. This, he is finding, is true of humans in general. Not just in books.

He tugs at his pants again. He thinks about how he will sit tonight. Up straight, back against the chair. He will use silverware. He practices sitting up. He closes his eyes.

"You look like Buddha."

Imms jerks. B has come into the room. Imms sometimes hates the noise on Earth. He hears so much noise all the time that he has gotten much worse at hearing important sounds. He's gotten worse at counting too. Numbers aren't solid in his mind anymore; they scatter and slide into one another when he tries to use them.

Hates. He is finding he likes to hate things. Hating is easier than he thought. On the Silver Planet, not-wanting was enough. But when he discovers something on Earth he doesn't want—and he has discovered many, many things in the two weeks he's been here—the scars on his chest seem to blaze open, and out leaps a much fiercer feeling, as though he'd rather die than let the thing he doesn't want get any closer. B says this is hate.

"Who's Buddha?" Imms asks. On Earth, B uses dozens of words that Imms doesn't know. They are almost all the names of things: laptop, spatula, Concord Street, raisins. Learning new words is not as exciting as it was on the Silver Planet now that Imms realizes just how many words are in the English language.

"Well, not really Buddha. You're too skinny. Buddha was a fat guy who sat with his eyes closed and meditated."

B is like this a lot now. Grinning, joking. Not at all the quiet, troubled man he was on the Silver Planet. B is glad to be home.

B still gets angry. Imms has become good at discerning when he is angry, and often why. In fact, Imms sometimes likes to make B angry. He can do this many ways. He can leave the stove on, or ask too many questions. He can bounce a tennis ball against the wall. He can take all the books off the shelf to look at them and not put them back. He can roll over in bed and pretend to be asleep before B can touch him. He feigns bewilderment when B's expression hardens, when red rushes to his cheeks. It is tough, sometimes, to keep from laughing.

Tonight, though, he doesn't want B angry. He doesn't want B to make everything a joke, either.

"What are you listening to?" B asks.

"*Northanger Abbey*. I want to learn about manners."

B laughs. "That's a pretty archaic portrayal of etiquette." Imms doesn't ask what *archaic* means. "But I see your plan. You're going to be terribly charming and polite at dinner, and make me look bad in front of my mother."

"No way," Imms protests as B kisses him.

"Yes, yes. You're a conniving creature. But it won't work on Mom. She'll see right through you."

"Will they hate me?" Imms asks.

B looks at him, really looks at him, for the first time since entering the room. "No," he says quietly.

Six buttons on his shirt.

B loops an arm around Imms, crushing him against his chest. "They'll love you."

"They're nice? Like Grena?"

B steps back. Twenty-eight light brown hairs in the space between his eyebrows. He has started shaving his beard down to prickles. "We've been over this, Imms. Not all women are—"

"I know," Imms says. "They're not just good or bad."

B goes to the refrigerator and takes out a tall green bottle. "Wine?"

Imms shakes his head. "I'll get sick."

"You had some the other night. You were fine."

"I felt sick. After you went to sleep."

"You'll at least *try* some of whatever my mother's made, won't you?"

"Yes."

"You can have all the apples you want when we get home."

Apples aren't quilopea, but they're good. Imms would eat them all the time if he could. If B didn't insist he "expand his horizons."

"Did you leave the oven on again?" B asks, looking at the dial.

Imms closes his eyes briefly. This time it really is an accident. He's fascinated by how hot it gets inside the oven—hotter and hotter without producing fire.

He gets up, goes to the oven, turns it off. The two of them stand there for a minute in the heat.

They drive to B's mother's house. B's mother has arthritis, so B's sister lives with her and helps her out. Imms likes cars. He likes to put his cheek on the window, feel the cool of the glass, watch the world fly by. He can't get used to lights on top of posts. Even at night, Earth is not dark.

As they drive, B sets a hand on Imms's knee, and Imms is grateful.

"Remember, this evening, we're just friends," B says.

"You don't love me tonight," Imms jokes.

"Don't say that." B clears his throat. "I just want to give them time to get used to you."

Imms knows. He and B don't love each other when they go to the NRCSE facility, either. Even when the psychologist asks Imms questions like, "Do you think B is handsome?" Imms has to pretend he has never thought about it.

Imms is allowed to tell NRCSE he considers B a close friend. He is allowed to say he doesn't want to live with anyone but B. He is not allowed to say anything about love or fucking or kissing. Nothing about being strapped to the table in the *Byzantine* lab, or about Joele burning him. The scars on his chest are supposed to be from rescuing B. The humans at NRCSE want to hear this story again and again. They want him to stand in the burned lab of the *Byzantine*—which now looks like a sad, tired old animal, not at all the towering emergency it was on the Silver Planet—and show them what happened. They call him a hero, but they seem afraid of him.

Imms turns the TV on sometimes when B's not around. People on TV are always talking about him. Last night, a blonde woman said that the presence of humanlike creatures on another planet proves the existence of God, and that the human body is the most perfect of all living forms. A dark-haired woman said this isn't true, that the existence of Silvers means the Bible is wrong, that Earth isn't anything special. She said the presence of humanlike creatures on another planet supports quantum mechanics. Infinite outcomes.

Nobody is supposed to have pictures of Imms. They're not allowed. Anyone who gets too close or asks questions or tries to take pictures gets in trouble. But B says Imms has to do his part.

Don't go anywhere alone. Don't talk to anyone B hasn't approved. Instead of a photo, the news channels display a drawing of him. It doesn't really look like Imms, but Imms likes to see it.

He has looked into mirrors and realized that he is ugly. The only things on Earth colored like him are machines. He looks at humans and feels shame. Not the same kind of shame he feels knowing he caused the *Byzantine* fire. That shame winds itself around his body so that sometimes he can't move without tripping over it. Shame over being ugly comes in jolts, gone so fast Imms is never sure it's real. He'd rather look at humans than himself. Humans have shining hair, colorful eyes. He likes overweight people. He likes how their bodies swing and wobble. He likes how soft they look.

B looks at him. "Would you quit picking at your pants?"

"Sorry."

"I thought those'd be more comfortable than jeans."

"They are."

"They look good on you."

Imms smiles. He puts his cheek against the window.

They slow down in front of a wonderful house. It's small, made of brick, with white trim around the door and windows and a circular plant on the door. Imms asks what it is.

"A wreath," B says. "It's tacky. Tell my mother that."

Imms won't because he can tell *tacky* means something bad.

For a moment, Imms can't move. He wishes they could turn around and drive home. He wishes B would call him Roach and hand him a package of dried fruit.

"Come on, slug."

Imms gets out of the car, follows B up the tidy walkway to the door.

The door opens before B can knock. A short woman with gray streaks in her dark hair takes B in her arms as they enter. "It's about time," she murmurs. Imms knows that B saw his mother and sister just after the *Byzantine* landed two weeks ago. Imms spent his first night on Earth with Grena at the NRCSE facility while B visited his family. But he can see from the expression on B's mother's face that this hasn't been enough. That she never wants to let him go.

She releases B and turns to Imms, extending her hand.

"Mary."

"Imms." He shakes her hand. "It is a pleasure to meet you."

She pulls him into a hug. He is surprised, but relaxes quickly. "I'm so glad you're here. B told me you like fruit. I made a fruit salad with yogurt dressing. There's chicken and potatoes, buttered sprouts, and blueberry pie for dessert."

"Sounds great," B says.

In the kitchen, a woman slightly younger than B sits at a round wooden table. She has short, dark hair and wide-set eyes. The flatness of her face reminds Imms of a cat. She has one leg up on the chair beside her. "Hey," she says when they come in. She looks past B and stares at Imms. "How's Earth treating you?"

"Fine, thank you," Imms tells her.

She snorts. "I'll bet. Plates are over here. We're rocking this buffet style."

"Imms, this is my sister, Bridique." B puts an arm around Bridique. She makes a face but gives his arm a squeeze.

"Pleased to make your acquaintance," Imms says.

"Sit through a goddamned dinner with me, then decide if you're pleased to make my acquaintance," Bridique says.

"Don't mind her." B claps Imms's shoulder. "Grab a plate."

Imms likes looking at the food. The colors and patterns fascinate him. But when it comes to actually putting it on his plate, he has trouble. He doesn't want the slick, sucking noises the potatoes make when he lifts the spoon. He hates how the fork tines nestle into the pale flesh of the chicken.

"Just take a little of everything," B suggests, reaching around him for something green.

B doesn't understand that food is more than taste. It has sound and color, and he thinks of its history and the way fire changed it.

Imms takes a little of everything and sits down.

"You want a little fruit with your entrée?" Bridique asks.

Imms looks at his plate. He has taken mostly fruit.

"Don't give him a hard time," Mary says. "What did you eat back home, Imms?"

"Quilopea," he replies. "It's a kind of fruit. A very good fruit."

"That's it?" Bridique asks.

"Yes."

"Don't you need, like, vitamins and shit?"

"Vitamins and . . . ?"

"Silvers only need quilopea," B says.

"What do you do for work?" Imms asks Bridique, racking his brain for B-approved questions.

"I work at a big cat rescue center. You know what lions are? Tigers?"

"He does," B says.

Bridique ignores him and waits for Imms's nod. "We take in cats that are sick, injured, or abandoned, and we fix them up. Give them a place to live out the rest of their days."

"Where do you get them?"

"All over. Zoos, circuses. People who try to keep them as pets, which is the stupidest thing ever. By the time they get to us, they're so fucked up." She shakes her head. "Humans are assholes. You'll learn this. Two divorces and a kid I only get to see twice a month. People don't have the slightest notion of how to be *kind*."

"Has B taken you anywhere exciting?" Mary asks Imms.

"It's damn near impossible to go anywhere, with all the gawkers." B wipes his mouth. "Our guard detail's outside right now."

The entourage. That's what B and Imms have started calling the group that follows them around and stays outside the house to protect them.

"He took me to the hardware store the other day," Imms says.

B swallows a bite of chicken. "I wouldn't call that exciting."

"Would you like some more fruit, Imms?" Mary asks.

"Dear creature," he says. "How much I am obliged to you!" This is how Isabella answers Catherine in *Northanger Abbey*.

Bridique bursts out laughing.

Mary laughs too, spooning fruit onto his plate. "No need to be obliged to me. What's my son been teaching you?"

"Not me," B says. "Jane Austen."

Imms discovers he hates people laughing when he is not. He sticks a forkful of chicken in his mouth. It is salty, and juice pours between his teeth. He feels a heat in his body that reminds him of fire. He sets his fork down. "May I be excused to the restroom?"

"Certainly," Mary says. "It's—"

"I'll show you where it is," B offers. He leads the way out of the kitchen and into the hall. He gives Imms's arm a playful punch. "You'd sound perfect if this was the 1790s."

"Yeah." Imms wishes they were home.

B catches his shoulder, turns him so that they're face-to-face. B studies him. "Hey."

Imms turns away. Eighteen squares of floor between his right foot and the kitchen.

"She wasn't criticizing you. She just wants you to be comfortable."

"It's fine."

"Imms?" Mary appears in the doorway. "I want to apologize. I wasn't making fun. It's been a long time since anyone around here has taken a stab at politeness. Look at this one." She nods at B.

Imms looks at this one and thinks, not for the first time, that even though many humans are beautiful, B's looks will always be Imms's favorite.

"Please," B says. "I'm not that bad."

Mary rolls her eyes. "You could learn a thing or two from Imms."

B turns to Imms. "You don't have to behave any certain way when you're here. Just be yourself."

Imms isn't sure who that is at the moment. "Okay." He tries to smile, to make it a joke.

Mary brushes a lock of Imms's hair behind his ear. "Good boy. I know."

Humans can do this, can pass judgment as easily as they issue a greeting. It scares Imms, and makes him glow, to be called good.

B says, "The bathroom's at the end of the hall, on your right."

The rest of the dinner goes smoothly. Mary asks Imms questions about the Silver Planet. About his family. About encountering humans for the first time. She listens attentively to his answers. Bridique is less attentive, twirling her hair on her finger, bundling herself into odd positions on the chair. Imms likes the lines around her eyes. They are like the lines in cartoon drawings that show something moving fast through the air. Every now and then, she snorts at something Imms says or shakes her head.

Once she mutters, "We're such awful creatures."

B jumps in once or twice to give his own perspective on one of Imms's stories, but most of the questions Mary asks are about life on the Silver Planet before B got there. She is especially fascinated by Imms's description of the water.

"It sounds just beautiful."

"It is." Imms is thrilled that she thinks so. He wishes he could show her.

Bridique talks some more about her job, about the big cats. She tells Imms she'll take him to visit the sanctuary sometime. B says only if Imms wants to.

"You can make your own decisions, can't you?" Brid asks Imms.

"Yes," he says. "I'll go."

B's body gets stiff. Imms senses he's done something wrong but isn't sure what.

"We'll have to get NRCSE's approval," B says.

"What, he has to get his permission slip signed each time he wants to go anywhere?" Bridique asks.

"Right now I'm the only one authorized to take him places. And yes, I'm supposed to check first."

"Well, get me authorized, too. Imms'll kill himself if he has to spend every minute with you."

It's a joke, Imms knows. He'd never shut off. He wants to spend time with B.

"Do you like big cats?" Imms asks B.

B throws an arm around his shoulder and kisses him quickly, unexpectedly, on the lips. "Sure. I'm just looking out for you."

Imms can tell by the way Mary and Bridique stare that B has kissed him in order to make them stare this way. Mary's expression shifts from surprise to a look Imms can't quite place. Bridique looks shocked for a moment, then like she's trying not to laugh.

Mary suggests B help her with the dishes while Bridique and Imms go into the living room and relax.

"I can do dishes," Imms says. "I'm good at it."

"That's sweet of you," Mary says. "B and I will manage."

Imms follows Bridique into the living room. It has green carpet and two bookcases built into the walls, little sculptures and framed photographs on the shelves as well as books. The curtains are thin and lacy.

Bridique flops on the couch. "Sit."

Imms sits in a rose-colored armchair.

"So spill," Bridique says.

"Spill what?"

"What's the deal with you and my brother?"

Imms doesn't know what the deal is, so he keeps quiet.

"Are you guys a thing?"

"A thing?"

"You do a lot of kissing?"

"Um—"

"Fucking?"

Imms isn't supposed to talk about fucking. But maybe it's okay, since Bridique is B's sister. "We used to on my planet. But now only sometimes."

Bridique stares at him for a long moment. He thinks maybe she's angry, because B is human and Imms is a Silver. But she says, "It's okay to talk about these things, you know. I had a therapist last year who said ninety percent of sexual hang-ups can be cured by *communicating*."

"Why?"

Bridique doesn't seem to hear him. "My first husband didn't think we should communicate about anything. Sex, money—certainly not the kid."

"Oh."

"And he's got her now, even though he knows about as much about being a father as I know about being grand vizier to the Ottoman sultan. What do you think? Do I look old enough to have been through two husbands?"

"I don't know."

"You'll like the cat sanctuary." She cradles one foot in her hands. "Do you hate me?"

He remembers Joele asking him the same question.

"No."

"Of course not," Bridique says. "You can't get pissed off. Right? That's what B says."

Imms nods.

"What if someone came up and socked you in the gut?"

"No."

"Do you have kids? What if someone socked your kid in the gut?"

"I don't have kids."

Bridique looks at the ceiling. "If I couldn't get pissed, I don't know what'd be left of me."

"It's how they stayed warm on the Silver Planet," Imms says, not sure why he's telling her, or if she'll understand. "B and the other humans. Being mad kept them warm."

Bridique rotates her ankle. "You let him boss you around? Tell you what to do?"

"He knows what to do."

"My brother?" Bridique shakes her head. "He doesn't know shit."

"What happened to your husbands?"

"They left. They got sick of me and left. Who can blame them? I talk all the time."

"That's not bad."

"Well, thank you, but with all due respect, you're from another planet. I sometimes think—" She sighs. "I'm not for anybody. And nobody's for me."

B comes in a minute later, his expression strained. "We should head out," he says.

Imms tries to shake Mary's hand, but she pulls him close and squeezes him. He offers his hand to Bridique. She slaps his palm. "Up top, bro."

He jerks his hand back. The slap didn't really hurt. She grins.

"You come back again soon," Mary says to them. B nods.

In bed that night, B unexpectedly defers to Imms.

"What do you want to do?" he asks. "Anything. Tell me how to make you feel good."

At first, Imms is relieved. He can tell B that what he wants is to be held, to curl against B until he falls asleep. Then he realizes that the desperate alertness he senses in B will grow worse if it's given no outlet. Imms will spend the night counting B's jolting, staticky breaths. So he says he wants B inside him. He says B can be a little rough, because B likes that, and sometimes Imms does, too—likes the way something they both want can hurt only one of them, and the way he can keep that pain a secret, pretend it's something else.

chapter
SIXTEEN

b takes Imms to NRCSE the next day, and Imms talks to the NRCSuckers—Imms is only allowed to call them that with B, never to their faces—in charge of his integration into human society. They ask him how he is adjusting, how his lungs and stomach feel, whether he misses the Silver Planet, and whether anyone has tried to talk to him or take his picture. They tell him that for now he has to stay in the city with B. He can't travel to other parts of the country. Dr. Hwong, who examined Imms when Imms arrived on Earth, does another blood test. The needle doesn't hurt much, but it's hard for Imms to hold still knowing the bite is coming.

"Why do they keep asking me the same questions?" Imms asks B on the way home.

"They don't know what to do with you. Whether they should give me a license to keep you or issue you a green card."

"I don't like the doctor."

"Me neither. We'll find someone else."

"I have to keep going to doctors?"

"Only when you're sick. *If* you're sick." He pauses. "Can you get sick?"

"I don't know."

"There's a lot here your body's not used to. I'm surprised—we're all surprised—by how well you've done."

"The doctor wouldn't stop watching my heart."

"He's never seen anything like it."

After a moment Imms asks, "Can we go to the park tonight?"

"I don't think the entourage likes us going out at night."

"Fuck 'em, though, right? You said you hate them following us around."

"I do. But we need them."

It's strange to see B so worried about doing what other people tell him to do. On the Silver Planet, he was the captain, the one in charge.

"What would humans do to me? If I wasn't protected? Besides take my picture."

"Hound you with questions. Stick microphones in your face."

"Would they hurt me?"

"Most of them, probably not. Not on purpose. But you never know."

Imms turns on the radio. He scans for a song he knows. Can't find one. He settles back and listens to one he's never heard before.

It goes:

Your love is all kinds of poisonous,
Your touch, the rush of heat
On this night,
It's right,
My body's lit with the delight of us. You're all kinds of poisonous.

"Can we please listen to something else?" B asks.

"Why?"

"Because this is god-awful."

"I like it."

"You like it because I don't. Turn it."

"No," Imms says.

The song ends and another starts. Imms thinks it's no wonder humans can't concentrate on anything for very long. Their lives are made up of snippets of sound, bursts of color. Three-minute songs, thirty-second TV ads. Billboards, supermarkets. B has tried to show Imms how to use the computer, but Imms hates it.

"You can read on it," B says. *"You can learn about anything you want."*

Imms doesn't trust it.

B turns off the radio. Imms wishes he'd turned it to a song B likes, because sometimes B sings, and Imms loves the sound of his voice. But if Imms asks him to sing, B won't. It has to be B's idea.

They arrive home, and Imms has a strange sensation he hasn't had before. At least, not so strongly that he's noticed it. He feels like he's entering a place he can't get out of. Like Tin Star in the jail.

"Can we work on reading?" he asks B.

B comes up behind him, winds his arms around him. Kisses his neck. "You sure that's what you want to do right now?"

Imms squirms. "I need to get better at it."

"There'll be time for that later." The stubble that used to be B's beard scratches Imms's neck. Imms laughs. "Right now, school's out."

B turns Imms to face him, and they kiss. It is almost like the first time they kissed on the *Byzantine*, like something neither of them expected to happen. Imms imagines they're in a competition to see whose lips can swallow whose first.

B undoes the buttons of Imms's shirt. Imms's heart glows so brightly it turns B's chin gold. B keeps his mouth over Imms's, moving his hand between Imms's legs. Imms feels his organ start to descend. Then it stops. This happens sometimes, and it usually upsets B. *"What's the problem?"* he'll ask.

B doesn't mind this time. He doesn't stop kissing Imms, and he moves his fingers back and forth very softly over the fabric of Imms's pants. The sensation makes Imms gasp. His organ comes out. Cock. He's supposed to call it his cock. B moves his hand to Imms's back and pulls Imms against him. He moves his body up and down slightly, so that their cocks rub through their pants. B grabs Imms's thighs, squeezing, digging his nails in. Imms whimpers into B's mouth.

It's over fast. B lets go, panting. Imms staggers to the sofa, sits down. His legs ripple like water.

They don't speak.

B returns to work later that week. He leaves a set of instructions for Imms: *Don't go out alone. If you need something, call Mary or Bridique. If you cook something on the stove or in the oven, TURN THE STOVE/OVEN OFF when you're done. Call my cell for emergencies. DON'T answer the door.*

Imms follows these instructions for three days. He stays in the house, soaking in a cool bath. It's hard to keep his skin from drying. The clear, thin water of Earth is ineffectual and sometimes seems to make things worse, but B has introduced him to lotion. It's slimy, but it helps. He listens to audiobooks and reads what he can of B's newspapers and magazines. He watches TV. His favorite is the local news with Elise Fischer. She talks about Imms a lot, but not in a bad way. Not like she's scared.

On the fourth day, he's so bored that he sleeps until B gets home. B is tired too, and they curl up together and don't fuck, just doze.

The fifth day, Bridique shows up carrying a bag with a picture of a lion on it and the words *It's a Roaring Good Time at Rose Sanctuary.* "You like movies?" she asks.

"Yeah."

"I brought some."

A couple of the movies are animated, which means they're made of paintings. Others have real people. They watch *Blue Valentine*, which Imms doesn't like. He knows that humans argue a lot, but it still doesn't make sense to him. Bridique's eyes are red by the end, but she doesn't cry. "That's what happened to me," she says. "My first marriage. I was so in love, and then it just collapsed."

"Why?" Imms asks.

"I don't know," she says. "I used to think it was his fault. He couldn't be happy anywhere, doing any one thing. Then I started thinking it was me. I didn't give him enough freedom, enough support. Now I think it was both of us. We were both idiots."

"Are you mad at him?"

She shrugs. "Not anymore."

"Where's your other husband?"

"I don't know. We're still married, technically. Just don't know where he is and don't care."

They watch *Pocahontas* next. Imms loves this one. "They don't show the end of the story," Brid says. "Pocahontas was a real person. She went with John Smith to England. She got sick and died of some disease." Bridique watches his reaction carefully. Imms thinks he knows why she showed him this movie, and it gives him a rubbery feeling in his stomach, the way she's looking at him.

"Could she really talk to animals?" Imms asks.

"I'm sure she could, but I doubt they talked back." Bridique stands. "You wanna go see the big cats?"

"Now?"

"Yeah."

"I can't leave the house without B."

"Oh, for Christ's sake, he's such a— Look, Imms. You can do whatever you want. You're a free soul."

"Free soul?"

"You've got as much right as anyone on this planet to go out and enjoy yourself."

"I can't go anywhere without the entourage."

"We are definitely not taking your goons. We'll slip out undetected."

They go out the side window in the den, which opens almost right into the hedge that separates B's yard from the neighbors'. Instead of going around to the front yard, they go through the hedge, across the neighbor's lawn, and to the street, where Bridique's car is parked. "Well done," she says, offering her palm for Imms to slap. He does, hesitantly. She shakes her head. "*Hit* it."

He slaps harder.

"Better."

Bridique drives differently from B, as though it is her own body sleekly cutting the air, not the car's. She keeps her eyes straight ahead. She goes fast.

"I'm really curious about what fucking's like for you and my brother," she says. "Not in a gross way. I used to want to be a sex therapist. I like learning about stuff like this."

"Oh."

"I mean, did you have to learn anything different?"

"Not really. Just—I think there's more to it, with humans."

"What do you mean?"

"Silvers just do it to breed. Humans do it—for what?" he asks.

"For pleasure," Brid says. "For revenge. To make up. To dispel tension. To reproduce. To boost or destroy a reputation. To pass the time." Bridique drums her fingers on the wheel. "Did you have a boyfriend? Girlfriend? Back on your planet?"

"No."

"How come?"

"One pair of Silvers is selected to breed once a month. I was never chosen." They pass a tall building with a familiar logo. "What's that place?"

Bridique glances at the building. "Local news headquarters. Bullshit central. 'Did you know your baby's pacifier could cause it to immaculately conceive? More at eleven.'"

"The news talks about me a lot."

"No shit. You are the news, big guy."

Brid has music playing, but it's very soft, and not the kind of music Imms would expect to hear in her car. No voices, just instruments.

"I guess I should thank you," she says.

"Why?"

"For saving my brother's life."

Something in Imms tightens. Pretending to be a hero to NRCSE is one thing. Pretending to Bridique is another.

Brid glances at him. "You ever sorry you pulled him out of the fire?"

Imms shakes his head violently. "No."

"I'm kidding. He's a good guy. He can be. He wants to be. He fucks it up sometimes." She pauses. "I should talk."

They arrive at the sanctuary. Bridique rolls down her window and waves her badge next to a machine. The light turns green, and the gate in front of them lifts. They drive into a lot with a sign that says Reserved Parking Only.

"Most of the cats here can never be released back into the wild," she explains as they make their way to the entrance. "They're too used to captivity. They wouldn't be able to survive. We've got two lions, a Bengal tiger, and a bobcat. And a liger. That's a lion-tiger mix."

Imms knows that different species on Earth are not supposed to breed. But sometimes, if the species are similar enough, they can mix. Like donkeys and horses. Lions and tigers. Dogs and wolves. It doesn't happen naturally, B told him. Usually humans have to create the hybrids.

Bridique greets a man at the entrance booth, and they chat for a minute. At the top of the gate, in letters that look like they're made out of sticks, are the words Rose Big Cat Sanctuary. Down the path, Imms sees a chain-link fence.

"Holy shit," the man in the booth says loudly. "Hey!"

Imms is wearing a sweatshirt with the hood up, and has his hands in his pockets, just like B taught him. He turns to the man, meets his eyes, then quickly looks at the ground.

"Holy shit. *Holy shit.*"

"Josh," Brid warns.

"No, this is— I can't— Okay," the man says. "Okay. Can he talk?"

"Yes, but—"

Josh addresses Imms. "What d'ya think about Earth so far?"

Bridique rolls her eyes. "Shut up, Josh."

"Well, I wanna know! It's not every day you—"

"Come on, Imms." Bridique takes Imms's arm and tosses a wave back at Josh.

She leads Imms to the first enclosure. It's big, not like the jail cell Tin Star was kept in. It contains grass and rocks and a small pool. Two animals drowse by the pool. "The lionesses," Bridique says. One gets up and walks lazily to the fence. The other follows a moment later.

"Kaya and Kaylee," Brid says, "meet Imms."

The animals have cake-colored fur and sharp amber eyes. Imms starts to put his hand to the fence.

"Uh-uh." Brid says. "Wild animals, dude."

Imms drops his hand. "Are you friends with them?"

"I guess so. As much as humans and lions can be friends. The bigger one, Kaya, she'll jump up and give me a hug if I go in there. Kaylee's shyer. They each eat eleven pounds of meat a day. Spend about eighteen hours sleeping."

Imms watches them a minute longer. Kaylee heads back to the pool. Kaya stares at him. He tells her she's beautiful.

"Is that your language?" Bridique asks him.

"Yeah."

"It's nice."

They meet Tommy next. Tommy is a six hundred–pound Bengal tiger. He does not get up to greet them, but lies on his side, his great belly moving up and down, his tail twitching. "He's pretty flabby," Brid says. "You ought to see him jiggle when he walks." Tommy is missing a patch of hair on one side. "He weighed three hundred and fifty pounds when we got him. Starved almost to death. Rescued from a circus. They made him jump through a burning hoop, and his fur caught fire."

Imms flinches. "Are circuses bad?"

"Don't even get me started. Circuses have this image of fucking family funfests, and the reality couldn't be further from that. Not just the way the animals are treated, but the people—at least, back in the old days—the people lived like shit too. There aren't many circuses anymore. Thank fuck."

They move on to the bobcat's pen, but she's sleeping in a hollow log and won't come out. "We do train the animals," Brid says. "Some of them. Just basic tricks. Nothing too strenuous. Jumps, sitting, rolling over like dogs. We travel around in the spring and summer and do educational performances. The admission proceeds go toward running the sanctuary."

"Do you train them?" Imms asks.

"That's mostly Margret's job—Margret Rose, she owns the sanctuary. And there's another trainer, Zane. But they let me help out some." She looks at Imms. "What do you think so far?"

"I love them." He watches the huddle of the bobcat in the log.

"Me too."

"There aren't really any animals on my planet. Except the snakes."

"Snakes? Of all the goddamn animals you could have, you got snakes?"

"They're nice, though. B says the ones here are venomous. Not the ones on my planet."

"Say the name of your planet. In your language." He does. Bridique shakes her head. "I hate humans," she says.

"Why?"

She doesn't answer right away. Finally she says, "You should speak your language as much as possible. So you don't forget."

Her phone rings while they're looking at Chess, the liger, who is the most beautiful of all the cats. Bridique turns away from the enclosure and answers the call.

"Hey, clown," Imms hears her say. "Not much. Imms and I are at Rose. Yeah. He wanted to get out, I wanted to get out. We're out." She pauses. "We'll discuss this *later*."

Imms wonders if B is mad. He focuses on the sand-colored cat. Her coat ripples as she paces, the faint orange stripes bend and straighten. She approaches the fence and presses her nose against the chain link. Imms knows she is safe. She won't hurt him. He puts his hand against the fence. Her rough tongue sweeps his palm. He laughs. Chess licks him again and again. He is still laughing when Bridique says quietly, "Imms. Take your hand away. Slowly."

He obeys. Chess gives him one last look, then turns and wanders off. Imms feels sad as she goes.

"My brother's already pissed I brought you here. Please don't make me take you back to him with a stump for a hand."

"She wasn't going to hurt me."

"A wild animal, Imms. Outside of her natural environment. You never know."

chapter
SEVENTEEN

the aboveground portion of NRCSE looks like a museum. Visitors can play interactive games, look at rocks and dust from other planets and read the fun facts listed on plaques. They can have pictures taken in a space suit on a surface painted to look like the Silver Planet. The NRCSE website has links for kids and adults, researchers and educators. NRCSE employees are available to speak in classrooms, at commencements, in prisons, and on talk shows. NRCSE has given tours to K–12 students, honeymooning couples, scientists, celebrities, and politicians. A river runs east of the complex, and a trail with lookout points runs along the bank. Photo opportunities.

Belowground, where the tourists never go, are simulation rooms, a biomedical research lab, a three-mile underground training complex, and a mission control center. They have stations that simulate the terrain and atmospheres of other planets. Offices, laboratories, and the barracks rooms—living quarters that have been fashioned from former cells in the now-defunct military prison NRCSE annexed. The barracks rooms still lock from the outside. The fields to the north of the facility, enclosed in chain link and barbed wire and once used as a fitness area for prisoners, are now used for training.

B is called to Kelly Hatchell's office Tuesday afternoon. Hatch likes cacti and has one particularly bloated, fat-spined specimen in an Aztec-looking pot near the file cabinet in her office, caught like a frightened performer in the spotlight of a standing sunlamp. B can only imagine the disaster in store should Hatchell one day forget to close the bottom drawer of the file cabinet and trip.

Hatchell wipes her glasses. "Howdy, Captain."

Human Spaceflight and Operations, the division of NRCSE B works for, strives to make its employees feel like a team, a family. HSO holds an annual holiday party and monthly raffles, and is the second-ranked team in the NRCSE intramural bowling league, behind Propellants and Fuels. Yet despite this constructed kinship, none of B's HSO colleagues have offered more than the briefest condolences. Few have said Joele's, Vir's, or Gumm's names out loud. B wonders if this is the result of NRCSE's professional heartlessness, its belief in necessary sacrifice for the greater good. HSO is probably more like a family than was ever intended, a group in which warmth, support, and loyalty are often overshadowed by fear, mistrust, and friction.

On Hatch's desk is a pile of news articles related to the *Byzantine* disaster. B has seen most of the articles before. "NRCSE Mourns Loss of 3 in *Byzantine* Fire." Mourns? Not the first word that comes to B's mind. "Back to Earth: A Survivor's Story." Unofficial, unauthorized, about Grena. "Foreign Aid: Extraterrestrial Saves *Byzantine*'s Captain from a Deadly Blaze." That one spun the straw of B's "no comments" into journalistic gold, painting B as speechless with grief, full of wordless gratitude toward Imms.

"Take a seat," Hatch says. B does. The cactus in the corner has what looks like a bulbous nose growing out of its main stalk. "How is it, being back?"

"Fine."

"And living with the, uh—with Imms? That's going all right?"

"Yes."

Hatch nods. "This is an incredible opportunity, you know, for us. To have Imms here."

"Of course."

"Though your reason for bringing him to Earth was, I guess, more personal than practical."

B's stomach tightens. Hatchell is stumbling through whatever she has to say, and Hatch isn't usually one to stumble. She's carelessly confident, an awkward optimist who kisses her bowling ball and whispers, *"Come on, baby, strike for me!"* before sending it down the lane.

"You bonded with Imms. Understandably so. It's really something, isn't it? That a creature lacking the capacity for emotion, with no obligations toward human beings, nothing to gain from aiding them—would risk its life to help you?"

B doesn't answer. Best to say as little as possible until Hatchell gets to the point.

Hatchell seems to interpret B's silence as the intrusion of some deep, abiding pain into B's memory. Her voice softens. "We're glad you made it, Captain. I know it can't have been easy, losing your people."

Vir, Joele, Gumm—B barely knew them prior to the mission. They are NRCSE's people more than they are B's.

"We're investigating exactly what went wrong with the ship."

B nods. If Grena's done things right, they'll never be able to tell exactly what went wrong.

"Captain, I'm not looking to make things any harder on you right now." Hatchell runs her fingers along the edge of her desk.

"What's the problem?"

"NRCSE is, as I said, grateful for the research opportunities the Silver provides. But the decision to bring it to Earth wasn't yours to make."

"All right," B says.

"It's something you should have discussed with us first."

"Imms wanted to come here."

"I understand that."

"What could be more valuable to NRCSE right now than to have him here as a resource? For future missions?"

"Yes." Hatchell's glasses are back on. "I agree. So does everyone else." She fires off her next words, as though they'll hurt less if they're shot into B quickly. "You're being asked to attend a disciplinary hearing. Just a formality. No one's really looking for blood."

"Christ. What am I looking at?"

"A month's suspension without pay. Best case."

B could yell. He could protest. But it won't help. He runs a hand through his hair. "A medal of honor and a month's suspension. Talk about mixed messages."

Hatch cracks a smile. "I hear you, Captain."

"What's worst case?"

"Worst case, we'd let you go."

Which would almost be a relief. B's not sure what he'd do for work instead. Something low stress, relaxing. Then it hits him, what this could mean. "And Imms?"

"Imms would remain the property of NRCSE."

"*Property?*"

"He would remain in our custody."

"I won't allow that."

"You wouldn't have a choice. You have custody of Imms now because you are an employee of the center. Because you know Imms best and can provide him with a more *human* environment than we can at this facility. But from what I'm hearing, Biomed isn't satisfied with the amount of access they have to Imms. Neither is Psychology."

"I bring him here once a week to be tested and interrogated. I submit reports—"

"Start bringing him twice a week. We'll see how that works for everybody."

And what happens when NRCSE wants three visits a week? Five? What happens if NRCSE finds out Brid and Imms are at Rose Sanctuary right now without permission or supervision? He clenches his hands into fists, not sure who he hates more at the moment, Hatch or Brid. "He won't live anywhere else. He *can't*—he trusts me."

"Twice a week. It's all we're asking. And I'm sure we'll find a way to show our appreciation."

B raises an eyebrow. "My hearing?"

"You'll get the month's suspension. A slap on the wrist."

"A fucking hammer to the wrist," B mutters. "I can't afford a month off."

"I'll see if I can't get it down to two weeks."

So it's like that. Hatch orchestrated this little pissing match to demonstrate to B that NRCSE is in control, and that B's act of subversion in bringing Imms here will be leveraged against him whenever NRCSE needs his cooperation.

"What does Biomed want with him?"

"That, I do not know. Take it up with Dr. Hwong."

"What about Grena? Does she have a hearing?"

Grena had agreed to bring Imms to Earth. She'd been nervous. She'd wanted to tell NRCSE before they left. Wanted to ask permission. But she'd agreed.

Hatchell hesitates. B suddenly hopes that someday Hatch will trip and fall into the waiting cactus. "She's agreed to work on the *Breakthrough II* mission," Hatch says. "Scheduled to depart late next year. She's helping train new crew members."

"So those who cooperate—"

"Escape with their hide." Hatchell offers a grin that looks sympathetic but isn't. "Twice a week."

"Twice a week. As long as Imms isn't hurt."

"Nobody's looking to damage the goods."

B will consider not shoving Hatch into her cactus his good deed for the day. "Is there anything else?" he asks.

"That's it."

B rises.

"You coming to bowling on Friday?" Hatch asks. "First match of the season."

B heads for the door. "I never did the team much good. You're better off without me."

chapter
EIGHTEEN

ridique drops Imms off at B's but doesn't come in. She says she
has to help Mary with dinner. Imms thinks she doesn't want to
talk to B.

B is in the kitchen on his laptop. "Hey. How were the cats?"

"Great." Imms can sense that B is trying not to seem angry, which
is almost worse than him being angry.

B shuts the laptop, stretches. "Surprised the entourage let her take
you out."

Imms hesitates. "We didn't tell them."

Something drops, or vanishes. Imms isn't sure how else to describe
it. One moment, a feeling is between them, a warmth, a relief at being
together that trumps even B's anger. The next moment, everything is
cold. They might be strangers.

"How did you get out?" B's voice is low.

"Through the hedge."

B says nothing. The shame Imms experiences now comes slowly,
an answer to the chill in the room.

"I didn't—"

"*Don't* do it again. That's all I want to say about it. Understand?"

"Okay," Imms says quietly.

"What do you feel like for dinner?" B's tone is normal now, but
it's the kind of normal that takes effort.

"Spaghetti. No sauce?"

"Just noodles?"

"Yeah. Do we have apples?"

"Sorry. I meant to pick some up, and I forgot. It's been a
rough day."

"How was work?" Imms asks.

"All right."

Imms gets a glass of water and feels B's eyes on him as he takes a cup from the cabinet.

"We're gonna start going to NRCSE twice a week," B says.

Imms looks up. "Why?"

"It's important that the NRCSuckers know more about you, to help you adjust."

Imms bites his lip. B hates taking Imms to NRCSE. He thinks Imms shouldn't have to go at all. Has he changed his mind? "Okay."

"They're starting to investigate the fire."

"What happens if they find out we lied?"

"They won't as long as we stick to our story. It's just gonna be a pain in the ass. They're gonna ask more questions. I don't want to answer more questions." B taps the table with one finger. "I'm not normally— I don't usually condone lying. Just so you know."

"Condone?"

"I'm not okay with it. I don't do it. But in this case, it's just better for you, for both of us, if we don't try to explain about you and Joele."

"Because you'd have to tell them I started the fire."

"Joele started the fire."

"Joele only had a small fire. I knocked it down. I made it grow."

"She was torturing you. But if I tell them that, they'll— I don't know what they'll do. They may not understand or believe the truth."

Imms sits at the table. "Vir didn't do anything. When the fire started. She didn't move."

"Vir wasn't well those last few weeks. Maybe not for a long time before that. Why're you chewing your lip?"

Imms stops. "I don't know." He never used to take his own blood, but now sometimes he likes using his teeth to peel fine layers of skin from his lip until he gets a sharp, salty taste.

B gets up and sets out dinner supplies. "How's Brid? She get on your nerves?"

"She was nice. We watched movies."

"Yeah? What?"

"*Blue Valentine*. And *Pocahontas*. I liked that one a lot."

"Which?"

"*Pocahontas.*"

"That's a kid's movie." B fills a pot with water and sets it on the stove. "It's for children."

"It was good."

"Like that trashy Western you like so much, that's something a ten-year-old would read a hundred years ago."

Imms is silent.

"If you want a place in this world, you really ought to act like an adult. You are, right? I mean, on your planet, you're considered fully mature. So what's with this sneaking through hedges and watching cartoon movies?"

For someone who doesn't want to answer questions, B asks a lot. Imms doesn't know why he bites his lip or likes kids' movies. He doesn't know the answer to Bridique's question, what fucking's like with B? Or Josh's question, how is he liking Earth?

B says, "I get what the NRC Suckers don't—that you are human, and you have a right to an independent life. But I brought you to Earth, and you're my responsibility." B breaks spaghetti over the pot. Throws the dry noodles into the boiling water. "I want to keep you safe."

"B?" Imms says uncertainly.

B turns and takes Imms's face in his hands, which are warm and moist from being over the steam. B looks into his eyes. "Why is it so hard to understand? I'm making sacrifices to protect you. Do you see why I might be upset when you put yourself in danger?"

"I wasn't in danger. Bridique just took me to see the cats."

B releases him and turns back to the stove.

Imms is silent. He wants to stay silent. He wants to go sleep by a lake where B can't find him. The scars on his chest hurt.

"Sorry," he finally offers.

"Don't be. I'm the one who fucked up."

B seems to relax over the next few weeks. Each Friday they go to dinner at Mary and Bridique's, and Imms looks forward to this. They go to the park. People stare, but Imms follows B's lead and doesn't look at them. The entourage keeps people from getting too close. They walk the wooded trails. The leaves are yellow, orange, gold, deep red, like blood. When he first saw the red leaves, Imms wanted to ask B if they were hurt. But he had a feeling that was a question that would make B laugh at him. Leaves can't hurt. That's why it's okay to walk on them. Now he knows that the color is from trapped glucose in the leaves. He has been reading about trees in a *National Geographic* book series B bought him. He's getting good at reading. He practices writing too, every day. Printed letters, and lovely, unbroken cursive.

He has to see Dr. Hwong at the NRCSE biomedical facility again. The doctor puts a cold metal circle on Imms's skin to listen to Imms's heart. The metal circle is connected by a tube to the doctor's ears. Dr. Hwong did this during the first examination too, but this time, he waits for Imms's heart to drift to different places in his body, and he listens to the heart in each place. He takes X-rays—big black-and-white pictures—of Imms's body. He puts them on a screen that makes them glow. He speaks to B, not Imms.

"I'd like to do an MRI."

Imms doesn't know what an MRI is, but looking at the way B frowns, he knows he doesn't want one. Three pockets in the doctor's coat. Two screws in his glasses.

"More sophisticated X-rays as well," Dr. Hwong continues. "CT scans."

"Ask him," B says.

The doctor glances at Imms, then back at B. His voice gets too low for Imms to hear him. Whatever he says makes B mad. B shakes his head, turns to Imms.

"Get dressed. We can go now."

They go to Mary and Bridique's that night. Mary shows Imms how to prepare the yogurt dressing for the fruit salad. Over dinner, Bridique describes people's reactions when the news broke that humanlike creatures had been discovered on the Silver Planet.

"People were happy?" Imms asks.

"People freaked the fuck out. The conspiracy theorists, the doomsayers. The fucking *vegans*, convinced we were going to enslave your race and, like, farm you . . . Did you ever wonder if there was life on other planets? Life that looked like Silvers?"

Imms shakes his head. "We knew there were other worlds. But we didn't want them."

"How did you know they existed?"

"Numbers," Imms says. "There's never just one of anything."

"I would argue there's never *two* of anything. Everything is unique, right? No two stones are the same. No two people—or Silvers—or worms, or planets."

Imms shrugs. "On Earth, there are all kinds of different creatures, and they look and behave differently from one another. But they want mostly the same things. You're not so different from B or Mary. Or from a big cat."

"Am I different from you?"

Imms focuses on his potatoes. "I don't think so." He wonders if he is wrong about that. Even nonhuman creatures on Earth are capable of anger, violence, and jealousy. Imms has seen animals on TV fighting over meals, killing each other to claim territory. Humans and Silvers are similar in intelligence, B says. But how smart can you be when you're missing so many feelings? Maybe Brid doesn't want to be compared to Imms, who is so limited in his ability to experience emotion.

But Bridique just asks, "Do Silvers believe in God? Or gods?"

"Not the way humans do."

Bridique turns to B. "This is the kind of stuff people want to know. NRCSE won't give us anything except press conference bullshit about how they're proud to welcome a Silver to Earth. People want to hear from *Imms*."

"We think it's best if Imms stays out of the spotlight."

"We, or you?"

"We," B says.

"Right, because then people will just forget he's here."

"NRCSE agrees he needs some semblance of a normal life."

"Why don't *you* do an interview? You'll have to now, won't you? Now that they're giving you the Golden Fuel Tank for bravery or whatever." Brid puts a forkful of corn in her mouth. "Isn't it something? You get a medal, when Imms is the one who saved your ass."

B shrugs. "Guess so."

Bridique serves herself more corn. "Have you talked to their families? Since the bereavement calls, I mean?"

"Families?"

"Joele's? Vir's? Gumm's?"

"Why the hell would I?"

"I just asked."

"I don't know them, they don't know me. Why would I talk to them?"

"Imms, honey, you mixed this dressing just right," Mary says, taking a bite of fruit salad.

Imms tries to eat what's on his plate so that he won't waste. But B's quick, hard movements beside him are distracting. B swipes his mouth with a napkin and stares at Brid. "I did try to save them."

"I know. I was kidding."

"It's not something to joke about. I don't want to give a goddamn interview. And Imms shouldn't have to parade in front of the media."

"That's fine," Brid says. "But people need more information than NRCSE's giving."

Mary sets her fork down. "Why can't we just accept what is? Why can't we be glad that Imms is here and that B is home safe?"

"Because I'm curious," Brid says.

"Be curious some other time. Not during dinner."

Bridique points at B with her fork, then at Imms. "Does NRCSE know you're banging him?"

"*Enough*," Mary says.

B won't say anything, but heat pours from him.

"I'm excused," Brid says, getting up. She leaves the kitchen.

B gets up too. Imms thinks he might follow Brid, but he goes to the sink and rinses his dish for a long time. Humans use a lot of water, even though they're supposed to be conserving it. B says humans will always find ways to waste what ought to be precious to them.

Mary gives Imms's knee a gentle squeeze under the table.

Imms thinks that if someone were to take his picture with a camera right now and put it on the news instead of that drawing, everyone would see that he is not a hero. That he will never rescue anybody.

chapter
NINETEEN

NRCSuckers love to apply the word *adaptable* to Imms. They are amazed by how quickly his lungs learned to breathe Earth's air, how effortlessly his digestive system adjusted to human food. He told them about the Cosmic Granola Bars on the *Byzantine,* and they laughed. They want to know how he became fluent in English in so little time, having never known of the *existence* of other languages before humans arrived on his planet. Imms isn't sure he picks the best way to describe it, but he tells them that when the humans came, he felt *ready.* Like he had empty places inside of him that didn't even know to feel empty until he saw what he was missing.

He doesn't usually mind going to NRCSE. Sometimes he feels uneasy being away from B, but other times it's nice—the break, the different people. He hates seeing the doctor, but B is always with him then.

The psychologist at NRCSE has a colleague from Sicily who is going to come in once a week to teach Imms Italian. The NRCSuckers want to study how he learns. They have asked him to try to teach them the Silver language, but it is difficult, because the Silver language doesn't have words for a lot of what exists or happens on Earth. Also, the NRCSuckers are even worse at the language than Grena and Vir were. He doesn't get to see Grena, and he hates that.

One day the NRCSuckers take him to a part of the building he's never been to before, a huge room with lights all across the ceiling. Most of the room is taken up by a rectangle of water with only a frame of ground to stand on. The water is bright blue, not clear like most human water. There are thick black lines running through it, and ropes dividing it lengthwise into five strips. The NRCSuckers call it a swimming pool.

Imms loves the tests they do that day. He stays at the bottom of the pool for as long as he can without coming up for air. He swims back and forth across the pool as many times as he can until he gets tired. A NRCSucker attaches a device to his chest and has him go underwater again and stay there until he has to come up to breathe. The black lines, he discovers, are not part of the water but are painted onto the floor of the pool, which is smooth, unlike the bottom of a lake. A NRCSucker named Violet Cranbrim is impressed by his ability to hold his breath for so long and offers him the peach she brought for lunch. He declines because sometimes it's good manners to refuse things you want when they are offered.

Every time he goes to NRCSE, he swims in the pool. Occasionally the NRCSuckers have him pull heavy weights through the water. They start taking him to a small room full of metal machines and have him lift weights with different parts of his body. They encourage him to follow a special diet. They want to see if his muscles are as adaptable as the rest of him. He is supposed to put a powder in his drinks, take vitamins, and eat more fish. One day they ask him to run as fast as he can around an indoor track. The man timing him whistles as Imms completes the lap. Then all the NRCSuckers except Violet Cranbrim huddle together to talk.

Violet stays with Imms. She smiles at him and says, "You're really fast."

Soon Imms is going to NRCSE three days a week. Monday and Wednesday are swimming and weights. Thursday is meeting with the psychology team and Italian lessons.

"You spend enough time at that place, you might as well live there." B gives a half smile, like he means it as a joke, but his voice and eyes are too dark for joking.

"I don't want to live there," Imms says immediately.

"Well, they didn't exactly have to apply thumbscrews to get you there three days a week."

"What're thumbscrews?"

B tells him, and Imms wants to go throw up his powdery drink.

Exercising while humans watch him feels strange—lonely. Except swimming. When he's swimming, he can disappear underwater. He doesn't have to see or hear humans. He can watch the black lines at the bottom of the pool, and the way the light comes through the water. The NRCSuckers take his pulse. They watch his heart. They feel his arms and legs, poke his chest and belly. They seem surprised, confused.

"Humans' bodies change depending on diet and exercise," Violet explains. "Their muscles get stronger the more they work out."

Imms already knows this. B has big muscles that he got from using machines and running in circles. "Mine don't," Imms says. He looks at his arms, which are still long and thin, and remind Imms of the dull gray pipes that go across the ceiling of B's basement. He's only been in the basement once and hated it.

"Exactly." Violet nods. "We're trying to figure out why. You're strong. You just don't look it."

That night Imms wakes with his heart circling his stomach. His head pounds, and he feels both thrilled and afraid. He lies in bed for a moment, confused about why he's here when just seconds ago he was in a huge white room in the basement of NRCSE. He sits up, shaking. The NRCSuckers had said the only way he could travel was strapped to the table. This idea frightens him a lot, but it will be worth it. He just has to get back to the room.

"B," he whispers, shaking the sleeping form.

"Hmnn?"

"B, wake up."

"What?" B opens his eyes and looks at the clock. It is 3:06. Imms just checked.

"How did we get back here?"

"Back here?" B's eyes drift shut again.

"We were at NRCSE, and they showed us that room—"

B yawns. "What are you on about, pardner?"

"The room," Imms says. "You were there. They have a secret room, with a ship—not as big as the *Byzantine*—and it can go to the Silver Planet quickly, and then it can come back. The NRCSuckers said if I went, I had to travel strapped to the table. But they said you could stay with me. I was trying to tell them yes. You shouldn't have brought me back here. I wanted to go." Imms's voice rises.

B grinds the heel of his hand against his eyes. "You had a dream."

"What? No."

He has to make B understand. He knows all about dreams, though he's never had one himself. Sidewalks turn into snakes, and people fly or breathe underwater or forget to wear pants to work. Dreams can be silly or terrifying or beautiful, but they are all lies.

What happened before Imms arrived back here in the bedroom was real. Imms can still smell NRCSE's sterile halls. He can see the faces of the NRCSuckers who showed them the ship. And B was there, brusque, doubtful, and none too thrilled about returning to the Silver Planet but willing to accompany Imms. *So what do you say, Imms?* one of the NRCSuckers had asked. For just a second, he'd been too afraid to reply, imagining being strapped to the table again. But he'd reminded himself it would only be for a few minutes, and he'd been just about to say yes.

B nestles against the pillow and smiles. "You can dream. You're a real boy, Pinocchio."

"It wasn't a dream. I don't know how we got here, but we need to get back there and tell them yes, we want to go. I know you don't like my planet. And I won't stay there, I promise. I just want to see it again. Just one more time?"

"Imms." B is awake now. "I know it seemed real. But it was a dream."

"No." Imms shuts his eyes. Maybe he'll pass out again and wake up back in NRCSE's underground room. He doesn't care if B comes with him. He just needs to go, quickly, to the Silver Planet, just to see it. Then he'll come back to Earth.

"Come here." B tries to pull him nearer, but Imms resists. "I know it's confusing."

"I know what dreams are! They're lies. This was real, I *know*—"

"They can seem very real," B says. "Sometimes more real than life. Believe me."

"I want you to believe *me*."

"I believe that it seemed real to you at the time."

Imms's eyes sting, feeling like fists are behind them, pounding to get out. He gets out of bed and looks around the room for any sign he's been away. He's naked. His clothes from yesterday are in the hamper where he left them. His shoes are—

His shoes. He always sets them neatly side by side in the closet. Now one is upside down, and the toe of the other rests on the exposed sole.

"My shoes!" he says triumphantly.

"Come on back to bed."

"My shoes aren't put away right."

"I threw mine in there before we went to bed. They probably knocked yours out of line. That's all."

"Do you not want me to go?" Imms asks. "Is that why you're pretending it wasn't real?" Though Imms hopes this isn't the case, he understands why B might try to trick him.

B sighs. "Do I want you to go back to the Silver Planet? No. But that doesn't mean I'd hold you back if there was a way you could pop over for a visit. But there isn't. No ship can take you there in seconds, Imms."

"I saw it."

"You were *dreaming*. It's three a.m., and I have to be at work in a few hours. Let's go back to sleep."

"I know what I saw."

"Fine. We went to NRCSE in the middle of the night, where they unveiled a miraculous spaceship that'll go from here to the Silver Planet in a heartbeat. But I didn't want you to go, so I knocked you out, dragged you back here, threw your shoes into the closet, and pretended the whole thing never happened. Sorry about that." B flops back down and shuts his eyes.

Imms grabs some clothes, slips his shoes on, and leaves the room. He goes downstairs and dresses in the living room. He'll go to NRCSE by himself. B can't stop him. He'll find the room, find the NRC Suckers who . . . Already he can't remember their faces. Can't remember what they said. The whole scene is fading, becoming smoke, drifting away from him. He remembers going to bed last night, but he doesn't remember waking up to visit NRCSE. He was just—there, suddenly. What did he and B talk about on the way to the facility? Which halls did they travel to get to the secret room underground? Why did the underground room have windows at the top, letting in sunlight?

"Don't go," he whispers to the memory as pieces of it drift away.

He sits on the arm of the sofa. The place, that secret room, feels far away. It's flat, half-formed, uncolored. All that remains immediate is his terror when he was told he'd have to travel strapped to the table. His desperate hope that Joele wouldn't be on the ship, wouldn't find him.

But Joele is dead. She couldn't be on the ship.

So why was the possibility of her so real in that room? Because it was a dream.

He's wanted to dream for a long time, but now that he has, he hopes he never does again. It is too cruel, the tricks the mind plays when it slips out for the night.

His throat tightens.

A creak on the stairs. Footsteps crossing the room. B sits on the couch beside him.

"You were right," Imms says hoarsely. "I was dreaming."

It takes B a moment to answer. Imms listens to B's nails scratch skin—probably his arm. Imms has memorized the sounds of different movements against different patches of skin. Has counted all of B's moles and freckles and scars.

And what does B memorize of Imms? The number of times Imms keeps him from sleep or work or the privacy of his own thoughts by being foolish, by not-knowing? The endless list of things B must explain to Imms, or watch Imms fail to understand?

Of all the human feelings he has learned about, longed for, shame is the worst.

"Sounds like it was a pretty good dream," B says finally.

Imms shakes his head. He's been wrong about lies. They are not thin and easy to sweep away.

B puts a hand on him. Imms pulls away. "Please. Not now?"

The more real B and this room and this moment become, the falser the feelings of hope and mystery from the dream.

"I used to have nightmares so bad I'd stay up all night just to avoid them," B tells him. "If I got myself tired enough, sometimes I could make it through a night without dreaming."

"What did you dream about?"

"Could never remember once I woke up." Imms listens to the tiny *glick-glick-glick* as B rubs his nose with the back of his hand. "Come upstairs?"

"Not yet," Imms says. "Sorry. I just need—"

B nods. He heads for the stairs.

Imms stays there for a long time, listening to the hum of the kitchen through the doorway. He wonders what B dreams about. What Bridique dreams about, and Mary. NRCSuckers. He wonders what secrets he keeps from himself. None, he decides. Probably the reason his dream seemed real is that the dream was as simple as he is. No hidden meanings, no symbols, no magic. Just a silly desire to travel through miles of space, wave to those he left behind, and return to Earth. A fantasy that he might hold on to both worlds and bounce between them on a whim.

He shivers, no longer afraid, but cold.

When he returns to the bedroom, B will be asleep.

Imms will lie beside him and still be on his own. Even if B appears in Imms's dreams, he can offer no protection. He's not real in the dream world. This is what Imms fears most about staying on Earth—what he will have to face by himself. He came here to avoid Alone, but Alone is under his skin and branches through all of him.

He returns to the bedroom, where B breathes slowly. Imms settles beside him. He has already pushed B away twice tonight. A third chance seems—but, it turns out, is not—too much to hope for. B's arms wind around him, and Imms sinks back, relieved. B sings into his neck, his beard stubble scratching Imms's smooth skin. Imms laughs quietly, because B is half-asleep and the song has no real words. But it is still music, and it's still the best sound on Earth.

On the local news tonight is a story about people who dressed as Imms for Halloween. Children and adults painted their skin silver and some used contact lenses to distort their eyes. One boy put a flashlight underneath his jacket to simulate a drifting, glowing heart.

"Look, B," Imms says as B passes through the living room.

B stops to watch the montage of trick-or-treating Silver imposters. "Don't let all this attention go to your head."

"Go to my head?"

"Don't let it make you think you're better than you are." He tugs a hank of Imms's hair.

"Ow, I won't."

B kisses him behind the ear.

Elise Fischer interviews Michael Huffman, the boy who put the flashlight under his jacket. "That was a very cool effect," Elise says.

"It worked pretty good." Michael rubs his nose. "Except I ran out of batteries after, like, an hour."

"What made you decide to dress as the Silver for Halloween?"

"I dunno. I just thought it'd be cool. I knew a lot of people were gonna be doing it, so I tried to make my costume extra good. The Silver's kind of mysterious, you know? Like a superhero."

"Thank you so much for joining us, Michael." Elise turns to the audience. "The Silver, Imms, inspiring a number of Halloween costumes this year. Coming up, it's available in eight yummy flavors, but what'll it do to your kids' teeth? A sticky Halloween treat that's better left in the bag."

Imms reads *Pride and Prejudice*, most of the Nancy Drew mysteries, and *Gulliver's Travels*. He especially likes the latter, because he loves the idea of islands—little bits of land surrounded by water. It would be hard to dry out on an island.

He can't read all the time, though. Reading never grows boring, but B promised him he'd find lots to do on Earth. Imms spends almost all of his time at home or at NRCSE. Just the thought of what else is out there is enough to make him restless.

"Can we go to the park?" he asks one Saturday afternoon. He wants to get out of the house, which feels too small to hold the two of them plus the shadows that surround B.

"Don't you get tired of people gawking at you?"

"I like the park."

"I'm staying in," B says. "I've earned a lazy day." So Imms makes do with a movie Bridique lent him.

The next day they go to NRCSE. Imms doesn't have to see the doctor, but the psychologist gives him tests. She makes him count things. First, objects in the room: wooden blocks, toothpicks, pores in the acoustic ceiling panels. She has him solve math problems on the computer. She quizzes him on colors. She shows him a chart of human faces with different expressions and asks him to pick the face or faces that best demonstrate how he's feeling. She shows him a movie where cows, chickens, and pigs are killed and made into food for humans. Afterward, she makes him pick faces again.

B drives him home, and Imms nestles under a pile of blankets on the couch, trying not to remember the animals being killed. It is not just Silvers that humans cut into. It is not just each other. Anything that breathes and has blood. Anything that isn't quick enough to escape.

B's phone rings, and B answers it in the odd, too-happy voice that means the caller is someone he hasn't spoken to in a while. B keeps using the word *no*, as though he's afraid whoever is on the other end might hang up suddenly. "No, I'm good." "No, that's great. It was great." "No, I'm glad to hear from you." He thanks the caller and says, "You too," before hanging up.

Imms curls deeper into the blankets. B had a life before—and now has a life outside of—Imms. B has his friends, his coworkers, his enemies. Imms's only friends are Bridique and Mary, and they belonged to B first. No one is his except B, and B is so hard to wrap tight and claim.

There are the NRCSuckers. Maybe Violet Cranbrim is his friend.

He waits and listens to B's footsteps, hoping B will come to him. B goes to the bathroom, humming to himself. Imms listens until the flush of the toilet drowns out the sound.

Two days later, Imms goes to the park. He waits until B is at work. A goon patrols the hedge, but Imms watches until the man turns his back, then slips out the window and through the shrubbery.

Soon he's running so fast that even if the goon sees him, the goon won't catch him. He slows when he reaches the street, and he pulls the hood of his sweatshirt up. He walks to the park, keeping his head down, but unable to stop himself from glancing at the people—on bicycles, walking dogs, holding children by the hand. Frisbees soar through the air. Couples sit on blankets and shiver.

Imms wants to get to the woods, where he will be safer with—fewer people. He would love to sit and watch the people in the park, but they might try to talk to him, and he's not allowed to answer their questions or ask any of his own.

He's not sure if he's walking the right way to get to the wooded trails. His sense of direction is not as good on Earth as it was on his planet. He is walking along the line of trees, looking for the trail entrance, when he notices a man sitting on a bench, wearing a hooded sweatshirt like Imms's. Imms nods at the man as he passes. He has learned this is another way of saying hello.

"You Skaggs?" the man asks. He's pale and thin, and his leg never stops moving. Imms turns. "What's wrong with your face, man?"

Imms doesn't answer.

"Whatever you're lookin' for, I got it."

Imms nods, wanting to keep going, but not wanting to be rude.

"What you lookin' for?" The man's leg bounces up and down, rattling something plastic in his pockets.

Imms shrugs, not at all sure what the man is talking about. "What's the best?" he asks.

"This ain't a fuckin' restaurant, man. Let's do this quick." He hooks a finger in his pocket and lifts out a small bag—just the corner of it, just so Imms can see it. "Shit kicks like a mule. One-fifty."

Imms takes a dollar and fifty cents from his pocket.

A voice says, "Don't move. Hands where I can see them."

A police officer approaches from the trees, hand on his holstered gun. Another officer follows. The man on the bench bolts. Imms does the same, but instead of running toward the park, he goes through the trees into the cover of the woods. One of the officers chases him. "Stop," the officer yells. "Freeze."

Imms runs until the trees end and he reaches the road. The police officer is still crashing through the woods behind him.

Imms recognizes the road toward downtown. Lots of people are always there, and it will be easier to lose himself. He speeds up. A siren whines nearby. Suddenly two more officers come from a different direction. "Stop!" they yell.

Imms reaches downtown's Main Street. The crowd parts for him as he pounds down the sidewalk. One man reaches out and tries to grab his jacket, but Imms is too fast. He dives to the ground and presses himself as hard as he can to the pavement. For an instant, he thinks it will work, that he'll slip under the surface. Then somebody grabs his elbow and hauls him to his feet. His hands are yanked behind him, and his body is shoved against the brick wall of an antiques shop.

Imms is shaking so hard that breath can barely find its way into his lungs. A crowd gathers, and the people who have identified Imms make such a commotion that the officer shouts at them to shut up.

The officer pulls Imms around to face him. His eyebrows go up. "Fuck. Get him to the station," he says to the other officer. He addresses the crowd. People have their phones out and are elbowing each other to get closer. "No pictures! Photographing the Silver is not permitted." The officer extends his arms, shielding Imms, as Imms is led to a car and urged inside, behind a cage wall.

"Did you hear me? *No pictures.*"

At the police station they take computer pictures of Imms's fingers. The woman who puts his fingers on the scanner looks disgusted by them. An officer asks him what he was doing in the park, what he was buying from the man on the bench. Imms is too terrified to speak. Finally, they call NRCSE, even though Imms asks them to call B. The station is loud and ugly, the fluorescent lights harsh. Imms's head throbs. He tries to think like Tin Star, who never complained when he got in a jam, who was always brave and always clever. But he is not Tin Star. He is Imms, and he wants B.

They make him wait on a bench. One of the officers sits beside him, offers him water. Imms takes it gratefully, but after the first sip, the cup slips from his hand.

The officer picks it up.

"Can you call B?" Imms asks.

"NRCSE called him," says the officer. "He'll be here soon." The officer claps Imms on the shoulder and leaves.

After 2,049 seconds, B walks through the door. Imms runs to him, throws his arms around him and hides his face in B's neck. B gives him a quick squeeze and whispers, "Not here."

Imms falls away, too relieved to be hurt by the rebuff. B talks to the officers for a while. He signs a paper. Imms has to sign it too. Then they are allowed to go.

In the car, Imms waits for B to start yelling or at least lecturing. He knows he deserves it. This is a new concept to get used to, submitting his actions for judgment. On his planet, a Silver might refuse to do his or her share of pollinating or break the rule about not having contact with humans, but the consequences were always simple: flowers died, flesh tore. Silvers passed no judgment on one another.

Human society seems to consist entirely of judgments, with elaborate systems of reward and punishment. When B doesn't speak at all, just drives silently home, going five above the speed limit, something cracks inside Imms. He feels a heaviness behind his eyes, a tightness in his throat. His breath stops on its way to his lungs. B glances at him and pulls the car into a fast-food parking lot. He passes his thumb under Imms's eye. Holds it up so they can both see the wetness on it. He removes his seat belt, then Imms's, and pulls Imms across the console into a tight hug.

chapter
TWENTY

he anger comes later. "Do you like living with me?" B asks. He has just come home from work, bringing with him a hard, frantic energy.

"Yes," Imms says. "Except for your night farts."

B slams his keys on the counter. "Because the NRCSuckers think you might be happier and safer living at their facility."

"I don't want to."

"Well, you need to tell them that next time we go."

"I'd rather die."

"Don't say that." B studies Imms, his breath moving his shoulders. "I'm sorry," he mutters finally. "It's just I'm getting hammered for the park incident."

"You didn't do anything."

"No, I didn't. I should have. I should have done more to drive it into you that *you cannot go out alone.*"

Imms presses against the sofa cushion. "I know."

B tosses his jacket over a chair. It misses and hits the floor. "The fact is, they're never going to treat you like a human. They're always going to treat you like a test subject, which means that if they don't think I'm taking proper care of you, they will take you away."

What Imms is most ashamed of, thinking back on the park incident, is crying. A strictly human thing to do. He wonders if it makes him less Silver. "I won't do it again."

B comes to the couch. He kneels in front of Imms and takes both of Imms's hands in his. "I can't lose you," he says. "You're all I have right now."

B's words have a fuzziness, a bit of static that blurs their meaning. Needing is not the same thing as loving. Imms knows this. B is afraid, lost, floating. B is not quite as anchored as he thought he'd be now that he's home.

"I love you," Imms says. He likes to practice breathing the words the way he imagines characters in books do. He likes to watch B's eyes follow the words in the air.

B squeezes his hands. "Promise you're staying with me. No more adventures in the park. Or anywhere."

"No more adventures."

"And I'll do better," B says. "I'll listen when you tell me you want something. We'll go to the park more. Whatever you want."

"Well," Imms says, in his best imitation of Jenny Feathers, the girl Tin Star loves. "You can start by buyin' me flowers. And we'll see from there."

"God." B flops onto the couch next to Imms. "Haven't you found a book you like better?"

"I want to meet a cowpoke."

"There aren't any cowpokes anymore. Just rednecks who wear cowboy boots and drive big-ass trucks."

"Let's meet them."

"No thanks."

"I want to walk around the whole Earth."

"That'd take a while." B looks at the ceiling. "What if we moved? Started looking for a big piece of property, somewhere isolated. We could lose the goons. Have an unlisted address."

"I like your house."

"Our house."

"Right."

B jostles him. "What would you think about that? You could pick where we go. We can look at places all around the country."

"What about NRCSE?"

"NRCSE, NRCSE." B sighs. "Fuck NRCSE."

"NRCSE is shit," Imms agrees.

"NRCSE is a big ol' fucking shit turd. With boogers on top."

Imms laughs. "I like the word *boogers*."

"It's a good one."

"Can we live in Antarctica?"

"No."

"Canada?"

"The Southwest, how about? That's where the cowpokes used to live."

"In the desert?"

"It's not all desert."

"It's too hot," Imms says. "We'll burn up."

"You're impossible." B tickles him under the arms. The sensation fascinates Imms—the catch of his breath, the spill of uncontrollable laughter.

"I know you are. But what am I?" Imms asks.

"Bridique teach you that?"

Imms nods. "She's teaching me to win arguments. She says it's a skill I'll need with you."

B tickles him again. "You think you can win this one?"

Imms gasps. "Okay, okay."

"That's what I thought. Don't take any advice from my sister. She's crazy."

"That's what she says about you."

B raises his hands.

"No!" yelps Imms. "I mean, she says you're—you're the greatest. You're always right. And you—you—"

"And I what?"

Imms looks at the tiny razor nicks on B's chin and neck. "*Non si può radere.*"

"Huh?"

"It's Italian. It means 'you cannot shave.'"

B pounces on him, nibbling the place where Imms's neck meets his shoulder. Imms laughs until he can't laugh anymore. B kisses him softly on the cheek. "Pardner. Don't go anywhere."

"I won't."

"I mean it." B gives Imms's arm a squeeze that's almost too hard.

Imms breathes out. Looks at the color in B's eyes. "I'll stay right here."

Bridique brings Imms newspaper clippings. "I thought you might like to see what the world's saying about you."

Imms glances at the headlines: "E.T. Flees Cops." "NRCSE Makes a 'Hash' of Silver Dealings." "Silver Tongue: How the Creature from the Silver Planet Talked Its Way Out of an Arrest."

"You're a sensation," Brid says.

"Yeah." Imms turns from a tabloid cover that reads "'I Only Wanted to Make the Pain Go Away': Alien Spills Truth about Life on Earth."

"You could hang them on your wall. Or make a scrapbook." She eyes him. "Hey, what's wrong?"

"Nothing." Imms tries to smile.

Nothing is what's wrong. An empty place is inside him, an arena that memories enter, one after another, like performers in a circus. Flames, leaping like acrobats. The cool water of a silver lake, as mesmerizing in its grace as a dancer on horseback. A black sky, once the only thing Imms knew. Now that sky is temporary, the darkness between acts. He spends nights waiting for the curtain to rise, the lights to come up. The distractions to begin.

"Mary and I need some help clearing gutters. Think we could borrow your muscles?"

"I should ask."

"I called Captain Universe. He says it's fine. I promised I wouldn't let you buy weed or bone minors or anything like that."

"Oh."

Bridique looks at him closely. "I'm just teasing." She sits at the table. "It must have been rough, huh?"

"It was fine."

"I'm sure it wasn't."

"I thought I—"

"What?" Bridique asks.

"Never mind."

"Spit it out, rock star."

"I wanted to do something alone." He looks at her. "B thinks I did it because he wouldn't take me to the park. But I just wanted—"

"I know," Brid says. "Believe me." She drums the table. "We all need to fuck up on our own terms. You wouldn't be hu—well, you'd be a rare bird if you didn't."

"I don't want to be alone anymore. It sucked. The big one."

Bridique laughs. "Next time'll be better. How about some gutter-clearing to get your mind off it?"

Imms likes the work. He scoops handfuls of wet leaves, enjoying their slickness, their smell. He wonders how it must feel to be washed from place to place by rain. When it rains, Imms always stands outside. He knows B wants to tell him not to, but B keeps quiet, letting Imms soak.

Mary and Bridique's neighbor helps, too. His name is Don Welbert, and Imms likes him. He doesn't stare at Imms's skin or ask questions about the Silver Planet. He mostly talks about sports, and when they all go in for a break, Don turns on the TV and explains the rules of baseball to Imms, Mary correcting him now and then. She knows more about the game than Don.

Mary serves blueberry pie, and Imms tells her about the book he's reading—*Tom's Midnight Garden.*

"You ought to meet my son," Don says to Imms around a mouthful of pie. "You two would get along. He likes books."

"Your son's half-wild," Brid says.

"Better half-wild than half-witted," Don says. "He'll be home from school at Thanksgiving. I'll have him give you a call."

"Okay." Imms is pleased that Don's son will call just for him, not B. He looks around the table and wonders if humans' capacity for cruelty gives weight to their kindness. They carry each other. They make each other laugh. They are not even as insignificant to their ecosystem as Imms once thought. They don't pollinate, but Mary has shown Imms her garden, and the compost heap. She keeps containers in the house where he throws cans and bottles so they can be recycled.

"Earth to Imms?"

Imms looks up. Don waves at him. "I asked if anyone's taught you to play poker yet."

They play for M&Ms, and soon Imms has a huge rainbow pile in front of him. He doesn't like chocolate, so he divides the candy between Don and Brid and Mary gives him two Gala apples instead.

"A health nut," announces Don, who's working on his third beer. "A born poker player, but a goddamn hippie."

"Don," Mary says gently.

Imms isn't sure about Don anymore. The white parts of his eyes have pink spots.

"Your throat's shiny," Don says to Imms, taking a last swig of beer.

"That's his heart," Brid says. "It moves around his body."

"That's nuts." Don turns to Mary. "You got any more of this stout? Or'd I drink it all?"

"There's more," Brid says. "You know where the fridge is."

"I'll get it." Mary starts to stand.

"No, Mom. You've been on your feet all day. Let Don get it."

"Least you haven't been climbing roofs and digging rotten—" Don burps "—leafs outta gutters."

"Geez, Don, how about a glass of water instead?" Brid says.

"What I wanna know—" Don wobbles to the fridge and removes another beer, popping the cap on the counter "—is why you"—he points at Imms—"came here. If the captain's anything like these ladies, he could probl'y talk you into goddamn anything." Don switches to a high falsetto. "'Oh, Don, please come help us clean the gutters. It'll be fun. Oh Donny, there's a couch we can't lift.' They got these charming little smiles. What wouldn't a man do for smiles?"

Bridique shoves a bottled water toward him. "Don, shut up."

"What about the captain? Did he smile and say, 'Please come to Earth with me, Imms. It'll be fun?' Did he say, 'What would I do without you?'"

"Ignore him, Imms," Brid says.

Mary is silent, staring at the blueberry tracks on her plate.

"That's right, ignore me. Ignore me until you need something."

"Don," Mary says. "We have a guest."

"Yeah," says Don. He stares at Imms until Imms looks away. "I see that."

chapter
TWENTY-ONE

"I've been working on a new trick with Chess. It'd be nice for her to practice in front of an audience." Bridique knocks Imms's shoulder with the back of her hand. "How about it? Want to watch?"

They go to the Rose Sanctuary. Brid has Imms sit on a metal bench outside a round enclosure with a small platform in the center and round stools spaced evenly around the circle. Bridique stands on the center platform, holding a long, thin whip. She explained to Imms that she doesn't use the whip to hit the animals, just to give cues. Margret Rose, who runs the sanctuary, lets Chess into the enclosure and shuts her in with Brid.

"Chess, circle." Brid holds the whip straight in front of her. Chess runs around the perimeter of the enclosure, her movements powerful and effortless. Brid rotates in the center with the whip out straight, like a clock hand. "Take your seat," Brid says. Chess leaps onto one of the stools and sits. It seems too tiny for her, and Imms laughs. Chess looks over at him, and he thinks maybe she laughs, too. "Okay," Brid says to Imms. "This is the one I've been teaching her." Brid stands in front of Chess but not too close, and flicks the whip upward three times quickly. Chess doesn't move. Brid repeats the gesture. Chess yawns.

"Chess," Brid says. Her voice is loud, but she's not angry. Chess turns her focus back to Brid. "Come on, gorgeous. Let's give Imms a good show." Bridique flicks the whip up again, and this time Chess rises onto her hind legs, her enormous front paws swatting the air. "Smile," Brid says, and Chess shows her long yellow teeth, then sinks back onto the stool. Brid tosses her a hunk of something—Imms would rather not know what. "Good girl."

J.A. ROCK

"She's about got it," Margret Rose says. She shoots a dark look in Imms's direction, and at first Imms thinks she doesn't want him here. Then he realizes she is eyeing the entourage.

Brid rejoins Imms outside the enclosure. "The crowds like that one. They want to see teeth and claws. They'd probably like it even better if the cats actually used them on us."

"She listens to you," Imms says.

"Sometimes."

"Always," Imms says. "Even when she didn't do the trick right away, she was listening."

Brid looks surprised. She nods.

They leave Rose and drive downtown. "Hungry?" Brid asks.

"Not really."

"Well, I'm starving. Prepare to watch me eat." She parks in a public lot, and they walk to Main Street.

They spot a group of protestors outside the county annex. The protestors have signs about Imms, and sometimes they shout in unison. Protestors can generally be divided into two groups: those who are concerned for Imms, who believe NRCSE is mistreating him, experimenting on him—and those who fear him, who want him sent back to the Silver Planet or killed. Imms is not sure which group this is, and Brid only glances at them a moment before shaking her head and hurrying along.

"Assholes," she mutters. So maybe it's the second group.

Brid takes him to a restaurant called Past the Gums. The tablecloths are checkered red and white, and each table has a candle in a round glass jar. Imms tries not to look at the candle.

The waiter asks what they want to drink. Imms says Kool-Aid. He knows this is wrong as soon as it's out of his mouth, but it's too late. The waiter looks at him, and Imms sees the flash of surprise, the quick, nervous swallow.

"Um, we don't have Kool-Aid. Just Pepsi products. And iced tea and lemonade."

Imms keeps his head down, wishing his hat covered his whole face, like the black masks robbers wear in movies. Now the waiter knows who he is. And maybe the waiter, like the protestors, wants him gone from Earth.

"Lemonade. Please."

"For you, ma'am?"

"I'll have Coke," Brid says.

"Pepsi all right?"

"Sure."

The waiter retreats to the kitchen.

Brid sticks her finger in the glass jar and moves it back and forth through the candle flame. For a second, Imms is too stunned to react. Brid pinches the flame between her thumb and forefinger and draws it up, out of the jar, then releases it. She starts to do it again.

"Don't," Imms says.

"It doesn't hurt."

B teases him like this sometimes, when Imms worries that B's doing something dangerous. B will do the dangerous thing again and laugh, and Imms will feel embarrassed because it is not very Silver of him to be cautious, to worry on someone else's behalf. Earth has made him this way with its countless dangers and the way those dangers camouflage themselves as ordinary. Right now Brid looks like she might laugh and pinch the flame again, just to tease him.

"The trick is to grab the flame by the top, not the center. Here, I'll show you." She reaches for his hand. He pulls away, knocking the table with his wrist. The wax in the candle jar sloshes, dousing the flame. The candle goes out.

Now Brid stares at him with those eyes that are like the cats' eyes and lets out a very soft breath that might also be the word *oh*.

He holds his wrist under the table. It doesn't hurt, but for a second he wishes it would. Sometimes pain makes things just a little bit clearer to him, jars him from the torpor of his Silver mind, which never knew pain or fear, was never prepared for danger.

Brid glances at the menu. "You want cheez stix? We could split an order. The fact that stix is spelled with an *x* makes me think we need to."

"Yes," he says, wanting to go along with her. This is how the cats must feel about Bridique. She has a loud voice, but inside, she is kind. Inside, she understands you and where you hurt and uses her stronger self to draw the pain out. You do as she asks because you *want* to, not because you fear her.

Imms would not be surprised if fire doesn't burn her, the same way big cats don't bite her.

"Chess's trick is good," he says.

"She's a smart girl. She'll be ready to do it in the show this spring."

"You said you don't like the shows."

"It's not totally exploitative like a circus. The cats don't do anything they don't want to do. We don't ask them to do anything unsafe. It's . . . kind of silly, but overall, I think it's a good thing. It's a chance for us to teach people about the cats. And it gives the cats something to do besides lie around and wait to be fed. Still, if I could, I'd release every one of them into the wild. It sucks that they're in cages. Even fancy-ass boutique cages."

"They feel safe," Imms says.

Bridique looks at him. "What?"

Imms wonders if he should keep his mouth shut about something he doesn't really know. But what he's about to say is true. He knew it when Chess looked at him today.

"They don't always mind being in cages. Because they're safe. You keep them safe."

"Yeah. I mean, they wouldn't have a clue how to survive on their own in the wild."

The waiter brings their drinks, and Brid orders the cheez stix.

"Stop jumping every time he comes over," Brid says when the waiter's gone. "And take your hat off."

"But people will—"

"Recognize you? Yes. And they'll deal with it."

Imms takes his hat off. One of the entourage shifts slightly, watching him. Bridique laughs. "Poor goons. Drinking bad coffee and waiting for our next move. We should offer them some stix."

"B says they're used to stuff like this."

"You're a celebrity," Brid says, pushing ice cubes down in her glass with the straw. "Gotta protect you from the paparazzi." She frowns.

"What's wrong?"

"Nothing." She sighs. "I don't like that you have to pretend not to exist." She picks up his hat, shakes it. "This." She motions to the entourage. "Them. How long is the world supposed to pretend you're not here? You saved B's life. Everyone knows who you are, but they're scared shitless to know more than that."

"B says—"

"I don't care what he says. How do you *feel*? Safe in your cage?"

The waiter brings the cheez stix. "Do you know who this is?" Brid asks him.

The waiter glances at Imms, then looks at the floor. "Yeah. Why, you want free stuff? I'm not supposed to give out free stuff unless it's someone's birthday."

"We don't want free stuff. I just wanted to introduce you. You're—" Bridique looks at his name tag. "Jeff. Jeff, this is Imms. Imms, Jeff."

"Nice to meet you," Imms says.

"Uh, yeah, you too."

"Now shake hands," Brid says. "Like gentlemen."

Jeff thrusts out his hand. Imms takes it. Jeff's skin is warm and damp. They shake.

"Am I gonna get arrested now?" Jeff asks, only half joking.

"I don't know, Jeff. A polite introduction is some pretty heavy shit. But I'd say since our secret service hasn't opened fire yet, you're probably okay."

"The news says we're not supposed to talk to it."

"'He,' not 'it.' And no, you shouldn't go up to Imms on the street and hound him. But a little consensual conversation never hurt anyone."

Jeff nods. He looks directly at Imms. "Our salad dressings are listed with the drinks. It's weird how they don't put them with the salads. Do you know what you want, or do you need a few minutes?"

"A few more minutes, please," Imms says.

"Sure." Jeff hurries away.

"Look at that," Brid says. "You made a new friend."

"I don't think he wants to be my friend."

"I don't think he's a very interesting person. You can do better."

The door to the kitchen swings open, and from the kitchen they hear someone say, "It *talked* to you?"

Imms is uncertain about cheez stix. They are greasy, messy—and delicious, he decides after the second one. He won't dip them in the sauce, though. It looks like blood.

When Bridique is done with her steakhouse salad, Jeff brings them two thin slices of chocolate cake. "On the house," he says. Then, to Imms, "Thanks for dining with us. Come back soon." He looks to Bridique as if for approval.

Imms thinks Brid will probably say something to Jeff that will embarrass him. But she just says, "Thank you."

He leaves them their check.

The manager comes out a minute later and thanks them for dining here. He looks right at Imms.

"I'll pay for my lemonade and half the cheez stix," Imms says when the manager is gone. Brid sets her credit card on the black plastic tray. "I have some money."

"Don't be silly. I've got it."

"You should let me pay for what's mine."

She shakes her head. "You owe what, like three dollars?"

Imms gives her four as Jeff picks up the plastic tray.

"For tax and tip."

"Listen to you."

"Why?"

"Arguing money. Eating cheez stix. Chatting with the waiter. You fit right in."

He feels warm pleasure, but it fades quickly. Maybe Bridique is teaching him tricks. Things he can do to charm an audience, like shake hands with a waiter or offer to split the bill, to pass the time so he doesn't just lie around and wait to be fed. Maybe this show is silly, undignified. That's a bad thought, because he likes so much about being on Earth, about learning to be human. He makes choices, he reminds himself. Like how Chess doesn't always do what Brid says—though she always listens—Imms can act independently, refuse orders.

He takes out two more dollars and slides them to Bridique. "Jeff should get a big tip," he says. And just like that, he's done it. He's decided that one human being's behavior is especially commendable compared to others'. He has passed judgment.

He loves cheez stix but hates the candle. Loves Bridique and hates protestors.

Loves and hates Earth at the same time.

He thinks Chess is more beautiful than the other cats.

That Jeff's hair could use a wash. That the paintings on the wall are ugly but fun to look at.

"The free cake was nice." Bridique looks at Imms like it's him she's pleased with, not Jeff.

When they get home, Bridique comes in with him. Imms tells B about the restaurant. B pretends to be happy, but he and Brid go into the den to fight. The door is shut, but Imms can still hear them. B calls Brid irresponsible and selfish. She calls him a controlling dick. B brings up the park and NRCSE and regulations. Brid laughs and asks if he hears himself.

"You are holding him *prisoner*," she shouts. She opens the door and storms out. Imms thinks he should do something to make it seem like he wasn't listening, but Brid doesn't even glance at him as she leaves the house. B comes out a minute later. He does look at Imms, but he doesn't say anything either. His face is red, and he's breathing hard. He turns and goes back into the den and shuts the door.

chapter
TWENTY-TWO

"—has the right to dictate what we can and can't do," a man with short gold hair is saying when Imms turns on the news. "It is an absolute violation of our freedom to say, 'No one can approach this extraterrestrial. No one can speak to it. No one can take its picture.' What is this thing, Muhammad?"

The screen splits, and a woman with a heart-shaped face says, "Jim, I think more disturbing is the government's unwillingness to share what it knows about the Silver's intentions. How do we know that it hasn't come to Earth with an agenda? They tell us there's humanlike beings on the Silver Planet, and one has been brought to Earth, and then—nothing. We know there are armed guards at the house where it lives. There's obviously some fear it might—might—"

"You're saying you don't feel safe with this thing around?"

"Not really, no. How can anyone, unless the government comes clean about what's going on?"

"So how do you feel about this whole story where it saved the captain's life?"

"I think there's a lot of possibilities, and not all of them are savory. What if it's trying to build our trust, so it can—?"

"And you know," says the man. "It's not just a matter of our rights as citizens, but—forgive me for going a little hippie here—this—this creature's rights. I mean, they say it's got a basically human brain. How do we know they're not experimenting on it?"

"I find it hard to worry about that."

"They must be, right? Why else would they bring it to Earth?"

"Why only one? Why this one specifically?"

Imms changes the channel, finding a satire news show he likes. The show is doing a segment called "Alienable Rights." The host jokes that the government has just adopted a puppy; it's cute now, but soon it will be crapping everywhere and stealing steaks off the counter.

"I don't even like steak," Imms mutters.

He turns off the TV and stretches out on the couch. B should be back by now. Imms can't tell if he's grateful for the time alone, or if he misses B. Making sense of his feelings is increasingly difficult. He never used to have so many. He sinks into the darkness, imagining it is water. He watches the light from his heart move across the ceiling. He finds that sometimes, if he follows a certain thread of thought, he can create a spark in his mind. Not a flame, not a fire, but an attempt at one. He can make himself almost-angry.

First, he thinks about the lakes on the Silver Planet. He reminds himself that he will never see them again. He thinks about all the colors and noises of Earth—too many of them—the way they slip under his eyelids and into his ears. He thinks about B getting annoyed at him for little things like biting his lip and liking cartoons. He thinks how unfair it is that Tin Star gets put in jail when the bad things he did were just things the Rough Rider Committee made him do. Finally, he thinks about being on the table in the *Byzantine* lab, about the glass rod against his skin. He remembers that over and over again, until the scars on his chest heat up. Then he thinks very quickly about all these things together: the lakes, the noise, Tin Star, burning, and especially B's irritation.

A spark shoots up, small and orange. It starts to fade, then glows bright again. It touches something else in Imms's mind, and then—a flame. Imms shakes his head, afraid. The flame dies.

He is not angry. He is still a Silver. He is not turning human.

B comes home. Imms listens to the rustle as he sets grocery bags by the door. "Why are you in the dark?" B asks.

"I was watching TV. But I got tired of the noise."

"I brought you something."

Imms listens to B approach the couch. Thirteen steps.

B's holding something in his arms. A dark shape that moves. Imms sits up.

It is a dog. A small, black dog with bent-back ears and a stubby tail.

"Her name's Lady," B says. "God-awful name, but a sweet dog. A friend at work can't keep her anymore."

Imms takes the dog carefully. She is very warm, and as Imms gathers her against his chest, she wags her stumpy tail. "Is she a baby?" Imms asks.

"No, she's two. Grown-up, in dog years. She's a miniature pinscher. That's as big as she'll get."

Lady puts her paws on Imms's chest and licks his face. "I love her!" Imms strokes her. She is so smooth. B switches on a light, and Imms looks at Lady more closely. She is perfect—sleek, delicate, with tan patches on her muzzle, her chest, and above her eyes. Her eyes are much kinder than human eyes. Imms laughs.

"I thought it might be nice for you to have some company around here while I'm at work."

"Yes!" Imms says. "Yes, yes, I love her." Lady's tail wags furiously.

"You'll have to take care of her. She needs to be walked at least three times a day. I'll let the entourage know. Stay on the property."

Imms turns his face, trying to get away from Lady's tongue. He can't stop laughing.

"This is the best present, B." Imms leans forward and kisses B softly on the cheek. Lady is immediately between the two of them, licking chins.

"It's important to me that you're happy."

"I am," Imms says. He cocks his head. "Are you?"

B gives him a soft smile. "I'm a lot better since I met you."

This makes Imms shiver. He's not sure why. "B? I killed the people on your team."

"No, you didn't."

"I knocked the fire onto the floor."

"It wasn't your fault."

"I hated that they died. But then, after it happened, I was happy it was just me and you. And Grena." He's never shared this before, and doesn't know if it will make B mad or not.

"Me, too." B is not looking at Imms anymore.

"I didn't want the fire to happen," Imms continues. "But I didn't feel that bad about it afterward."

"You can't feel bad," B says, almost sharply. "You're incapable."

"Silvers can feel bad."

"What, like guilty? When did you feel guilt before we came to your planet?"

Imms shrugs. Lady has settled on his lap and looks back and forth between him and B. "I don't know. But I've felt it before."

"You don't need to feel that way."

"You would tell me if you were mad about the fire?"

"I'm not mad," B says.

"You'd tell me?"

"Yeah, I guess so." B stands. Lady's ears prick up. "What are you thinking for dinner?" He heads for the kitchen.

"Dunno."

"I need to teach you how to cook," he calls.

"Okay." Imms looks at Lady. He still feels happy to have her, but a dark feeling is underneath the happiness.

Imms shifts. The dog jumps off his lap and stands looking at him. He gets up and goes to the kitchen. "Let's not eat yet," he says.

"Not hungry? Do you—"

Imms shuts him up with a kiss. He pushes his fingers through B's hair. He doesn't leave B any room or breath to kiss back. He tugs the front of B's shirt, and is surprised when B follows him willingly to the bedroom. Imms undoes B's pants—rare, B usually undresses both of them. He attacks B's shirt, fingers moving deftly down the line of buttons.

"Turn over," Imms whispers, unbuttoning his own pants.

"Why?" B asks.

"I want to fuck you."

B stares at him for a moment in the darkness. Imms's heart pounds somewhere behind his stomach. It thumps against his spine, making his tailbone shudder. "Okay," B says at last.

B lies facedown on the bed, arms folded under his head. Imms moves his hand from B's neck down to B's thighs, enjoying the feel of warm skin under his palm. B has to adjust to accommodate his organ's rising. Cock. His cock.

Imms enters B very slowly. Once inside, he takes his time. He explores as he would any new place. B groans.

"Shh," Imms says. He wants silence except for the slick, crinkling noises of their fucking. Except he's surprised by his own inability to hide how much he enjoys this. B is almost always quiet during sex, so Imms feels he should be too. But he can't stop himself from making noise, and soon B is answering him.

The dog enters the room. B notices first. "Get her out of here."

"Why?" Imms asks.

"So she doesn't see this."

"She would be doing it too, if she had a mate."

B pulls away from him, yanks his pants up. The dog backs out of the doorway. B puts a hand on the door, as if to close it. He turns to Imms. "Let's start dinner," he says. "I'm hungry."

chapter
TWENTY-THREE

b shouldn't be surprised the old feelings know where to find him. He left them here in this house—in the wrinkles in his sheets, the dust on the curtain rods, the pipes under the sink. He left Earth, left behind boredom, the sharp-sticky mess of love, and that deep despair that kept him awake but unmoving at night, finding solace in the ink of the universe until even the trajectory across infinity grew lonely. The Silver Planet was a distraction, but it made him colder than ever. He still slept poorly millions of miles from home.

Now he is back and has brought a new mess to set on top of the old one.

He arrives home one evening while Imms is at Mary and Bridique's. He hasn't had the house to himself for a while, and he tries to savor it. He dials Grena, but she doesn't answer. B wants to talk to her, make sure they're still clear on their story about the fire. NRCSE is starting to ask more questions about the fire, about Imms, about Project HN.

B thinks, as he sometimes does, of the tears in Imms's flesh when B first found him—healed now, barely threads of scars where Joele's belt fell. B wonders if some of his hope for what the two of them could be didn't fall into those wounds, if the skin didn't heal over them. What B feels now is a restless aggression, a snarling desire to use his time on the Silver Planet as a shield against the life he left behind. *Look what I saw, look what I conquered. Look what is mine now.*

He turns on the TV and sees that horrible drawing of Imms. A woman with dark hair is talking to local news anchor Elise Fischer. B recognizes her. Veronica Stuart, the planetary integration specialist hired by NRCSE. The media face of Imms's assimilation to Earth.

Veronica Stuart has the tense, over-smiled look of the consultant on one of those shows where a finicky client struggles to find the perfect house or wedding dress or spouse. She has met Imms only once and was afraid to shake his hand.

B changes the channel and is almost relieved to see images of a flood in the southeast—anything but Imms. He mutes the TV and tries to concentrate on other people's disasters.

The world is watching. B feels people staring when he walks down the street and hears the clicks of covert cell phones. The entourage crouches like video game heroes surrounded suddenly by enemies from all sides at once, and they battle the gawkers while B continues forward. He thinks the media could be a valuable ally. They love the story of Imms's heroics. If NRCSE continues to fight for access to Imms, turning to the public for support might be an option worth considering.

The trouble is, he doesn't want his life with Imms to be a constant struggle to either fend off or ally with outside forces. He wants the two of them bound by something neither of them understood, like they were on the Silver Planet.

The moving idea is a good one. He and Imms can make a choice together about the future. B won't have to look at this damn carpet or any other badges of failure this house wears—the house itself is a badge of failure. It seems a shame, though, to move too far from his mother and Bridique. They are good with Imms, good *to* Imms— better, probably, than B is to Imms.

Money is a problem. NRCSE hasn't offered B a hero's salary. They provide a small stipend for Imms's care, but B dislikes this. It binds Imms to NRCSE, gives NRCSE leverage over both of them. So far NRCSE has agreed that Imms benefits from living in B's custody. They want to see how he does living a "normal" human life. But B knows it is only a matter of time before the NRCSuckers decide what they really want to do with Imms is exactly what B and his team did to other Silvers—take him apart. They'll see it as a wasted opportunity to let Imms live in domestic bliss, or an imitation of it, with B.

Dr. Hwong, for instance, wants to look at Imms's brain and heart. He wants to be the one who solves the mysteries of a mind that can't hate and a heart that moves. He's planning an invasion, slicing Imms open, gawking, prodding. He wants to attach a tiny tracking device to Imms's heart so he can search for patterns in its movement. The doctor says he'll put Imms under. Imms never even has to know what's being done. He's willing to pay B for the opportunity. B's supposed to "sleep on it."

It's not right. B can't offer Imms up for procedures he won't understand. And if he says yes to this, it's a slippery slope. NRCSE won't take no for an answer anymore. Any part of Imms they want, they'll take.

Then there's the fire. B spends each day waiting for a call. From Hatch, from the investigators, saying they know how the fire really started, that B and Grena lied, that Imms isn't really a hero, and so humans don't owe him any kindness. The call doesn't come. What B does get are unsolicited messages from magazines and tabloids. Once, the superintendent of a local elementary school calls and wants to know if B will give a talk at a career-day assembly.

B's phone rings now and he jumps, but it's not Grena or the investigators. It's Matty. Maybe B should be surprised, but he's not. Matty kept in touch for a while after the breakup. Said he wanted them to stay on good terms and meant it. On some level, B's been expecting him to check in.

"Hey," says Matty. His voice reminds B of being outdoors.

"Hey," B says.

"Wanted to call and say I'm glad you're home safe."

"Thanks. How've things been?"

"Good, good. I'm living with someone."

That was Matty. Blunt as hell when he wanted you to know something.

"He treat you well?" B asks.

"Sure. He's a—whatdyacallit, a cyclist."

A whatdyacallit? "That's great."

"I understand you're living with someone too." B hears the grin in that mud-and-cliffs voice.

B can't think of anything to say. Finally he says, "Yeah."

"I really am glad you're home safe."

"Thanks."

"We should have coffee sometime."

"Sure."

"B?"

"Yeah?"

"You sound just the same."

"Be careful, now," B says, a general warning, not a response to Matty's statement. He feels like a parent cautioning a child. He always felt that way, just a little, with Matty.

"Same. Stay cool."

Then Matty's voice is gone. B is left, eyes closed, remembering this kitchen with their mutual smoke rising from a skillet, their laughter, Matty trying to cover the skillet with a lid while keeping his arms around B's waist. B imagines Matty and the cyclist on some absurd bicycle for two, Matty's arms around the cyclist's waist. People come and they go. Some trace your bones for a while, some taste your skin, kiss your eyelids. But they dig beneath fences. They slip under.

Memories of Matty slide into memories of Imms. Those nights by the rocks. The moment B started to go into the ground with Imms and was surprised to find his fear wasn't really fear at all, just the knowledge that he *should* be afraid. The fear he feels now when he looks at Imms, needs Imms, maybe that's not real either. He thinks he should be afraid to love someone not human. He needs to let go, go deeper. He has to *want* to go deeper.

That is what he wants, he realizes. He just has to get better at letting Imms know.

He is still smelling smoke when Imms gets home. He is smelling smoke and smiling.

Today the NRCSuckers have a surprise. They're going to let Imms swim in the river. It is still warm for fall, but Violet Cranbrim warns him the water will be chillier than the water in the pool. Imms doesn't mind. A river is much more like a lake than the pool. A NRCSucker named Devin drives them to the river in a jeep. Violet rides in the back with Imms.

The river is thin and has a strong current until it flattens out into a wider pool. The water is kept calm by a dam there. If Imms swims too far down the wide part, the river will get skinny again, and the current will pull him downstream too fast for the NRCSuckers to catch him. So he has to be careful.

They park the jeep at the beginning of the wide part. Violet tells him to have fun. Imms jumps into the greenish water and strokes through the murk. He pops up in the middle of the river. He swims up the dam, touches it. It's cool and rough against his fingers. He can feel the water, angry and pushing on the other side, forced into ineffectual ribbons by the stop logs.

He swims down the river's center, then dives under, coming to a rest on the silky bottom and reaching out to feel the rocks and plants. After he's been still for a few minutes, the mud settles, and he can see better. A big fish with whiskers swims by. Catfish—he's read about them.

When he looks up, he sees bugs skating along the surface.

He swims farther. Eventually he becomes aware the water around him is stirring. Chilly bursts of it knock the sides of his head, and he feels himself tugged forward. He must be close to the thin part of the river where the current is strong. Straight ahead, the river seems to deepen and darken. He grabs a plant on the river's floor and stays in place for a few minutes, feeling the water try to tug him with it as it rushes forward. He likes this—waiting on the threshold of danger.

He sees a rock a few feet away and releases the plant, letting the current push him toward the rock. He hugs it and sticks his head out of the water, grabbing a breath. The river splits to go around his rock, the twin streams flowing fast, joining each other in a powerful white sash that rushes as far ahead as Imms can see.

He hears a sound above the rushing and knows it's the NRCSuckers. Over his shoulder, he can see the dark dots of them running along the bank, waving their arms. He turns around and swims back into the fat part of the river. He has to fight the current for a moment, and this is exciting. When he returns to the bank, the NRCSuckers all talk at once, asking him what he thought he was doing, and didn't they tell him to stay away from the current? Devin whispers to Violet, "Well, I guess that's the last time they let him in the river."

On the drive back, Violet asks if he has any idea how long he was out there swimming. He says no, and she shakes her head. A long time, she says. "Didn't you get tired?"

He never gets tired of swimming.

"You need to listen when we tell you something, Imms," Violet says sternly.

Violet never speaks to him that way. Imms sits a little farther from her.

chapter
TWENTY-FOUR

b is pleased to see how Imms has bonded with Lady. Imms walks the dog around the property every few hours, plays with her, feeds her, and teaches her to shake. B is adamant that she sleep in a crate, not in bed with them, and Imms accepts this. Once, B catches Imms speaking to Lady in the Silver language.

"You're on Earth," he says to Imms. "There's no need for that anymore."

If Imms has any hope of living a normal life on this planet, he's got to dedicate himself completely to being human. Maybe it bothers B on a personal level, too, that he can't understand Imms when Imms speaks his old language. That it is a way of shutting B out, excluding him.

Imms looks at B uncertainly, as though he wants to protest. Imms is doing more of that lately, arguing with B over little things: the television volume, how long to cook pasta—Imms likes it almost a mush—what color lawn mower to buy. B documents these incidents in the weekly reports he turns in to NRCSE. But now Imms doesn't argue, just stops talking to the dog. He scratches her ears and sits with her for a silent half hour, until B kisses him and suggests they go to the park, Lady, too. Imms says he's tired.

They buy plants—an indoor herb garden, a bonsai tree, three succulents in fancy pots. They make plans to do an outdoor garden in the spring: vegetables in the backyard, and some flowers in the front. B knows Imms will like that. Imms gets into music—heavy metal, classical, R&B. His tastes are eclectic, and he and B sometimes pass entire evenings cooking and singing at the tops of their lungs or curled up on the couch, Imms reading and B dozing or working on his laptop. B doesn't ask Imms many questions about the Silver Planet, afraid of making Imms homesick. He likes that they are here now. He likes that the past fades.

Sometimes he puts an arm too tightly around Imms, and Imms expels a short breath, almost a whimper. But he'll grab B's imprisoning arm and squeeze right back. B wonders if there's any miracle as fucked up and fantastic as loving someone who doesn't have an ounce of bad in him. Someone whose adoration isn't soured by anger or jealousy. B's never had love like that before. Such a big part of being with Matty was feeling the barbs of Matty's disgust with him. Their mutual disappointment in each other, and how it hurt at first but then became as natural and unremarkable as the slightly egg-ish smell of their home.

Dr. Hwong calls one morning while Imms is in the shower.

"Have you thought any more about my offer?" the doctor asks.

"You're not cutting him open."

"Have you asked Imms?"

"I don't need to. It's not necessary, and it's not safe." B grips his phone hard.

"Tracking his heart will help provide a better understanding of it, which may aid in future medical treatment, should it ever be necessary."

"I'll talk to him. He needs to know he has a choice."

"Do hurry," Dr. Hwong says. "Or I'm afraid I'll have to ask NRCSE's permission, not yours."

"It's his choice," B repeats. "Not mine, not NRCSE's."

B hangs up, heat moist on his face, like he's leaned over a pot of boiling water. He watches Imms emerge from the bathroom, towel draped over his shoulders instead of wrapped around his waist, his silver skin glistening. B studies Imms's smooth groin. His cock tucked up inside him. Hairless. Sexless. Yet still so beautiful that B's nerves bristle. B's gaze travels down Imms's legs, to those strange ankles. Then up to the wet, dark hair that Imms is toweling. B meets the cracked-glass eyes. They used to repulse him. Now they are like looking at a wonderful accident.

"What?" Imms asks.

"Nothing. You look good, that's all."

Imms grins. "What's my best feature?"

B shakes his head slowly. He's not in a mood to play or to explain. "I don't know. You just . . . look good."

Imms sits on the bed beside him. "What's wrong?"

"Dr. Hwong wants to do an operation."

"What kind?"

B explains about the tracking device. "Okay," Imms says immediately.

B shakes his head. "We're not going to do it."

"Why not?"

"Because it's your heart. Nobody has the right to mess with your insides. Not unless you say so."

Imms tilts his head. "But I said it's okay."

"I don't think you should let him."

"Is it dangerous?"

"It could be. For humans who undergo surgery, the risk is small, but it's there. For you, who knows?"

Imms puts a hand over B's. "If I didn't want to do it, I'd say no. I'd like to see where my heart goes."

"That's a stupid reason to let him have his way." B's not sure where the anger is coming from. It's probably directed more at Dr. Hwong than Imms, but he's in no mood to be precise. "You said you don't like him."

"I don't."

"Then why are you on his side?"

"I'm not. I just—"

"That's what my team did. Cut you guys open, tried to track your hearts. And you know what happened to those Silvers, don't you?" B is pleased to see Imms flinch. "I try to do a decent thing for you—"

"I appreciate that," Imms says.

"You appreciate that. Good. I'm glad you *appreciate that.*" B leaves the room, a gust sweeping his mind, flattening his thoughts. When they spring back up, B knows this is not about doing the right thing, protecting Imms. It is about how fiercely he wants Imms's heart for himself. It is what makes him a hero, not the captain of a fumbled mission. The man who brought the first Silver to Earth. Who bonded with a wild creature.

Who kept that creature.

In the kitchen, he punches the coffeemaker on. He ignores Lady, who wanders near his feet. *No,* he thinks. *That's who I'm afraid of becoming. A captor. A possessor. If he's mine, it's because he wants to be.*

And I want him, too.

The nuances of a language may be lost in translation, he thinks. Doesn't it stand to reason that the nuances of love are lost when it is forced through two atmospheres? When it hangs in space for days, weeks on end? When it arrives at last on a planet that jangles and screams and is crushed in color?

Imms comes in and slinks around him, grabs an apple. Imms is missing the pieces necessary to make this a true tragedy. They cannot battle one another. B rages and Imms dodges. In the end, they will have an epic avoidance, a wailing Greek chorus of across-the-room silence. The two of them will die, not with knives in their breasts, but shivering, each trapped beneath the ice of the other. For just a moment, B sees this. It stops him from going to Imms, from putting his arms around him, from saying he's sorry. It drives him through the door, to work, and at lunchtime, spurs him to take out his phone and call Dr. Hwong.

chapter
TWENTY-FIVE

d on Welbert's son, Dave, arrives home toward the end of November—earlier than expected, according to Mary and Bridique, who mutter about motivation and grades one evening while Imms is over. Bridique is right. Dave is half-wild. And Don is right. He and Imms get along well.

"You on Earth for good, man, or just a little while?" Dave asks.

"For good, I guess."

"So what have you *done* so far?"

Imms tells him about the big cats, books, learning to cook a little, gardening, and clearing the gutters.

"Dude, okay," says Dave. "That's cool. Here's what's cooler. Beer. Video games. The cliffs. Say it with me."

Imms says it with him.

Beer is horrible. Video games are fun, especially the ones that involve singing and playing fake instruments. Imms hates the ones about wars. Two of Dave's friends come over, and they all hang out in the Welberts' basement.

The cliffs are the best. Dave, his friends, and Imms leave the city and drive to the state forest, where they hike a long, inclined trail until they reach a section of the mountain face with several uneven ledges leading up to a plateau. They race to see who can climb to the top the fastest. Dave wins. Then the boys show Imms the correct sequence for jumping down the ledges. One particularly steep jump makes Imms's heart hold still. They dare each other to try different things on the way down—spinning as they jump, slapping each ledge with their hands as they land. They do the cliffs until they are exhausted.

B seems happy about Imms's new friendship, though he reminds Imms he doesn't want to get stuck walking Lady while Imms is off playing video games. Imms has tried to stay on B's good side since the argument about the tracking device. Especially after how nice B was when Imms got scared in the MRI tube last week. It reminded Imms of being tied to the table on the *Byzantine*, and for a moment he thought he'd lose control, tear the tube apart to get out. But B's voice through the intercom was gentle, and soon Imms was so relaxed he could have fallen asleep. Imms thinks B likes him best—maybe *only* likes him—when he is helpless.

Imms also thinks he sometimes likes to make B just a little angry because he enjoys the contrast when B is kind later.

Imms hasn't told B that the real reason he said yes to the MRI and CT scans, and to the tracking device, wasn't that he likes the idea of pictures of his brain and heart, or that he wants to defy B. He simply knows they shouldn't make Dr. Hwong mad. The doctor is not a good man. He told Imms during an early visit, when B had to leave the room to take a call, that if Imms didn't cooperate during these exams, he wouldn't be allowed to stay with B. He'd have to come live at NRCSE. Imms isn't sure if Dr. Hwong really has the power to make that happen, but he won't take the chance. He would rather they stay on decent terms with the doctor.

"That's cool, man. Just bring your dog here," Dave says when Imms explains about Lady. So Lady becomes the official basement mascot, finishing off their pizza crusts and whining along to classic rock songs. Imms works on liking beer and saying things like "man" and "cool." One night, after a few beers, the boys ask Imms questions about his planet. Questions like Bridique asks, about alien sex. They laugh, and Imms laughs too. Imms says the Silver Planet should be more like Earth. He says this is what life is all about, right here, and he gestures to the basement, spilling his half-finished beer. Lady comes over and licks the fizzing carpet. The boys clink their bottles in agreement, and Imms slumps against the couch, a cheering crowd paused on the TV screen, and closes his eyes.

He wakes in the guest room at Mary and Bridique's, a large silver bowl by the bed. Bridique sits in a chair in the corner, reading. She looks up when Imms shifts.

"He's awake," she calls.

The sound of her voice is like Joele's belt falling against Imms's brain.

Bridique says to him, "You were drunk off your ass."

"Nonsense." Mary comes in, carrying a stack of towels, which she sets on the dresser. She moves to the bed. "David said he had less than half a beer. Honestly, those boys. Do they even *think*? Has he even had anything like that in his system before?"

"Alcohol's a natural element, Mom. They probably have it on his planet."

Mary brushes back Imms's hair. "How are you feeling?"

Imms opens his mouth and suddenly his stomach wants to erupt.

"Bowl," Brid says, and Mary steps back as Imms leans over the edge of the bed and vomits. "I can't believe you have anything left to puke up. You hurled twice last night."

Imms waits miserably for the last strings of liquid to fall from his mouth.

Mary whisks the bowl away, and Imms is ashamed that she is cleaning up after him. Bridique says nothing, but Imms feels her looking at him. He tries to concentrate on the ceiling. Mary comes back with a new bowl.

"Thanks," he whispers.

She hands him a glass of water. He drinks, even though it doesn't seem like a good idea to put anything else in his stomach. She passes a hand over his forehead.

"Jeez, Mom, relax," Brid says. "It's his first hangover. It's a rite of passage."

"He's running a fever. You rest now," she says to Imms. "You sleep all you want. No one'll bother you."

"B?" he asks.

"At work. I called him last night to let him know you're here."

"Where's Lady?"

"I'll bring her up. She's been lying on the kitchen floor, won't move. She's worried about you."

Mary brings Lady to Imms, and the dog wriggles with delight as Mary sets her on the bed. She cleans around Imms's mouth with her tongue, then curls up next to him.

"If that isn't the cutest thing I've seen in a while," Mary says.

"Put it on your Christmas cards," Bridique mutters. Mary leaves the room and Brid says, "If you wanted to get drunk, you should've come to me. There's an art to it. I would've done it better than those losers."

Imms can't make himself answer. He's glad when Bridique leaves. She is especially sharp today, and the way his head throbs and his stomach churns, he can't take sharp.

He wakes in the late afternoon, the sun watery and gray behind the trees. He hears voices down the hall—Mary's and a man's. It takes Imms a second to realize the man is Don Welbert.

"—not something I want to discuss right now," Mary says.

"When will you want to discuss it?"

"You need to stop coming around when you're not invited."

"So it's fine when you need my help—"

"We don't *need* your help. You offer it, and we appreciate it, but if this is going to turn into—"

"Hey, no, no, you got it. I'm out. I'm goin'."

There is a pause. "You said you were leaving."

"You want my help. You want my help now, I know. You want me to bring her home. Tell me where you think she is. I'll go get her."

"You're drunk, Don. And when you're drunk, I don't want your help. I don't want your company."

"You think she's snorting up in a bathroom somewhere? You think she's back on that road?"

"Please go."

"I could stand here all night. What would you do about it?"

"I'll call the police."

"I'll come back tomorrow."

"That isn't funny."

"No," Don agrees. "It's not funny. We're neighbors. Neighbors don't kick neighbors out."

With effort, Imms gets out of bed. The room tilts and spins. When it stops, he walks down the hall to the kitchen.

Don laughs. "Lookie here. My son got the alien wasted. How was it?"

Imms doesn't need to start the flame in his mind, because it's already burning. Don's laughter pops in his ears.

"How are you feeling?" Mary asks Imms.

Imms keeps his eyes on Don. His scars pour heat like blood. "Go," he says to Don.

Don laughs again. "Golly, but don't you look wrecked."

"Imms," Mary says. "You shouldn't be up." She moves to help him.

Imms lurches forward, away from her hands. He's propelled, not by anger, but by purpose. He wants to physically alter this situation, wants to change where Don Welbert is. He goes to Don, who looks mildly surprised. "She wants you to leave," Imms says.

Don holds up his hands, as though in surrender. Imms catches his wrist.

"Go," Imms repeats. He squeezes Don's wrist. Nerves tremble there, little vessels skitter beneath the skin. It is a powerful feeling, to have hold of someone.

Don yanks his wrist from Imms's grasp, so hard that Imms staggers backward. Don crumples his beer can, tosses it into the sink. "Good for you, Mary. Got yourself a new man of the house. Or a—something of the house." To Imms he says, "You ask her sometime 'bout the shoes you gotta fill to be the man of this house." He turns and lumbers toward the door.

Imms shuts his eyes against a spike of pain. He can still feel Don Welbert's wrist in his grip. The bones delicate even in a big man. The scars on his chest have cooled. He doesn't know why he's standing here except that Mary has been so kind to him, and she wanted Don out of her kitchen.

Mary helps him back to bed. "I'll put it down to the fever," she says brusquely. "I've never known you to stick your nose where it doesn't belong, Imms."

The heat of shame mixes with the sweat of fever. She sounds unhappy with him.

"Who did he want to find?" Imms asks.

"Sleep," Mary says once the covers are pulled up to his chin. He does.

B comes in the evening. Imms is glad to see him. B kisses his forehead, says, "You stink," and helps him sit up. Imms is dizzy, and the dizziness doesn't go away. He's scared he'll vomit again and lies back down.

"Let him stay here," Mary says. "He's in no shape to move."

"What sucks most?" B asks.

"My stomach," Imms says. "I keep puking."

"He's burning up," Mary says.

Imms hates when she says that. He is not burning. "You want to stay here?" B asks. Imms nods.

"If you stay, you have to try to eat," Mary says. "I have plenty of apples."

"I'll stop by tomorrow morning before work," B promises.

Mary leaves the room with him, and Imms hears their voices getting farther away.

The next day is worse. Imms can barely open his eyes when B comes. He sleeps, aches, does whatever he's told. Sit up, drink this, sleep now. He's dragged to the toilet, then back to bed. When he wakes, he feels Lady beside him and strokes her. "Don't let me fall back asleep," he mumbles to her as he drifts off again.

chapter
TWENTY-SIX

gray light slips into the room, and he is alert, on edge. He wants to get up, wants to talk to Mary and Bridique. He wants to smell better and eat apples, and maybe even run. Something is wrong, though. Lady isn't on the bed with him. His heart speeds up. B might have taken her home. Mary or Bridique might have gotten up early and taken her for a walk. Still, he's restless and doesn't like not knowing, so he rises and takes a few steps. He is weak, but his skin doesn't burn, and his head doesn't throb. He goes down the hall to the kitchen. No one there, but he finds a tea bag on the counter, sitting in a small greenish pool, and a packet of sugar ripped open and empty. He checks the living room and finally looks outside. Then he hears a murmur below the floor. Someone is in the basement.

He has never been to this basement before. Somewhere he's been thinking it might be too much like the lab on the *Byzantine*. He doesn't know why the Welberts' basement doesn't bother him. Maybe because it has a TV and carpet. This basement has always seemed colder, darker. It is dark, but it is also tidy, with curtains on the windows. A couch and an armchair.

Bridique sits on the couch, Lady in her lap. The dog jumps off her and runs to Imms.

"You're better," Brid says. She is staring straight ahead, eyes hollow and red, body rigid. "The miracle of drugs. Mom agonized over whether or not to dope you. I told her if your body can handle her chicken divan, it can handle NyQuil. Thanks for letting me borrow your dog."

"Are you okay?"

"Fine," she says. "Just having one of those completely lost moments."

"Oh." Imms feels sure he knows what a completely lost moment is.

"I never cry. This is my version of crying."

He sits next to her, almost afraid to move the cushion, to jostle that perfect pain.

"Do you cry?" she asks.

"I don't think so." Imms thinks guiltily of the ride home from the police station, after the incident in the park. He shouldn't be able to cry. He is a Silver.

Bridique takes a deep breath and pushes her hair behind her ears. "It only gets harder and harder," she says, "to know if anything I'm doing is right. Either it used to be easier, or I used to not care as much."

"What don't you know if you're doing right?"

"Everything. Every decision I make—where to live, where to work, who to love, what to fucking do with my hair . . ."

"Your hair is nice," Imms says.

"I'm thirty-two years old, and I live with my mother. There's nothing I do that fulfills me, no way that I contribute to society."

"You help the big cats."

"I clean pens. That's what I do at Rose, Imms. Scoop shit."

"And teach Chess tricks."

She grumbles something Imms doesn't catch.

"You take care of Mary," he says.

"There is nothing worse than taking care of your own mother. You know why? Because I've been hoping for the last God knows fuck how many years that she'll start taking care of me again. Like she did when I was a kid. That she'll tell me what to do."

Imms says nothing.

"It's pathetic. It's the most pathetic thing to wish for. Especially for a woman to wish for. I ought to take care of myself. I ought to make *myself* happy." She wipes her nose on the back of her wrist. "Don Welbert would fucking love to come over here and take care of us. But we don't need him."

"Why does Don—"

"I feel like I'm trying to get in line at a checkout, and people keep coming up with their arms too full and they look like they're about to lose their grip on all their shit, so I keep saying, 'Oh, after you, after you.' It's like, when's it my turn? When do I get what *I* need? And yes, I'm aware that I sound like a whiny loser."

"You don't. You sound human."

"When I was a kid, I wanted to be out from under everybody's thumb. To be a grown-up." She runs her fingers up and down her throat. "It's fucking humans. We overnurture our young. If I were a lion, I'd have been fending for myself by age two." She shifts so that she's partly facing Imms. She shakes the hair out of her eyes. "What's it like on your planet? How do Silvers raise children?"

"Silver children stay underwater," Imms says. "They can hold their breaths much longer than adult Silvers. They only have to come up for air about once a month." Bridique looks at him, quiet and expectant, and he continues, "The water on my planet, I've told you, is silver. Like the shiniest metal you can think of. The children go underwater after they're born. Their parents don't see them again until they resurface. In human time, that's about eight years later."

Bridique's mouth falls open. "What do they do underwater for eight years?"

"No one knows. I don't remember much from my own childhood. What I do remember is all silver. I just drifted. Sometimes the water was darker. Sometimes I could see light, and that meant I was near shore. I remember how welcome the black sky was when I came up for air. Just a moment of cold. A moment without the heaviness of water. I could see that the world was still there. Then I'd go back under."

Bridique wipes her eyes, though they're not wet. "I wish we could do that. I wish my little girl could go on her own underwater journey for eight years, without anyone to yell at her or tell her what to do. I wish she'd surface with eight years of mysteries locked away in her brain. That's what I wish." She shoots a quick, sharp glance at Imms. "Maybe I only wish that so I wouldn't have had to try to be responsible for her. I fucked that up pretty good."

"That's an okay reason to wish that. Maybe Silver parents don't realize how lucky they are."

"Do you really think that? Do Silver moms not miss their babies?"

"I don't know."

"I get to see my little girl this weekend."

"What's her name?"

"Cena."

"She'll be glad to see you," Imms says.

"No." Bridique shakes her head. "You know how Chess at the sanctuary came right up to greet us? And Tommy, the big tiger, didn't budge? She's Tommy. With me. She can hardly spare a glance."

"Oh," Imms says. He wishes he knew more about humans, so he could tell her what Cena's behavior really means.

"She's very grown-up. You know? The way she acts. She's one of those kids who makes you feel like . . . like she knows more than you. I hate it sometimes."

Imms doesn't answer.

"Can I see your heart?" she asks. "Please?"

They're both quiet a moment. Then he unbuttons his shirt. He's not sure where his heart will be, but he is suddenly sure that he can will it to where she's looking. Sure enough, it drifts up, settling just left of his breastbone, where a human heart is supposed to be. It's glowing bright. He pulls his shirt away and lets her look.

"It's so fucking perfect." She glances up. "Sorry. I'm always telling the kids who come to the sanctuary on field trips, 'This is not a zoo. These cats are not here for you to gawk at. They are beautiful creatures who belong in faraway places.'"

"I'm not a beautiful creature," Imms says quietly. "I'm an ugly creature, from an ugly place."

"Modesty doesn't suit you."

"I'm just saying gawk if you want."

She looks again at the glowing spot beneath his skin.

"Does it give off heat?" She puts out a hand. "May I?"

He smiles. "I'm a wild animal. Be careful."

She places her palm over the glowing spot. Her fingers are cool, small, smooth. They search the skin around the heart. "It's not any warmer than the rest of you," she says.

Her touch is strange and makes him miss B.

"What happened here?" she asks, tapping his crossed scars.

"I got burned."

She laughs. "Sorry." She puts a hand over her mouth.

"What?"

"Humans use 'burned' as slang sometimes. Meaning, I don't know, betrayed, usually."

"Betrayed?"

"Like, when my first husband left me. I think I actually told the next guy I dated that I wanted to take things slow because I'd been burned before."

"Oh," Imms says.

"But that was awful of me to laugh. How'd you get burned?"

"I don't know." He hopes this sounds like the truth. "It was during the fire. But I don't remember what happened." He starts to button his shirt. Bridique puts her fingers on the scars again. Imms swallows. Her eyes meet his.

She looks like she might say something else but doesn't. Imms finishes buttoning his shirt. "Are you okay?" he asks her.

She nods slowly. "Better. Thanks."

She gets up and goes upstairs. Imms doesn't know whether he should follow her.

Mary is furious that he's out of bed. "I don't care how good you feel. Your body has not recovered, and you shouldn't push it." She changes the sheets while he's up and lets him have a bath. She insists on sitting with him, though, in case he passes out in the water.

"I can hold my breath a long time," he tells her.

"Is that so?" she asks dryly.

He hopes she's forgiven him for the incident with Don.

She hasn't mentioned it again.

He soaks in the warm water, and she stares out the window. He imagines she's counting the things she has to do. Imms doesn't count much anymore. He is growing lazy.

"I'm done," he says, once he's rinsed the shampoo from his hair.

"Don't rush on my account. You stay in as long as you want."

Imms sinks back, watches the way his skin becomes shinier, more metallic, the longer it stays under water. "What was B like when he was young?"

Mary glances at him. "Just how you'd imagine."

"I don't know how I'd imagine," Imms confesses.

"Very serious. Bright. Commanded an army of neighborhood boys. Only one who wouldn't take orders from him was his sister."

"What was she like?"

"She was . . ." Mary sighs. "She was very bright as well. And caring. She took good care of . . . people."

Imms swirls the bathwater with his finger.

"Never easy to tell what either one was thinking. They get that from their father."

"Is their father dead?"

Mary shakes her head. "No. He isn't. But he's not coming back."

"You're a good mother," Imms says.

Mary looks surprised. "How do you know?"

"You take good care of people."

Mary looks, for a red and hollow-eyed instant, like Bridique did this morning. "That's sweet of you. But you don't really know. Maybe if I'd taken better care of my son, he wouldn't have traveled light-years to get away from home. If I'd taken better care of my daughter, maybe she wouldn't look for men who'll push her away once they get what they want. Maybe she wouldn't need whatever she puts in her body to make herself feel better." She pats her knees, stands up. "But that's my burden. Not yours."

"I like to know," Imms says. "Sometimes I don't understand B. I wish I did."

Mary gets a towel from the cabinet and places it on the counter. "Does my boy take good care of you?"

"Yes."

"I'm glad. You've been good for him. I can see the difference."

"He was sad on my planet. He's glad to be home."

Mary nods. She looks as if she has wandered into the room and forgotten what she meant to do there.

Imms pulls the plug from the drain and lets the warmth swirl away. Mary helps him out of the tub, puts him back to bed. Being human means a lot of different cages, Imms thinks. Caught beneath covers, between walls. Bounded by yards, towns, regions, countries. Even the human heart is shrouded in ribs. He supposes his Silver body was a sort of cage too, until Joele opened it up, let the blood out.

Now he knows what it's like to be opened and to close again. To bleed and to heal.

He lets himself be surrounded. Tries not to miss the black sky, flat bright land, a world without walls. That is a part of him that bled away when he opened. He has healed around the loss. He is home.

chapter
TWENTY-SEVEN

"**h**ave you seen these?" Hatch asks. Hatch has Vir's journals, three of them that Vir kept during her time on the Silver Planet. Two are filled with field notes, and the third is a personal diary. Hatch lets B stay in her office, reading them while she goes to lunch. B keeps glancing over at the cactus, which seems like it's watching him.

The first few entries in Vir's diary read like her field notes. She documents her surroundings. Her body's reactions to the unfamiliar place. She tries to use neutral prose to mask some of her astonishment over the discovery of the Silvers but quickly loses the battle. For the first two months on the planet, Vir is in love. She writes about her interactions with the Silvers, teaching them English, showing them photographs, learning about their society.

Then something happens. She doesn't write directly about the violence her crewmates perpetrate on the Silvers, but she hints at it. The words "cruelty" and "unethical" come up. Gradually her writing stops making sense. Entries end midsentence. Words appear on the page with no apparent order or reason. Even her handwriting unravels, the neat, tight cursive becoming a loose, drifting scrawl. She draws pictures.

She draws fire.

B sees flames eating letters, eating people, eating a crude cartoon of the *Byzantine*. Comets with long, burning tails and walls of flame separating people.

She writes that she is cold. At first B thinks she means physically. Then Vir writes that she is *just like the rest of them—I don't feel.* B hopes that by "the rest of them" she means Silvers with their limited emotions. But he knows she means him. And Joele and Grena and Gumm.

She visits the Silver in the lab during Project HN. It speaks to her. She never learned the language well enough to know what it's saying. She knows she could let it go, but she doesn't. If she were truly human, she would. If she were human, she'd use any means necessary to put an end to this violence.

Then, abruptly, the handwriting tightens again. The sentences aren't hard to decipher. The entries become clinical descriptions of the way Silvers bleed, the way they die. Vir says someday the Earth will get so hot, it will burst into flames. Then the Silvers will rule the universe.

B takes the journals to a nearby office and makes copies of certain pages. He sits in Hatch's office and tries not to think how unlikely it is that Silvers will ever rule the universe. The best Silvers can hope for is that humans will leave them alone. But that won't happen.

That won't happen because of B.

B has cut into Silvers and, in doing so, has invited everyone else to do the same.

He doubts drinking beer with Dave Welbert is what made Imms sick. More likely the illness was the result of whatever leaped into Imms's body when Dr. Hwong made an incision in Imms's chest and put a small tracker on his heart, so that the doctor can monitor the journey the heart goes on. Imms goes to Biomed once a week so the tracker can beam his heart's trajectory right to Dr. Hwong's computer. B imagines the doctor analyzing the organ's path, sticking pushpins into a map on his wall like a military strategist.

Hatch is gone nearly an hour. When she comes back, she smells like onions.

"Well?" she asks.

B hasn't thought about what to say. "It was hard for her there" is what he finally goes with. Stupid, empty words.

Hatch accidentally knocks her rubber band ball off the desk, and B sees her decide it would be undignified to try to retrieve it. "Did you know she was slipping?"

"Not like that."

"You think she could have set the fire?"

"What?" B is genuinely surprised.

Hatch sits at her desk. "The wire that sparked—don't ask me for details; I don't know anything about this stuff—but apparently the way the insulation was worn away didn't look like an accident."

"Of course it was an accident."

Hatch picks up the notebook. "Vir was crazy. You read this. She'd lost her damn mind."

B doesn't answer.

"I've known you a long time, Captain. I'm not your lawyer. You don't have to tell me anything. But it might help if you did." Hatch leans forward. "Are you covering for her?"

This time B can't answer. He stands. "Vir didn't sabotage the ship."

"No one's saying she did." Hatch pushes her glasses up. "Yet. The investigators want to talk to Imms again."

"He's told them everything he saw."

"He's the only witness. They want to make sure they haven't missed anything."

"Christ. Fucking hell, Hatch."

"You trust Imms, I take it?"

B stares at Hatch. "Imms saved my life."

Hatch looks at her cactus as though for guidance, or maybe to share a moment of pity for B. She turns back to him. "Do you have a lawyer?"

"Do I need one?"

She shrugs. "Even if you were covering for Vir, I'd understand, to some degree. But—"

"I'm not covering for Vir." This, at least, is true. "If Vir wanted to set a fire, how could she guarantee it by—what, messing with a wire?"

"She could have messed with it before setting the fire. To make the fire appear accidental."

"She *died* in the fire." B's temper is rising. "What did it matter to her if the fire looked like an accident or not?"

"Let the investigators talk to the Silver."

"Does *he* need a lawyer?"

"All I want is to keep this as quiet as possible, Captain. I was happy to give you and Grena medals and call the whole thing a tragic accident. Now I've got this." She motions to the journals.

B didn't go into Vir's room after the fire. Couldn't. He didn't go into Gumm's, either. Just Joele's, in case she'd left anything incriminating— matches, bloody clothing, pickled Silver livers. He wishes now he'd gone into Vir's room and found these journals, destroyed them.

B doesn't know what exactly he tells Hatch. He needs a walk. Fresh air. He goes out to the exercise compound and walks along the fence, dragging his hand along the chain link, making it rattle.

Imms is about to go into the conference room where members of the *Breakthrough II* mission are waiting to ask him questions about the Silver Planet, when Grena arrives with two NRCSuckers. Imms is too surprised at first to speak. Grena is talking to the NRCSuckers and doesn't notice him right away.

"Grena!" he says when he finds his voice.

She looks at him. Her expression changes too quickly for Imms to read it well. He recognizes only the smile she ends on.

"Imms." She walks over and hugs him.

He throws his arms around her, and for a second he doesn't want to let go.

She steps back. "How are you?"

"I'm good." He wants to tell her everything—about B and Bridique and Mary and Lady. About Don and Dave, the park, the cliffs, being sick, and how he and B might move to where the cowpokes live.

"I, um. We have to go in now. But maybe we can talk after?" She glances at the NRCSuckers. "If that's okay?"

One of the NRCSuckers nods. They all go into the room. Imms has been nervous about the meeting, but now he's excited. He can barely focus when the head NRCSucker introduces Imms to the team. He keeps looking at Grena in the back of the room. She is mostly the same but thinner. He can't tell what she's thinking. Once, she smiles at him, and he thinks he's going to turn in circles like Lady does when she's happy to see Imms.

Imms answers the team's questions as best he can. Some are formal—questions of logistics, survival. Some are personal. Team members want to know about Imms's experience growing up on the Silver Planet. The more questions Imms answers, the stranger he feels. He is describing a place that used to be his home, a place he is never going back to. This room has white walls and harsh fluorescent lights. Is this what's normal now? He is telling these humans how it will feel to go to the Silver Planet. He is helping them figure out how to interact with Silvers.

But what if their intentions aren't good? The NRCSuckers have told Imms this team is not going to harm Silvers. They're just going to learn more about them. But Imms suddenly can't shake the feeling he's betraying the Silvers.

"Why did you come here?" one man asks him.

For a second, Imms can't remember. Why would he come here when he could have a place without walls, without lights, without people asking him questions? A place where he fits, where he is not a stranger?

Then he remembers being forgotten. He remembers Alone, and B saving him, and wanting to be different from every other Silver. But he can't talk about B here.

"The same reason you're going there," he says finally. "I wanted to see what it was like."

"Do you miss home?" the man asks.

"I . . ." He looks at Grena. She looks back at him. He swallows. His body is tense, and his mind is stuck.

Imms turns to the head NRCSucker. "I miss it sometimes." He feels dizzy, confused. The NRCSucker doesn't respond. Probably because Imms meant to address the answer to the man who asked the question. He gets it wrong again when he turns to his audience and says, "I don't want any more questions."

That's what he should have said to the NRCSucker.

"I don't want any more questions!" he shouts at the floor.

He doesn't know what to do now. He feels like he's swimming, like the current is rushing past him, like there's nowhere to set his feet. He jerks away when someone tries to touch him. Then Grena is beside him and she's telling everyone else to get away. She walks him into the hall, where it's cooler and darker.

"Imms," she says. "Look at me."

He tries. He would rather go into the ground.

"Imms. I've been talking to NRCSE about getting you on the *Breakthrough II.*"

Now he does look at her. "What?"

"There might be a way back. If you're unhappy here. If you need to go home."

For just a second, everything inside him stills. He might be able go home. Back to his clan, the lakes. Grena might rescue him.

But he can't. He *does* like it here. He does love Mary and Brid and the big cats and Dave and Lady. And B.

He can't leave. B can't even know he wants to.

And the truth is, he doesn't want to. Earth might not truly be his home, but neither is the Silver Planet, not anymore.

He shakes his head. "No," he says softly. "I don't want that."

"You can think about it," Grena says. "If you decide you want to, I'll do everything I can to help you." She pauses. "This isn't good for you, Imms. What they're doing to you here."

"No," he says again, not sure if he's agreeing with her or still protesting the idea of leaving Earth.

She touches his shoulder. "Think about it."

Now the NRCSuckers are crowding around, assuring Grena they'll take care of Imms. At some point, Grena is no longer touching him. Then she's gone.

Matty brings B a casserole the day before Thanksgiving. Imms is out with Bridique.

"We made two, but there's gonna be so much food at Greg's parents', and now our fridge is crammed. Something had to go. It's good, though. Really good."

"Thanks," B says. So that's the cyclist's name. Greg.

"Where's your friend?"

"Out," B says.

B has been trying to get information from Imms about his talk with Grena. Grena still won't answer B's calls, and B knows she said something to Imms that's upset him, but Imms won't say what. Imms says they just talked about how he's doing on Earth.

"I get so much crap from everybody. 'Have you seen your replacement? He's out of this world.' Greg was like, 'It'd be bad enough if you'd turned him straight, but this . . .'"

B doesn't laugh. "He's not your replacement. What makes you think he and I—"

"Why does everyone assume I drove you away?"

B stares at him. Matty doesn't know. *Couldn't* know.

Only B's mother and Bridique know what Imms is to B. No reason to panic. "My mom and sister don't. They blame me."

"Well, that's something."

"It was my fault," B says, nodding at the wall. He says it to Vir and to Matty, to Imms and to NRCSE.

"Nah. It takes two."

Matty never did understand. He would have been happy forever with this house and the ugly carpet and every evening the same. Matty's never wanted to leave town, let alone leave Earth. B knows he's probably every bit as afraid of being alone as Matty. The difference is that B can't be with someone who's already decided once and for all who he is. Who can't even imagine himself in a life, a world, other than the one he occupies.

Matty thanks B for taking the casserole off his hands. He says they should get coffee sometime. He goes back to Greg the cyclist. For just a second, the past is spread out on the floor, like the instructions for assembling a piece of furniture. B is on his knees, throwing rivets, cursing manufacturers. He will never build anything that stands using these blueprints.

chapter
TWENTY-EIGHT

Imms isn't sure he wants to go back to the Welberts'. He is afraid Don will still be mad about Imms telling him to leave Mary's and grabbing his wrist. Dave assures him it will be fine.

"My dad never remembers what happens when he's drunk. Seriously, I bet he hasn't given it another thought."

Dave is right. Don—sober, flannel shirt, checking the status of some items he's auctioning online—is as friendly as ever. He asks if Imms is feeling better, asks after Mary and Bridique. He has a quiet ease in his voice and body when he's sober that flees when he drinks.

"Don't give him any more booze," Don tells Dave, with a wink at Imms.

"Yeah, man, that was rough," says Dave. "We'll be careful."

They go down to the basement and play an old Mario Bros. game while they wait for Dave's friends. "Can you believe this shit used to be, like, state of the art?" Dave makes Mario jump onto a flying turtle shell. "Why do you think your people never invented stuff like this? I mean, you're obviously pretty smart."

"We didn't need to."

Dave nods, eyes on the screen. "Makes sense." Mario runs off a cliff. Plunky music plays as the screen goes black.

Imms is Luigi, wearing green. He runs through a world of flat-topped trees. He bounces on clouds. Plants with teeth leap from pipes, and strange creatures throw fire at him. He has to keep jumping, dodging, stepping on heads. The world moves as he does, so he can't always see the next obstacle, and can't go back if he misses a coin or one of the boxes with question marks on it. The screen edges him into the unknown, toward the finish.

"Do you know what you'll do?" Dave asks. "Are you gonna get a job or anything?"

"I don't know," Imms says.

"My dad could probably get you a job at the plant, if you want."

"Plant?"

"He works at the meatpacking plant. I dunno. It's kind of sick, but you could make okay money."

Imms pictures a plant with teeth—like the ones that keep shooting out of pipes in the video game—putting hamburgers into a suitcase. "Where's your mom?" he asks Dave.

"She died when I was a kid."

"Sorry," Imms says. That's something he's learned on Earth. It's good manners to apologize when somebody is dead.

Dave shrugs. "I don't really remember her."

"Is your dad in love with Mary?"

"Dude." Imms isn't sure what the "dude" means. He waits, and after a moment, Dave says, "Naw. I think he's into Bridique."

Imms is so surprised he runs Luigi into a turtle.

"Bridique?"

"Yeah, hey, you don't have to tell me. But, yeah, they're kinda— they used to see a lot of each other. Not like—I don't think they ever—but yeah."

"Does she like him?"

"I dunno. I try not to think about it. I think she sort of encourages him because he promised to help her get her kid back. 'Cause like, he was in law school before he dropped out. And I'm prelaw. So Dad thought between the two of us, maybe we could help her. And Brid knows it's like, a joke, pretty much. But still."

"Why can't she have her kid back?"

"Ask her about it, man. I don't want to go spilling stuff that's not my business."

The pounding upstairs means Dave's friends have arrived. Imms hears them exchange greetings with Don. Dave calls to them to get their asses down here. They put in a war game. The next few hours are crashes, explosions, electric sparks of gunfire. Imms pretends to want to kill. He tries not to think about Bridique and Don.

Thanksgiving is at Mary and Bridique's. Imms asked if Grena could come, but B said she didn't pick up when he called. Imms likes the smell of the food, especially the baked apple cobbler Dave made.

"You *bake*?" Brid asks.

"Yeah, I'm not half-bad in the kitchen," Dave says.

They go around the table and say what they're thankful for. Mary is thankful B is home safe. She's thankful Imms is here. Don is thankful he has such kind neighbors, and for his new washing machine. Dave's thankful for the break from school, and Bridique is thankful for the fucking food and could they hurry up please she's starving.

B squeezes Imms's knee under the table and says he's thankful for his time on the Silver Planet, but he's glad to be home. Imms doesn't know what to say. On the Silver Planet, nobody says what they are thankful for. If you are thankful for someone, you curl up next to them. You take their hand.

In the Silver language, Imms tells them, "I'm thankful for all of you. And Lady."

"In English," B says.

The others look at him.

Bridique says, "Why the fuck can't he be thankful in whatever language he wants?"

"He can. But if he'd like to communicate with us—"

"He's right there," Brid says. "Tell him."

B turns to Imms. Imms tries not to let anything show on his face. If B is mad, it'll be worse if nobody takes B's side. B will sit through the meal with his anger balled tight, and later it will come unraveled. "We didn't understand what you said."

"We don't need to," Brid says. "It's up to you, Imms."

"I said I was thankful for all of you," Imms says.

"There we go." Don slaps the table lightly. "Doesn't matter how you say it. It's the thought that counts."

Dave reaches for the turkey. "Let's dig in before Bridique wastes away."

The food is good. Imms eats a lot of turkey and tries not to think about it having been a live bird. After dinner, they go into the living room and turn on the TV, but nobody really watches. Dave takes off for another dinner at a friend's house. Imms sits next to B, who slings a casual arm around him, and Imms can tell that he's not mad, but he is frightened. His heart races. Imms imagines he can see through B's clothes and flesh into some uncertain hollow, a place where B is lost, or hidden, or wounded and cold. B is trying to be a son, a brother, and also to belong to Imms. He is trying to be home. But he might as well be beneath a black sky with no stars.

So Imms puts a hand on B's ribs. Over the worst tear in the curtain that hides that empty place. He keeps his hand there until B stops talking to Mary and looks at him. B doesn't understand exactly what Imms is doing, because B isn't even aware of the hollow. He has lived with it so long that it has become part of him. He thinks of it not as an empty space, but a growth, a burden. Something in B's face softens as he looks at Imms, something in his eyes apologizes—not just for his words, but for what is missing inside him. He lets Imms touch him.

Later they play a board game called Scrabble. Imms wins twice.

"English isn't even his first language," Don grumbles.

Imms wants to tell him it's not just about the words. It's about counting the spaces, seeing where each tile will be best utilized. Looking at other people and figuring out what they want to do, then thwarting them. When Imms and B go home, B is quiet. They get ready for bed on opposite sides of the bathroom. They go to sleep, and B takes almost no breaths that Imms can count before B reaches for him. Imms curls closer, stroking B's skin, the satisfying lines of his muscles. Imms holds B until the sleep breaths start. B needs this.

This is one way Imms can rescue B.

Bridique tells Imms to meet her at the picnic shelter in the park. The entourage follows him, dressed to blend in, their weapons concealed. When Imms reaches the picnic shelter, Bridique is there with a little girl. The girl has Bridique's wide-set eyes, and the tilt of her jaw reminds Imms of B.

"This is Cena," Brid says. She looks down at her daughter. "Say 'hi.'"

"Hi," Cena says.

"Hi," Imms replies. "I'm Imms."

"You're gray." Cena turns away to watch the kids on the swings.

"Tell Imms how old you are."

Bridique is not herself. Her voice is higher pitched. She seems desperate for the girl's attention, and for Imms to approve of her and her daughter—the two of them together.

Cena doesn't answer.

"She's almost eight." Brid jostles Cena's hand.

"Right?"

Cena doesn't look at her.

"I'm sorry." Brid turns to Imms. "She's sort of in her own world."

"You have nice hair," Imms tells Cena. She does. Loose, reddish-brown ringlets.

Cena swings her head toward him. "Thanks."

He counts thirty-five stickers on her backpack, which is blue plastic with astronauts on it. She has one hundred and sixty eyelashes on her left eye. When her thumb goes into her mouth, her lips pulse around it twenty-one times before Bridique says, "Stop. You're way too old for that."

They walk around the playground, but when Bridique asks if Cena wants to swing or seesaw, Cena shakes her head. It's too cold to be out long, but they walk downtown, past the shops decorated for Christmas. Bridique asks Cena questions, and when Cena doesn't answer, Bridique proceeds with the one-sided conversation as though she has. Imms wonders if he should also try to ask Cena questions. If between the two of them, they could get Cena to open up.

"What do you want for Christmas?" Brid asks.

Without looking at her mother, Cena replies, "A bike."

"What kind of bike?"

"Blue."

"A blue bike," Brid says. "Maybe we should look for one while we're out."

"I already asked Daddy." Cena sounds bored. She sounds like she has a hollow like B's, but nothing has hardened around it because she is soft and small.

Cena sees a friend from school out with her family. They all go into a toy store. Bridique watches as Cena runs off to the back of the store with her friend.

"Do you want her back?" Imms asks.

"Would it make me a horrible person if I said I don't know?" Brid folds her arms across her chest. "I used to. For sure. Now I kind of . . . I feel safer, knowing she's not with me. I love her so much. But I think maybe I just want to be able to call someone so special mine without actually having to take care of her. I should be strung up, right?" She doesn't wait for Imms to answer. "It runs in the family. It's how my dad felt about my mom."

It is, Imms is fairly sure, how B feels about him.

Cena returns to them, a stuffed animal in tow, and Imms knows why the girl doesn't answer Bridique's questions. She is smarter than Imms. Smart enough not to give her heart to someone who will always maintain a distance. Who cannot—will not—protect it.

Cena tugs Imms's hand as Brid pays for the stuffed animal. "I'd like you to come to my house sometime, so I can draw you," Cena says solemnly. "You can say no, but the offer's on the table."

"You draw?" Imms asks.

"Yes. I'm good at it. And you have an interesting look."

"I'd love that. When could I come to your house?"

"Imms can't go to your house, sweetie," Brid says, joining them. She herds them toward the door. "He can only go certain places."

"Like you?" Cena asks.

"I can go anywhere."

"Not to my house."

Brid is silent as they exit into the chilly air. "I want to go home," Cena says.

"I'll have you again in two weeks," Brid says. "Imms can come over to Grandma's. You can draw him then."

"I won't have my easel."

"Bring it."

"You said—"

"I know what I said," Brid snaps. She closes her eyes for a moment. "That was a long time ago. It was hard, because you kept trying to drag everything you owned back and forth. Bring the easel. Bring anything you want."

"We'll have to ask Daddy."

"No. It's my weekend with you. It's not up to Daddy, it's up to you, and to me."

Cena turns to Imms. "I'll draw you in two weeks. But you have to hold still."

"I can do that," Imms says.

chapter
TWENTY-NINE

december rolls by. Imms keeps his fingers crossed for snow, but it doesn't come. Bridique takes him Christmas shopping. "B wouldn't go into a mall if it was the last place on Earth to get a cheeseburger," she says.

The lights and music and the swarm of voices are a lot to take in, but Imms likes the decorations.

"Hasn't B put anything up at home?" Brid asks.

"No," Imms says. "He says he doesn't know how to decorate."

"I was being sarcastic. He hates holidays. Still, he should've made the effort. It's your first Christmas, for Christ's sake."

"Your house looks nice."

"Yeah. I used to work in a flower shop doing arrangements and stuff, so I can Christmas it up pretty good. We'll get some stuff while we're here, then sneak back before B comes home and make your house look like Christmas fucking exploded in it."

Imms gets a lot of looks as they shop. He hasn't been anywhere this public before. One boy approaches and asks for Imms's autograph before his mother pulls him away. "I feel like I have a disease," Imms says.

"Better a government-declared leper than chum in open water," Brid says. She has two bags of toys for Cena and some gardening gloves for her mother. She helps Imms pick out some wall prints for Mary. Imms can't find anything for B.

"He's impossible to shop for," Brid says. "I always just get him something stupid from the joke store. Fart sirens. A fairy-catching kit. It's right here, let's pop in."

The store is called Crown's Gags. Imms browses aisles of fake vomit, rubber spiders, glow-in-the-dark dildos. Playing cards with pictures of naked women. Edible socks. Bridique goes to look at gargoyles in the back. A silver ball hangs in the middle of the store, refracting pink, blue, and silver light. The music thumps and growls.

Imms flips through a rack of posters. Mostly big-breasted females in bikinis. A few movies and TV shows. He comes to a poster that makes him stop. It has a black background and shows the top part of a glowing silver sphere with two blue flowers on its surface. A gray, humanlike figure stands on the sphere, staring straight ahead, while a muscular human man charges up behind it with a net. The gray figure's thought bubble reads, "The truth is out there."

"Hey." Bridique's voice makes him jump. She notices the poster. "Oh. Oh, that's tasteful."

"I want it," Imms says. He can't explain why.

Bridique raises an eyebrow. "Into irony, are we?"

The young man at the cash register keeps glancing at Imms, then looking away. He bites his lip to hide his grin as he bags the poster. "Cool, man," he says. "Happy holidays."

"That's how Christmas shopping used to go for me," Brid says, nodding at Imms's bag. "I'd come home with all this shit for myself and nothing for anybody else."

"I don't know what to get B."

"I have an idea," Brid says. "There's a place downtown called the Potter's Wheel where you can throw your own pottery. They'll help you. It's like a flat fee for two hours, plus a little more for each additional hour. You could make him something."

"Throw pottery?"

"Basically, you use a giant rotating wheel to make things out of clay—pots, vases—it's really, like, relaxing and soothing. I'll go with you if you want to try it."

"Okay. But what would I make?"

"Anything you want. That's the great thing about handmade gifts—they don't have to be useful. Just the fact that you made it will score you major points. I can make something for my friend in New York while we're there. It'll get broken in the mail, then she can use the shards in one of her weird-ass collages."

"Are you going to get anything for Don?" Imms asks.

She looks at him sharply. "Why would I get something for Don?"

"I thought you were friends."

She shakes her head. "I can't be one of those people who buys shit for the neighbors, the mailman, my hairdresser . . . I'd go broke." She stops walking. "Who's telling you stuff?"

"No one. I just—he came to Thanksgiving. And he's kind of your friend, isn't he?"

"Well, I'm not going to get him a present. My mom can do that, if she's so inclined."

They are in the center of the mall, next to Winter Wonderland, where children wait in line to sit on Santa's lap. Enormous, sparkling packages rest on mounds of cotton snow. On the far end, a plant dangles from the ceiling. Couples pose beneath it, lips locked, while someone dressed as an elf takes a picture.

"What's that?" Imms asks.

"Mistletoe Junction," Brid says. "They started it a few years ago, but had to stop for a while because too many teenagers—and adults— were kissing less than chastely. Now it's back, but there's a set of friendly rules to follow. No tongue."

They watch as a young couple, both dark-haired, press their lips gently together. The man's eyes dart toward the camera, and the woman starts to giggle. The elf snaps the picture. "Beautiful," says the elf. "Merry Christmas. You can pick your photo up at the Holly Table."

"Want to do it?" Bridique asks. Imms turns to her, startled "Just for fun." She tugs him toward Mistletoe Junction. "Come on. You need to experience Christmas in all its commercial, capitalist, gag-me-with-a-snowman glory."

He follows her. They wait in line to kiss.

After shopping, they stop at B's so Imms can drop off his loot and pick up Lady. Then they drive to Brid's. Dave is home for winter break, so after saying hello to Mary, Imms and Lady head over to the Welberts'. The smell of smoke is heavy, and the sky is already fading to black, even though it's barely dinnertime. Imms is surprised to see a thick clump of orange flame hovering in the twilight in the Welberts' backyard. He picks Lady up and holds her close, staring at the fire.

Don steps out from behind the flames, a beer can in one hand, poking at the fire with a stick. The fire is in a steel barrel, Imms sees as he comes closer.

"Hi," Imms says.

"Burning trash," Don says. "Not really supposed to around here. But Mary don't mind, and there's no one on the other side to complain."

A flurry of sparks shoots up, and suddenly Imms is back on the table in the *Byzantine* lab. Joele holds the glass rod in the flame until it glows red. Lady growls against his chest.

"That's a cute little dog," Don says. "I never get to see her. You boys always hog her when she's over." He steps closer, hand out, and reaches for Lady. His beer can pops. Lady growls again, then snaps at Don's hand.

"Ow!" Don pulls back. The can falls to the ground. "She bit me."

The lab disappears. Imms can breathe again. He tries to look at Don's hand. "She's never done that before," he says, feeling Lady tremble against him.

Don mutters something Imms can't quite hear. He catches the word, "Bitch."

"She was scared," Imms says.

"Of what?" Don holds his bitten hand close to his chest, the way Imms is holding Lady. "She knows me." He walks back toward the fire. "Gonna have to call animal control."

"What?"

"She bit me. Got to report it."

Imms starts to panic. "She won't do it again."

Don looks at him with something like pity. "I know she didn't mean it. But once an animal shows signs of aggression, it's real likely they'll go for someone again. And what if it's a kid next time?"

The look is not pity. The look is careful, deliberate. It's a grin behind a wall. This is not about the dog. Don remembers exactly what happened the day he wouldn't leave Mary's.

"What'll animal control do?" Imms asks, holding Lady so tightly she whimpers.

"It'll be a strike against her. Two strikes, three strikes, I forget. Then they put her down."

The back door opens and Dave comes out, jacketless. "What's going on?" he asks.

"The dog bit me," Don says.

Dave laughs. "Lady? You must've really wound her up."

"No, she got me good. Look." Don thrusts his hand at Dave, who comes closer to the fire to see. "All I did was try to pet her."

"Oh, yeah," Dave says. "'Bout tore your pinky off, huh?"

"She drew blood."

"Like, a drop."

"I'm gonna call animal control."

"Bullshit you are. I'd bite you too. You smell like a hobo. Come on in, Imms. I've got something to show you."

"What if she bites a kid next time?" Don demands.

"A kid's not going to stagger out from behind a barrel of flames like fucking Gigantis."

"You've got no regard."

"I know, Dad. Come on," Dave says to Imms. Imms follows him inside, still unsure whether he and Lady are safe.

Dave shows Imms his new mountain bike, a red twenty-one speed. "Early Christmas present." Dave doesn't say from whom. "You learn how to ride a bike yet?"

"No."

"I'll teach you. Then you can use my old one—it's a good bike, but nothing like this one—and we can go riding in the state park. There's great trails there."

"Cool," Imms says.

"What's up, man? You look freaked out."

"Is he really going to call animal control?"

Dave snorts. "He'll forget all about it after a couple more beers."

That's what Dave said before, that Don would forget about Imms grabbing his wrist at Mary's. But Don hasn't forgotten.

B is on the couch, reading, when Imms gets home. He has been dark lately, quiet and unhappy and restless. But tonight he seems calm.

"Hey," he says. "There's coffee." Lady races for the couch and leaps onto his lap. "Hey, little Lady."

Imms sits beside B. "She bit Don."

"Really?"

"There was a fire. Don was burning trash. I was holding her, and she could tell I was . . . I didn't like the fire, so when Don reached out to pet her, she snapped at him."

"She draw blood?"

"Just a teeny bit."

"Was Don upset?"

"He wanted to call animal control."

B rolls his eyes. "Good grief."

"Dave stopped him."

"He'll forget all about it by tomorrow."

"I think he's still mad at me about something I did."

"What'd you do?"

"It was when I was sick," Imms says. "He was in Mary's house. I heard them arguing. She kept telling him to get out, but he wouldn't leave. So I grabbed his arm."

"You grabbed his arm?"

"Yeah, his wrist. And I squeezed. I wanted him to listen."

"Yeah? How did you feel?" B seems more curious than anything.

"I don't know. My scars hurt. Mary said not to tell you."

"Because she knows I have to report it."

"When you write about me for NRCSE?"

B nods. "If you felt anger or something like it, the NRCSuckers will want to know."

"How many strikes do I get?" Imms asks quietly.

"Strikes?"

"Don said Lady would get two with animal control. Maybe three. Then they'd put her down."

B sets his mug on the coffee table and draws Imms down so they are lying side by side. Imms breathes the familiar smells of the couch, of B. Lady lies on top of both of them. "Well, they're not going to put you down. But my mother's right. NRCSE's on the hunt for reasons to get you out of here and into their facility. I'm sure they would have found some way of turning that around, saying I'm providing inadequate supervision or guidance, or whatever bullshit."

"Are you going to report it now?"

"I'm going to pretend I never heard about it." B pauses. "But let me know if that happens again, okay?"

"Okay."

"It's incredible, isn't it? I mean, a few months ago, you couldn't feel anger at all."

"I don't want to feel it."

"Earth's rubbing off on you."

"Don't say that." Imms settles his head on B's chest.

"What's wrong with that?"

It's strange how quickly B's embrace can become a barrier. Imms is no longer held—he's cut off from B and from that humans-only place of quick, uncapturable feelings. Lady hops off the couch, heading for her food dish. Imms takes a breath. B's arms relax around him. "Did you live somewhere else? Before here?" Imms asks.

"Grew up about twenty miles north of here. Mom and Brid and I lived in this tiny duplex with a tree house out back we couldn't use because the floorboards were rotted." He rolls onto his back. "When Brid and I were teenagers, we'd both blast our music at the same time in our rooms. I'm surprised Mom didn't kill us. Or herself."

"You don't mean that."

B laughs. "No. But it must have been rough on her. The walls in that house were about as thick as my finger."

"Did you and Brid fight?"

"Nonstop. She used fists. I was a gentleman. I used words. And superglue."

"Superglue?"

"I may have put superglue in her pockets. Once."

"Why?"

"She squirted water on my computer. What choice did I have?"

"Diplomacy," Imms suggests.

B's laugh fills the room. Makes Imms smile. "Would never have worked with her."

Imms lets his fingers drift to a button on B's shirt. He pinches it. "What happened? When you glued her hands?"

"She had to go to the ER. I was shut in my room while they were gone to 'think about what I'd done.' I spent the whole time wishing the house would catch fire. I'd stay in my room like I'd been told and die, and then they'd be sorry."

"Why would you wish that?" Imms moves his hand from B's chest.

"I didn't really. Just a stupid thing people think when they feel someone's been unfair to them. 'If something awful happened to me, they'll feel bad they treated me that way.'"

"But you'd be dead. You'd be burned."

"That's why it's so ridiculous. Like it's worth dying to teach someone a lesson."

"Oh." Imms laughs, too loudly, but his throat is still dry.

"See?"

"Kind of."

"I was so pissed they left me there. I wasn't thinking about Brid, wasn't even worried about her."

"Did she get revenge?"

"Dismembered my favorite action figure. And hid the limbs all over the house."

Imms grins, softening against B once more, "I like hearing stories like this. About you."

B is silent for a moment. "You have any good stories? About your family?"

Imms shakes his head. "Silvers are nice to be with, but they don't love like you do."

"Is that the moral you get from that story? That I love my sister?"

"I know you do."

"Yeah. I guess so. She's nuts, but I wouldn't have it any other way."

"What about your father?"

"What about him?"

"Mary says he's gone, but he's not dead."

"Might as well be."

"Where is he?"

B doesn't reply for a long time. When he does, he doesn't answer Imms's question, and he speaks quickly. "They moved while I was in college. The people who bought the old house painted it blue and had a boat. Mom and Brid moved into the house they have now. I was never gonna come back to this town, ever."

"Why did you?"

"Because it's home, and that's the easiest place to run to when you've been fucked over." He holds his hand up, flexes his fingers. They're both silent until B says, "I'm not an idiot. I know you miss it. Your home is where you make it, but it's also the place you grew up, the place you can't shake, that's got its head buried in your skin like a tick."

"I do miss it sometimes."

"I know."

"But I like it here."

"It's not so bad." B pauses. "Here, I mean. I hated it for so long, but it's not so bad."

"What did you want?" B looks at him. "Instead of here?"

"I just don't want to be trapped."

They're quiet a while. Then B continues, "Sometimes I want to know what I'd be like stripped of everything. My home, my family, my job. Kind of like you, I guess, when you couldn't go back to your clan."

"Why would you want that?"

"I don't fit anywhere. And I want to go somewhere I don't have to fit."

"You want to be forgotten?"

"I want to be lost for a while and have that be okay. I don't want to think about what's coming next."

Imms understands. B wants to close his eyes. He wants to be told it's okay to sleep, that someone else is standing guard.

B shifts, and Imms isn't sure anymore. Isn't sure about anything at all. B clears his throat. "That's why I think moving might be a good idea. We can make a home together, somewhere neither of us has been."

"What about Mary and Brid?"

"We'll visit. And they can visit us."

"What about NRCSE?" Imms has asked this before, but he needs to hear what B will say now. "What if they need to ask us more questions about the fire?"

Imms makes the mistake of looking at B's face and wishes he hadn't. The feelings there would take hours to sort through, to piece together. B sits up. He climbs over Imms and stands beside the couch, brushing the dog hair off his sweater.

"Sorry," Imms says.

"For what?"

"I don't know."

"No, you don't," B agrees. "I don't think you really know at all what it means to be sorry."

"What's wrong?"

B rubs his face. "NRCSE's never gonna fucking let us go. If we move, it's not gonna be a relocation. It's gonna be a fucking escape."

"Maybe that's okay."

"What'd Grena tell you, Imms, when you saw her? Did you talk about the fire?"

Imms shakes his head.

"So what? You told her everything was fine?"

"I just . . . I said . . . I was okay. Living here. We didn't talk about the fire."

"You don't even understand what we've done, do you?"

"We lied." Imms understands that much. "You said it was the only way."

"Maybe, maybe not. Now the fire's Vir's fault. Vir, the only one of us who gave a fuck about being decent. And Joele, the shithead, is a medal-of-honor hero. All because I thought I could keep you safe." B knocks on his own head, which strikes Imms as funny, though he knows better than to laugh. "There's no captain in here. Just a coward who'd let an innocent woman take the fall for a truly *cosmic* disaster."

"It's okay," Imms says. "I still love you."

"Jesus."

Imms isn't sure where B's mind is right now, so he waits.

B clenches his fist at his side. Releases. "I'm probably not the best fucking person you could love."

The shock and hurt of his words is so great that Imms can't even think about replying until B is already upstairs. Imms sits on the couch for a long time and thinks about Vir. That's what's causing B's darkness, guilt over the original lie and the lies of omission that followed.

Now people think Imms is a hero, that Joele's death is tragic, and that Vir was a criminal. When really, it's Imms who is the criminal.

Even if knocking the small fire off the table was an accident, he shouldn't have been near the lab in the first place. B told him to stay away from the ship. If he had, Joele never would have made the fire. She, Vir, and Gumm would still be alive. And B wouldn't feel guilty.

"I don't care," he says aloud. He's looking for the spark that flares into anger. He wants to see how high the flame will go. "I don't care. He shouldn't have sent me away. I wanted him. I went to the ship because I wanted him."

He feels something only halfway familiar, but he doesn't think it's anger.

Lady pads into the room and jumps up on the couch with him. She licks his face and fingers. "I'm probably not the best fucking person you could love," he whispers to her.

chapter
THIRTY

Imms gets an early Christmas present in the mail from Cena: an invitation to an art show at her school, where her drawing of Imms will be displayed.

Cena wouldn't let Imms see the drawing while she was working. When he was done posing, she said she was going to take it home and do some more work on the shading.

They all go to the art show together—Imms, B, Bridique, Cena, Mary, Don, and Dave. Imms wears a scarf and a thick cap pulled to just above his eyes, but people still notice his skin.

"Cool, the alien!" one child shouts.

Parents corral kids in their arms, stare at Imms in fascination, anger, horror. One mother offers him a tentative smile.

Looking at all the finger paintings and half-scribbled sketches in the room, it is clear that Cena is very gifted for her age. Imms thinks the portrait looks like him—not just the gray skin, but she has captured the broken surfaces of his eyes, the pale line of his mouth.

"Do you like it?" Cena asks. She folds her arms and stares at the drawing, head tilted to one side.

"I love it," Imms says. "It really looks like me."

"Thanks. I wanted it to show how you always look sad."

"I look . . . ?"

"It's great, sweetie," Brid says.

Cena watches Imms. "I should have made your nose bigger," she says softly.

The next day B gets a call, which he takes to the bedroom. Imms hears his voice, low and terse, behind the door. When he comes out, he says, "Apparently the school was off-limits to you."

"Why?"

"Beats the hell out of me. The kids were excited to see you, the parents were a little nervous, but everyone survived."

"I'm glad we went." Imms goes back to his book.

"Me, too. Except NRCSE's gonna add that to the list of reasons I'm an unfit handler."

Imms looks at the pine swags on the mantel, the red velvet bows. As promised, Bridique came over last week while B was at work, and she and Imms made it look like Christmas fucking exploded. Packages sit under a small tree, mostly from B to Bridique and Mary. *"I don't know where they come from,"* Brid said. *"It's like great whites mating—no one's ever actually seen him shop."* Imms's gift to Mary and a tiny box from Imms to Bridique—a necklace with a lion pendant— are also under the tree. His vase for B is still at the Potter's Wheel. It is almost done; it just needs another coat of glaze. He and Brid are going back tomorrow to finish. There is nothing from B to Imms, but Bridique assures him this is because B has gotten him something way too awesome to go under a tree.

"I don't want to live anywhere but here. I don't want to move." He knows it's true as he says it. It's not just that he doesn't want to live in a lab. He doesn't want to leave this house. This town. Mary and Brid.

He looks at B and thinks he sees something collapse.

But B nods. "Okay."

"I don't mean never," Imms says. "Just not now."

"That's fine." B picks pine needles out of the carpet.

"Will Brid ever get Cena back?"

B throws the needles in the trash. "I don't know. Cena's father wants to keep Brid away from her."

"Is Don helping Brid get her back?"

"Who told you that?"

"Dave."

"I don't know what's going on with Don and my sister. I don't care to."

Imms gets up and goes to the kitchen to make scrambled eggs. B usually compliments Imms when he cooks, says something about how this is the best human skill Imms could have learned, and how he'll have to keep Imms around a while. Imms hopes he'll say something now. He wants to do something nice for B. Scrambled eggs taste like puke, but B likes them, and Imms can swallow them without chewing.

Imms takes the eggs out of the fridge.

B walks in. "Eggs?"

"For you."

"I'm going to work for a couple of hours," B says. "So you can make something you like. Or I'll give you money and you can go get something with Brid."

Imms puts the egg carton back in the fridge. He sees a long day, alone and bored, and that frightens him. He wishes he and Brid were going back to the Potter's Wheel today.

"Stay out of trouble. I'll be back around eleven, and we can do anything you want—park, movie, you name it."

He shuts the door. Lady whines.

Imms could call Dave, but he doesn't feel like video games. He doesn't feel like lunch with Brid, or books, or movies. He curls up on the couch and tries to enjoy being alone with the smell of the Christmas tree. Somewhere on the street he hears carolers. He sits up. Turns on the TV.

"—caused quite a stir last night when it showed up at Plainview Elementary's art show," says Elise Fischer, Imms's favorite local news anchor. "The Silver was accompanied by the captain of the Silver Planet mission and the captain's family. We turn now to planetary integration specialist Veronica Stuart. Veronica, tell us, should the Silver have been allowed to attend the art show?"

"Well, Elise, the interesting thing about last night was how positively children reacted to the Silver's presence. There were no tears, no screams of terror." Both women laugh. "The only ones who looked worried were parents. And that may not have as much to do with the Silver's presence as with the rules posed by our government: Do not approach the Silver. Do not talk to the Silver. Don't come within x number of feet—"

"The Silver was recently spotted Christmas shopping at the mall, am I right?"

"Yes, I did hear that."

"So how do these rules apply to store employees? They're paid to provide customer service. That means greeting the customer, handing the customer change, *making contact*. How do the rules apply to those who might be interacting with the Silver in a professional capacity?"

"Well, I think that's a different story. The government is trying to prevent people from harassing the Silver and its handler. At the same time, the National Research Center for Space Exploration, which oversees Imms's integration into Earth life, has announced that it wants to observe Imms in more public interactions. So I think we're going to see more of Imms in places like the mall."

"Schools?"

"Given the lack of incident last night, I see no reason why Imms should be banned from community events like the art show."

"Thank you so much, Veronica. We have to take a break. Coming up: are the growth hormones given to chickens—"

Imms turns to cartoons. Cartoons are funny, colorful. Cartoons don't call him "it." Cartoons don't even know he exists. Except that's not true. This episode centers around the main character getting a pet Silver for Christmas. Imms turns off the TV. He is everywhere on Earth, and he is nowhere. He is in human thoughts, on their TV screens, in their conversations. He is in one small house. What is the point of coming to a new world if you are assigned only a corner of it?

He stands up. He makes scrambled eggs even though B is not here. He chews them. They wobble and come apart in his mouth and are not so bad.

B tried to ignore Imms's face when he told him he wasn't going to the Christmas Eve light show.

"Not really my thing," he'd said. "But you'll have fun with Mary and Brid."

He knows Imms wants them to spend Christmas Eve together, and they will. He just needs Imms out of the house for a few hours so he can set up.

He whistles as he rolls the five ten-gallon barrels into the bathroom. What he's whistling isn't quite a Christmas carol, but it has a bit of a "Jingle Bells" flavor. He pulls the barrel upright. What he's done will get him fired, probably worse, if anyone at NRCSE finds out, but it will be worth it. One of the perks of being a hero and surviving a tragedy is that people don't ask a lot of questions when they see you somewhere you're not really supposed to be.

He spends over an hour getting everything ready. Then he sits on the couch, intending to read until Imms gets back. He can't concentrate. He goes to the tree to investigate a slender, rectangular package to him from Imms. It is surprisingly heavy and rustles when he shakes it. Whatever's inside must be packed in plastic. He smiles, trying to imagine Imms and Brid Christmas shopping together. He's glad that Brid has taken such an interest in Imms, and that Imms isn't put off by Brid's . . . Brid-ness. He remembers how much Brid hated Matty at first. How nervous he's always been, introducing friends and boyfriends to Brid.

Mary calls when they are leaving the light show. Anywhere between fifteen minutes and half an hour, depending on traffic. B turns out the lights, so that only the tree and the pine-swagged electric lantern on the mantel glow. He puts Lady in her kennel. He goes into the bathroom and checks one more time that everything is perfect. He waits.

Imms comes in, excited. "B, you missed a fucking Santa that could twirl a Christmas light lasso . . . Why are you in the dark?"

"Spend too much time with my sister and your mouth'll rot." B pats the couch. "It's mood lighting. Sit down."

Imms does. "Mood lighting?"

"I know we're doing presents tomorrow at Mom's. But I'd really like to give you my gift tonight. There's, um, a couple parts to it."

B watches Imms's face carefully. Imms looks surprised, then pleased. "Okay. Should I give you mine, too?"

"Only if you want to. Mine needs to be just between the two of us." B kisses him. "I don't want you to think about, or worry about anything tonight, okay? Just let me—*give*."

"Okay," Imms says softly.

"Take off your clothes and lie down," B says.

Music is playing. Not Christmas music, not classical.

Both seemed wrong for this. B opted instead for an instrumental album Brid gave him years ago by some Bulgarian string group she was into. *"It sounds like what would happen if someone took all the fierceness out of the world, but left all the strangeness,"* she'd said. This is B's first time listening to it, and Brid's right.

B watches Imms remove the last of his clothing, then moves so Imms can stretch out on the couch.

"Facedown," B says.

No candles. B would have liked candles, but no fire. Not for Imms. The lantern light is close enough. B takes a moment to study what's in front of him. Imms's face is buried in the cushion. B takes in Imms's long neck, his slender shoulders, the vertebrae outlined under shimmering skin. His spine looks like a dinosaur tail. B's gaze lingers in that lovely hollow at its base, then follows both legs at the same time, like standing at a fork in a road and seeing two futures.

Imms's skin is slightly dappled in places but has no moles, no freckles or pimples, no hair. Imms's heart approaches B lazily like an old, happy dog. B puts a hand out and touches Imms's side where it glows.

A spell is in place; a feast is before B. A world unknown is waiting for Imms. B guides Imms into that world, massaging his nape, working his way down, going slower, deeper into the tissue. He imagines he is taking Imms apart, very tenderly, peering between Imms's joints, unscrewing appendages, and pouring himself into the holes. He feels Imms surrender, go completely slack. He nips the top of one thigh. Imms tenses and whimpers. B smiles. A reminder that the unknown world might not all be gentle.

Finally, he rolls Imms over. Imms's eyes are wide, asleep, confused. B crawls on top of him and kisses him. He makes it the kind of kiss you float on, dream in, the world knocks and you don't answer. Imms matches it perfectly.

"Come on," B whispers, holding out his hand.

B leads Imms into the bathroom. Watches him take in the tub of silver water and the champagne flutes filled with apple cider on the tub's ledge. B has pulled a standing lamp in to replace candles and wrapped a garland around it—messy, imperfect, but the best B could do. At the lamp's base is a Tupperware container enclosing a single wrapped package. "I didn't want it to get wet. You can open it at the end of the night."

Imms can't stop staring at the water in the tub. "Where did you get this?"

"I stole it," B says, kissing the back of Imms's neck. "Don't tell anybody."

They get in together. The water is cold, nothing B could do about that. Imms doesn't seem to notice, but B grimaces as he sinks into the opaque water. The two of them in the tub is a tight fit, and B thinks maybe their combined body heat will make it tolerable.

This water smells strange, almost sweet. Their conversation winds down until Imms rests with his head against B's chest, no sound except their slow, overlapping breaths and the occasional plinks of the water as their bodies shift.

"You're half-asleep," B murmurs. "Let's get out and go to bed. You still have to open your gift."

B stands and helps Imms up. Silver droplets fall from them. B is almost envious of the way Imms glistens. The water does nothing to B's own skin. They step from the tub, and B wraps Imms in a towel. Then B leans down to unplug the drain.

"No!" Imms says. "Leave it."

"Overnight?"

"Forever."

B laughs. "We can't keep using the same bathwater."

"Why not?"

"Because it's dirty." B reaches for the plug once more.

"No! Put it somewhere else. However you brought it here, put it back and keep it."

"I'm not going to keep fifty gallons of used bathwater in my house."

Imms pulls B's wrist. "Please."

"You're being ridiculous." B hates the words as soon as they're out of his mouth, because they aren't true. He understands exactly why Imms wants to keep the water, and the reason is not silly at all. But the water has a very different effect on B than it has on Imms. It reminds him of months of cold darkness, of loneliness, of not being human.

It reminds him of tearing Silver skin just to watch blood flow. To Imms, the water is something to cling to. A sad souvenir of home. B has tolerated it, appreciated the joy it brings Imms. Now he wants it gone.

He pulls the plug. The silver water is sucked down the drain with a gurgling noise.

Imms plows into him, grabbing the arm that holds the plug. For an instant, B is too startled to respond. He twists his arm out of Imms's grip, and puts his other hand out to keep Imms back. Imms lunges forward again. "Put it back, B. I mean it."

"Are you pissed at me?" B asks.

"Yes I'm pissed at you! I'm so pissed. You can't do this. You can't!" He pounds B's shoulder with a fist, not hard enough to hurt, but B feels the emotion behind the action. "If you don't give me that right now *I will bury you.*"

B almost smiles at what are undoubtedly Bridique's words coming out of Imms's mouth. But he is too disconcerted, almost frightened by Imms's genuine anger. He half wants to continue the argument, up the ante, just to see what Imms will do. But he can't do that, especially not on what's supposed to be a perfect night. "Easy, easy, easy," he says, holding up both hands.

Imms snatches the plug and kneels over the edge of the tub, shoving it in place as the water swirls around his wrists. He remains on his knees for a moment, hands in the water, breathing hard.

Imms takes his hands out of the water. "I'm sorry." His voice is as soft as the sound of water droplets rolling from his hand into the tub. "Sorry," he tries again, looking up when B doesn't respond.

"You scared me."

"I don't know what . . . I hate feeling this way! I want it to stop. I'm not mad at you."

"I think you are, a little bit."

Imms's fingers curl into fists. "Don't do that to me again, B. Do you hear me? Don't just go ahead when I tell you to stop. You don't get to make all the decisions."

"I know," B says. "I won't."

"It's not just this. You always do what you want."

"I know. I'm sorry. Wait here just a minute." B slips past Imms. He's just out of the bathroom when he feels a hand on his shoulder. He stops. Imms carefully winds both arms around his neck. Imms's touch never hurts. He feels Imms's cheek between his shoulder blades.

He turns to take Imms in his arms. He's feeling something he can't identify, some combination of shame, love, anxiety, and sadness. Months ago on the Silver Planet, he'd wanted to make Imms angry. He'd refused the possibility that a being so human could be so incomplete, naive, simple. Is that what this is about? That B has taken innocence and twisted it? Torture couldn't draw harsh, violent emotions from Silvers in Project HN. But B's disastrous attempt to love Imms, to protect him, has made Imms feel all the worst things a human can feel.

When they are in bed, still damp—an old Smuckers jar of Silver water hidden behind a mountain of socks in the bedroom closet—Imms opens the package. Inside is a book. The cover is black and glossy with pinprick silver stars. The pages are filled with pictures of the Silver Planet. Pictures of Silvers, of the lakes, of the blue flowers that turn to quilopea. A snake. The *Byzantine* nestled on the bright earth. Pebbles on the ground. A human's shoe print. A Silver holding a hand out as if to block the camera.

And among the pictures is writing. Scraps of paper with dates, notes.

The Silvers learn so fast, reads one scrap. *One in particular is already speaking English like a native. Loves* Tin Star. *Tomorrow will try*

Will try what? Imms wonders. Then he remembers—the next day Grena read aloud the scene where *Tin Star and Thunder Sam* are reunited, over and over until Imms had it memorized. Then they acted it out together.

"Grena and Vir's notes," B says. "And Gumm's pictures, mostly. A couple are mine."

I think they are smarter than humans. This note is in different handwriting. Vir's. *Even though they have not invented much, or created. They have created something out of just themselves. They don't need canvases or gadgets.*

Imms holds the book, afraid if he shuts it, it will disappear. Anything sour left over from their fight disappears. He lets the book slide from his lap as he throws his arms around B and squeezes, harder than he squeezed Don Welbert's wrist. "Thank you," he says into B's neck, letting the heat of the words blast back into his mouth.

"Merry Christmas."

Imms can't say what he wants to say. His own gift to B—his heart sinks as he thinks of it—is painfully inadequate, stacked against all this.

B eases him back on the bed, kisses him again. "Tell me your favorite things about your home."

Imms isn't sure he wants to talk about this at first. He remembers answering the *Breakthrough II* team's questions. But once he starts, he can't stop. Telling B is different than telling strangers. He feels like he's making B a part of his old life, like when he almost brought B into the ground with him that night on the Silver Planet. His stories maybe aren't as interesting as B's. He's never superglued anyone's hands to their pockets. But B listens, and B never stops touching him, and Imms's heart presses against the front of his chest as though it wants out through his skin.

When B is asleep, Imms takes the book into the kitchen and flips through it again. Once, twice. Three times. Then he goes to the living room. He tears the paper off his gift to B and opens the box. The vase is slightly lopsided. Brid says that gives it character. He doesn't like the glaze color he chose—reddish brown, like dried blood. He turns the vase over. He'd carved *To: B* in the clay at the bottom, on an impulse just before the vase went into the kiln the first time. The letters are clumsy and childish. The whole thing is ugly, inexpert. Not enough.

He takes it to the kitchen and grabs a plate from the cabinet. Holding the plate in one hand, the vase in the other, he counts to three and drops both at the same time.

They both break in big chunks, though the vase leaves some small, scattered pieces as well. Imms quickly sweeps the vase into a plastic bag, bundles it tightly, and throws it in the trash. He has just started sweeping up the plate when B reaches the kitchen.

"What's up?" B asks sleepily. "You okay?"

"Sorry." Imms lets B see the shards of familiar ceramic. "I broke a plate."

"You shouldn't clean up barefoot," B says, kicking his slippers toward Imms. He heads back to bed.

Imms finishes sweeping. He goes to the closet where he left the bags from Christmas shopping and finds the poster from the joke store. He takes it to the living room and slides it into the box. Rewraps the package. Makes a new tag.

Goes back to bed.

chapter
THIRTY-ONE

C hristmas Day begins with cocoa, but Bridique introduces a bottle of wine early on and they all partake. Bridique lied, she does have a present for Don—a watch. "Not very fancy," Brid says, "but it's waterproof. And it's got a stopwatch feature. For when you start running." Dave snickers. Brid doesn't look at Don when she talks. In fact, she hardly looks at Don at all. Don looks at her. A lot, thinks Imms. Don gives Brid a book about a lion that saved an African soldier's life and bonded with the man. The soldier and the lion are pictured together in the author photo.

Imms loves his gifts. A set of leather-bound classics from Mary. A gift certificate for a pottery class from Bridique. A Game Boy from Dave. "These things are like, antique," he says. "But you seem to like the older systems. And you can play it anywhere."

Don gives him a shot glass that says "World Poke-Her Championship," and a set of naked women playing cards.

"Classy," Brid says. "I'm sure he loves the titty pics. That's totally his jam."

"Yeah, well, I saw the picture of you two at Mistletoe Junction and figured he'd switched teams."

"What picture?" B asks.

"You didn't show him?" Brid hops up and runs with her wineglass to the kitchen.

"I shoulda got him a muzzle for this damn dog," Don says. Lady is curled in his lap, eyes half-closed as Don rubs her ears.

Brid returns with the photo. "Mom put it up on the fridge. How cute is it?" She thrusts it at her brother.

"What'd the photo elf say?" B asks.

"He said Merry Christmas—go buy a thousand fucking copies."

"Charming." B hands the photo back.

Imms's stomach sinks as B picks up his gift from Imms. He seems puzzled when the box lifts easily. "It's not much," Imms says hurriedly.

"Oh please," Brid says. "If you won't tell them how hard you worked on it, I will."

B tears off the paper, opens the box, and pulls out the poster. He unrolls it. Stares at it.

"What the—?" Brid says.

"Let's see." Mary motions B to turn it toward her.

B sets the poster down in front of him, holding it flat.

Everyone crowds around to look. Dave bursts out laughing. "Did you make that?" he Imms asks.

"No," Imms says. "I bought it."

"That's hilarious."

Imms stares at the figures—the oblivious Silver and the human stalking it. *The truth is out there.* It's a quote from an old show called *The X-Files*, Brid had explained to him. *"It means there's life on other planets."*

Don snorts. "I don't get it."

B doesn't laugh. Just stares at the poster. Finally, he looks at Imms and says, "Thank you." Nothing beneath the surface of the words.

"Imms, come get more wine with me," Brid says. He follows her into the kitchen.

"What the hell?" she demands. "What happened to the vase?"

"I broke it," he says, with just enough defiance that she'll know he means on purpose.

"*Why?*"

B enters. "I'd like a filler-up too, please." He squeezes Imms's shoulder. "Thanks for my present. It's funny."

"Hilarious," Brid mutters, jamming the corkscrew into a bottle of red.

Imms would like to disappear. Into the floor won't be enough. He'd like to vanish completely.

They return to the living room and finish off the presents. Brid squeals when she opens her necklace from Imms and ignores Don when he offers to help her put it on. She is much quieter when she opens a small box tagged *From Bill and Cena* and pulls out salt and pepper shakers shaped like dancing penguins.

Imms gives Don a gift card to a sporting goods store, and Don seems genuinely pleased.

Dave leaves to go to some girl's house, and the rest of them gather in the kitchen to eat. Mary didn't cook this time, but she has frozen lasagnas in the oven and Dave brought Christmas cookies. Imms tries to enjoy the meal, but all he can think about is the poster. Whether it's funny or not, it is certainly inadequate. After dinner Imms sits with Brid on the front steps. It is chilly, but they are wearing jackets and sitting close. They have switched from wine to brandy, because it's warmer. Whatever had made Imms sick after the tracker was implanted, maybe it hadn't been the beer. Imms's body has adapted to alcohol, as it has adapted to so many other things.

"I screwed up my first Christmas," Imms says.

"No, you didn't." Brid rests her head on his shoulder. "I love my necklace. Mom loved the prints."

"He gave me the most beautiful things last night. And I just thought—"

"You can make him another vase. At your class." Brid hiccups, then laughs. "You're not the only one who screwed up. Want to hear something horrible?"

"What?"

She leans close to his ear. "I slept with Don last night."

"No." The brandy makes him loud.

"Shhhhh!" She slaps his shoulder, then whispers, "Yes."

"You haven't before?"

"No, gross. He's almost Mom's age."

"Then why—"

"He was kinda drunk, I was kinda drunk . . ." Suddenly Brid is sobbing. And laughing. Imms can't tell which she is doing more. "Don't tell Mom. Don't tell anyone."

"I won't." Imms puts an arm around her. She lets him pull her close.

"You're the nicest," she says, "of anyone I know."

"You're nice," he says. It almost sounds like an accusation. "Sometimes you're nicer to me than B is."

"That's not saying much."

"Hey! You two drunkards up for Scrabble?" Don yells.

Brid sits up, puts a hand to her head. "I'm ready for a nap," she says. "Hey, don't tell anyone. Okay? What I told you?"

"Okay," Imms promises. He helps her up. They go in together.

That evening, at home, Imms has sobered up and waits for B's judgment. When it doesn't come, Imms is puzzled.

"B? Can I talk to you?"

B sits on the bed next to him. "What's up?"

"I made you something."

"Oh?"

"I made you a vase. At the Potter's Wheel. But I broke it."

"Last night?" B asks.

Imms nods. "I did it on purpose."

B waits.

"I did it because your present was so good. And the vase wasn't. It just—seemed like, if I was going to give you a stupid present, it should be a stupid present I bought, not a stupid present I tried to make."

"Would it be incredibly corny of me to say that it doesn't matter what you get me, because spending this Christmas with you is a gift?"

Imms's mouth falls open. "You were watching the Hallmark channel when I came home the other day!"

"I was not. I sat on the remote by accident. But seriously, I'm sorry that you thought I wouldn't like something you'd made me. I like the poster."

"It's mean."

"It's somebody else's idea of us. We know the truth. It's not out there. It's in here." He takes Imms's hand in his own and tries to place both on Imms's heart. "Here," he says as Imms's heart drifts away. "Here." B chases it again. Imms laughs.

"Hallmark," he pretend-coughs.

"Never." B clears his throat. "I want to make an addendum to my gift last night."

"Oh no." Imms flops back on the bed. "Don't give anything else. I'll feel worse."

"Hey, listen." B tugs Imms up. "I wanted to tell you that things are going to be different."

"Different how?"

"Better. Between us. I haven't been very good to you lately. I just want you to know that I'm going to try harder."

"To be in love with me?" Imms claps a hand to his mouth. "Sorry. I think I'm still a little drunk."

"I'm going to try harder to be there for you. To work with you. Not against you."

"Okay," Imms says. "Me, too."

"You have tried hard. I know it's not easy. I know you must miss home."

"I like it here."

"You can still miss home."

Imms stares at B's arm. The skin with its freckles and the light hairs that arc from it. Imms has never been as close to anyone as he is to B.

"I almost forgot." B reaches into the nightstand and pulls out a long, flat envelope. No return address. "This came for you in the mail. You got a secret admirer?"

Imms opens the envelope. Inside is a handmade book of cryptowords.

B is in the bathroom. Imms slips downstairs.

He stays up the next two hours solving all the puzzles, collecting letters and numbers, arranging and rearranging them. When he's done, he has:

59 QUEEN ANNE ST
BRIDGETOWN
IF YOU EVER NEED ME.

chapter
THIRTY-TWO

things do get better for a while. B tries to spend more time at home and less time at work. He takes Imms out with him when he goes to the grocery store, to the bank, to the post office. Imms gets as excited as a kid about errands. Once, at the grocery store, B puts his arm around Imms in front of a bin of cantaloupe. Just for a few seconds, but the way Imms looks at him, so surprised and delighted, makes B feels guilty. Pleasing Imms is so easy, and yet he so seldom tries.

Imms seems to enjoy his pottery class. He makes a vase for B to replace the one from Christmas.

Vir enters B's mind at the oddest times. He'll reach for a glass and remember her eyes as she told him that vivisecting a Silver was like chopping up a fucking manatee. He'll walk in the park with Imms and wonder when the last time was Vir saw snow. He'll think about her family—parents both living. No spouse or partner, no kids. No pets. He'll read a book and instead of the words on the page, he'll see Vir's scrawled journal entries.

Vir didn't sabotage the ship, didn't hurt anyone. But she was hurting, and B didn't notice. Or he noticed and didn't act. He has never been able to see past what he wants *right now*. That's why Imms is stuck on Earth with him. That's why Vir is a villain. That's why his sister thinks he is, among other things, a coward, a doubledouche, a total ass clown, and a fuckup.

He looks sometimes at the copies he made of Vir's journal entries.

Talking to Grena would help, but Grena wants nothing to do with him.

"Imms?" B says one night. He shakes Imms gently, and Imms's eyes flash in the dark. Imms yawns and his tongue gleams. He grabs B and curls against him, and B strokes his back. A Silver's body is lighter, more delicate than a human's. B remembers that from lifting Silver bodies, from throwing them into the lake.

"B?" Imms asks. "You all right?"

B doesn't answer.

"Don't be sad." Imms kisses the corner of B's mouth. "I have an idea."

Imms is awake now. He ushers B out of bed. B doesn't speak. He watches as Imms takes the comforter off the bed, then follows Imms downstairs and out the back door.

"Come on." Imms picks a spot in the center of the yard. He lies down.

B eases himself onto the ground, not liking the way his joints pop. He stretches out beside Imms. Imms pulls the comforter over both of them.

"It's cold," B says. The grass pricks the back of B's neck. "You've been scooping up after that dog, right?"

"B," Imms says quietly.

B shuts up. He looks at the sky.

"Imagine it's just us. You don't have to fit anywhere." B tries to imagine. No expectations. No guarantees. Nothing but the two of them surviving together.

The stars are bright, and when they blur together, when there's a sort of fuzz warping the sky, B wonders if it's because his eyesight is shot, or because there are some things humans just aren't meant to see clearly.

Two NRCSuckers come to the house while B is at work. Imms isn't supposed to answer the door, but he doesn't feel like listening to B today.

Two men, one tall with sandy hair, the other shorter and dark-haired, stand on the porch. They show Imms NRCSE badges and tell Imms he needs to come with them to a special session at the facility. Imms doesn't like them. They are in a hurry, anxious. Lady growls and hides behind Imms's leg.

"I'll call B," he tells them.

"He's already been informed," says the first man, Sandy-Hair.

"What's the special session?" Imms asks the men.

The NRCSuckers look at each other. "We're going to interview you," Sandy-Hair says.

Imms has already been interviewed dozens of times. He doesn't know why he needs to be again. "Will it take long?"

The man shrugs. "Depends on how quick you give us answers."

"I don't want to," Imms says.

"We want you to," Sandy-Hair replies. Dark-Hair nudges Sandy's ribs.

"What would B think if he knew you were giving us trouble?" Dark-Hair asks.

Imms doesn't know. B hates when Imms goes to NRCSE. But he doesn't like when Imms makes trouble.

"That's right," Sandy-Hair says. "I wonder if you're getting to be too much for the captain to handle."

Imms goes with them. They drive a blue car, which smells too sweet. A cardboard strawberry hangs from the rearview mirror.

The men lead him to a part of NRCSE where they have to use their thumbs to get through entryways. They go down a clean, white hallway lined with numbered doors. One door is ajar, and looking in, Imms sees what looks like a bedroom with dark-blue carpet and dingy walls. They turn right at the end of the hall, and Dark-Hair pushes open a heavy door with his shoulder.

The room they enter is darker than the psychologist's office or Dr. Hwong's office. Its walls are large blocks painted a shiny flesh color. One table is in the center with a metal chair. Sandy-Hair tells Imms to sit. The chair grinds against the floor as he moves it. The other, the quiet one, has a gun, and keeps putting a hand to his hip to draw attention to it. Imms tries not to be nervous. He wishes he'd called B.

"We're heading up the investigation of the *Byzantine* fire," Sandy says. "We have a few questions for you."

Now Imms can't help but be nervous. He has already answered questions about the fire, many times. Why do they need to interview him again?

"It's very important that you tell the truth, Imms. Do you understand that?"

He nods.

"If you don't, bad things can happen. You need to tell the truth, even if you didn't tell it before. Even if you think it will get you or someone else in trouble. Okay?"

Imms doesn't like the way the man talks to him, as though Imms is stupid or a child. "Okay."

The investigator starts by asking Imms what he was doing in the lab before the fire started. Imms has answered this question before. He tells them Joele was talking to him. They make Imms tell them what questions Joele asked him. B has prepared him for this. He tries not to recite his answers too perfectly, though, because B said that will make people just as suspicious as if he doesn't answer at all. The questions get harder. The man wants to know how far away Imms was from Joele. What the spark looked like coming out of the wire. How Joele reacted. How she moved. What her face was like.

Imms uses what he remembers of Joele's reaction to having the fire on her clothes. It hurts to remember that, and he wraps an arm around himself. Pretends it's B's arm.

The investigator wants to know what's wrong. What was Joele to him? Just a human, right?

"I didn't like seeing her hurt," Imms says.

"Why didn't you save her?" Sandy asks. Imms looks at him, surprised and confused. "Why did you save B's life, but not Joele's?"

"I tried. I couldn't find the hatch."

"Yet you found it when you got B off the ship."

"I found it." Imms echoes the man's words. "But she was already dead."

"You were sure?"

"Pretty sure."

"But not sure?"

Imms shakes his head.

"You knew B was still alive, though."

"Yes. He was just sleeping. I mean, passed out."

"He tried to rescue Vir." The man doesn't say it like it's a question, but he seems to expect an answer.

"Yes."

"Why not you?" the man asks. "You left Joele to rescue him, but he didn't try to rescue you."

This is not true, and Imms wants to say so. B did rescue him. B is brave, braver than anyone in a book. And B loves him. Loved him.

"Vir was more important."

"Why?"

"She was human."

"What did Vir do, during the fire?"

"Nothing. She sat there."

"Just sat there. She didn't move, or yell for help?"

"No."

"Did B instruct you on how to answer questions about the fire?"

Imms isn't sure how to answer this one. He shakes his head.

"He didn't coach you at all?"

"No."

Sandy glances at the pad of paper Dark-Hair is writing on. He tilts his head. Looks back at Imms. "Imms, you have a history of rebellious behavior. There was the park incident. And I heard you went swimming in the river and left your designated area. Is this true?" He steps toward Imms.

"I didn't know how far away I'd gotten."

Sandy is almost behind him. His voice comes over Imms's shoulder.

"Are you sure you're telling the truth, Imms? Think carefully."

"Yes."

"You're telling the truth about all of it? The fire? The rescue?"

"Yes."

"Bullshit," Sandy says calmly.

"What?"

"Bullshit. I don't believe you." Sandy motions to Dark-Hair, who gets up. The two turn to leave.

"Where are you going?" Imms asks.

"To get a snack," Sandy says. "I hope you're ready to tell the truth when we come back." They shut the door.

Imms stands and paces. He needs to talk to B.

B must not know he's here after all. B wouldn't let the NRC Suckers come to the house and take him. He would have told Imms first. Once again, Imms has been stupid. He has thought like a Silver, not a human.

He needs to get out of here. He tries the door, but it's locked. No number pad to open it. No windows. No hatch in the floor. He paces until he's exhausted, then sits in a corner. How long will they keep him here? He tries yelling, but the sound stays in the room with him. Maybe the men will call B. Maybe B will get worried and come looking for him. Maybe B is too angry to want him back.

He shouldn't be here. He hasn't done anything wrong. He has tried to be good since coming to Earth, but he has only caused trouble. He could have stayed on his planet. It would have been boring, lonely, but at least he'd never have gotten into a mess like this.

It is B's mess. B was never as strong as he pretended to be. B won't find him, won't rescue him here, because B doesn't have the power to protect Imms from NRCSE. Imms sees that in a nasty burst of clarity. Imms has been tricked. Tricked into coming to Earth. Tricked into believing he's human. He is not. He is something for humans to watch, to laugh at, to cut into. To fuck.

He feels it. The spark. His weak version of anger, half-real, half-pretended. It heats his whole body, pounds in his head. He is sick of feeling wounded. He is sick of being protected. He is tired of being told what to do. By the time the investigators return, he is not afraid of them. He looks them in the eye, looks at them with such hatred that Sandy stops on his way toward Imms and takes a step back. Then he grins.

"Don't like the chair, huh?"

"I don't like you," Imms replies.

Sandy turns to his partner. "How about that?" Imms digs his fingers into his knees. "Sit down. Let's finish our chat."

"Fuck you," Imms says. Bridique would be proud.

"That's not very nice, Imms." Sandy steps toward the corner. Imms growls like Lady. The man stops. "Are you going to come to the table? Or do I have to get you?"

Imms stands but doesn't leave the corner. Both men approach him from different sides. Sandy reaches for him. Imms spits in his face.

Sandy stops to wipe his cheek, and Dark-Hair grabs Imms's arm. Imms kicks him in the shin. Dark-Hair grunts but doesn't let go. He pushes Imms against the wall and throws his elbow into Imms's stomach.

"It's okay," Sandy says, still wiping spit from his eye. "Let him go. We'll come back later."

They leave the room again. Imms keeps an arm around his middle, trying to contain the pain. He is still too angry to worry about the consequences of what he's done—if he'll be taken away from B, kept at NRCSE forever.

They leave Imms in the room for a long time. He gets hungry. Misses B, and Lady, Brid, and Mary. Alone sits beside him, and his hatred of Alone is some small, strange measure of company.

When the door opens again, it is not the two men. It's Kelly Hatchell, B's boss, whom Imms met once. She's accompanied by a NRCSucker Imms doesn't know. She asks if he's all right. He nods uncertainly. She seems uncomfortable, like she doesn't know how to act around him. She tells him to follow her and leads him up to the aboveground part of NRCSE. The other NRCSucker walks behind them. Probably to keep Imms from running, which he wants to do. What if Kelly Hatchell is leading him to a place worse than the room?

Bridique is waiting near the public entrance. She looks Imms over, mutters a thanks to Kelly Hatchell. She takes Imms's hand and leads him out of the building. It's dark outside.

"They hurt you?" Brid asks as they drive home.

"No," he says.

She slaps the steering wheel. "People are no good. No good!" she yells at a driver who passes on her left.

Imms stares out the window.

"They weren't going to let you go. Don and Dave gave me some lawyer terms to throw at them. I made them let me talk to Hatch. I wouldn't leave."

"I was fine. You shouldn't have come."

"Don't be ridiculous."

"Where's B?"

"At home, Imms. At fucking home." She glances at him. Her voice gets quieter. "He's worried. Don't think he isn't. He just—"

"I didn't need him," Imms says. "They weren't hurting me."

Brid spends the rest of the drive talking about the new cheetah cub at Rose. She pulls into B's drive and starts to get out of the car. "Don't come in," Imms says. He doesn't want to witness another fight between Brid and B. Doesn't want to feel himself tugged back and forth as they shout at each other.

Brid nods. "Punch him where his balls should be for me." She backs away, her car's headlights throwing Imms's shadow onto the garage. Imms stares at the house for a moment, then walks up the drive.

B is in the kitchen. He gets up when Imms enters. Slowly, like his knees hurt. Imms thinks B is afraid of him. "You all right?" B asks.

"Fine," Imms says. "Hungry." He goes to the pantry and gets pasta out.

"There's some leftover—"

"I've got it," Imms says. He puts water on to boil.

"I'm sorry this happened. I wanted to go there and break down the fucking doors, but I didn't think they'd keep you long. I thought it would just be a few questions, and that if I went there, it would make things worse."

Imms doesn't answer.

"What'd they ask you?"

Imms shrugs. "Same old stuff."

"For nine hours?"

"They took a break for snacks."

B sighs. "Come here."

Imms wonders if B knows how wispy his concern sounds, how it dissolves in the air without ever surrounding Imms, engulfing him, making him feel safe.

Imms stays by the stove. "How was your day?"

B hesitates. "Awful."

Imms breaks handfuls of spaghetti noodles and throws them into the pot. B leaves the room. Imms takes a deep breath and lets it out. He wishes B had made him come to him. On the Silver Planet, B seemed to have so much power. Now Imms can knock him over just by holding still.

chapter
THIRTY-THREE

b has packed a bag. It's not much—a foolish attempt at foresight, like a Boy Scout's wilderness survival kit. In case he and Imms have to run. Just knowing it's there helps. It's a constant reminder life could shift at any second and dump them somewhere unexpected. Because if the NRCSuckers are going to come after Imms, if they're going to take him and keep him for hours at a time, if they can't let this investigation *die*, then B will redeem himself and the promise he made to Imms. He'll protect him.

They'll run.

B wants to tell Brid. He's afraid to tell his mother and upset her, but Brid might understand. His paranoia, his guilt. Vir's voice, singing him a fucking lullaby every night. She might understand that he needs to protect Imms, because he made a promise. Because he can't fail everyone in this world.

When B was ten, he ran away from school at recess. He wandered for a while, in love with a quiet world where most people were trapped in their offices or classrooms, but he was free. He remembers the sky that day, lint gray with a couple of patches of blue that looked like spills, accidents. He could almost imagine that no one would miss him, no one would find him, he would suffer no consequences for his actions. That this world would always be open to him. That he'd find ways to survive in it without anyone's help, and that his family would continue to love him but would accept he was gone. Wouldn't grieve for him.

The police eventually found him and drove him home. The school had trouble getting hold of his mother at work, but by the time B and the officers reached the house, Mary had heard what had happened and was on her way. Brid was already home, and their neighbor, Mrs. Anders, was sitting with her in the living room. As soon as B saw Brid, her pale face and huge eyes, her mingled anger and relief, he was terrified. His life, his actual life where he was bound to his family, to school, to karate lessons, to mowing the lawn to earn his allowance—that was all suddenly more real than the silent world he'd been king of that afternoon. He didn't want to see his mother's face when she got home. It would be ten times worse than Brid's.

But Brid sat with him and held his hand. *"It's not the end of the world,"* she said.

Where is that Brid now? The one who could tell him the world wasn't ending and make him believe it? Torn between the freedom he wanted and the past he was afraid to let go of, he's wound up in an unhappy limbo where he doesn't really know his own life anymore. He has the outline of it, but nothing colors it, nothing fills it. Except Imms.

And he's failed Imms. Failed him in ways that haven't even made it past the surface to show themselves to B. He's done something strange to trust, made a mangled sort of event of it. Heroes in movies can sell tickets to their promises: *Watch me save the world.* But B neglects people so casually. Because letting them fall is easier than devoting his whole self to catching them. When you live in one big dream about the future, you can justify your disdain for the present. And the dream of the future ends at achievement, at gratification—it never goes as far as consequences.

Somewhere the man who dug a Silver out of the ground and took him into his room instead of the lab exists. Who fell for the Silver moment by moment, who lived in the danger and the suddenness of that love. Who envisioned a future that simply included staying together and staying safe, and didn't take into account the strain of everyday existence. And somewhere the boy who walked away from the playground and into the world he wanted still exists. Who didn't take into account how much his absence would frighten those he cared about.

It often takes as much courage to do the foolish thing as it does to do the right one.

But every day that passes without Hatch calling B into her office, without anyone coming to cart Imms away, makes B feel stupider for packing a bag.

Something strange is happening to Imms's heart. Dr. Hwong says it just circles, day in and day out, like a fish in a bowl. It doesn't seem unhealthy. Just . . . bored. That's what B thinks when Dr. Hwong tells them. Imms's heart is bored.

By midwinter, Imms has slipped away somewhere. He lies on the couch, not reading, not watching TV, hardly moving. He eats less than usual. B wakes in the night sometimes to find Imms's side of the bed cold.

"It's snowing," B says one day. "Want to go to the park? I'll brave it if we can get coffee afterward."

"No, thanks," Imms says quietly.

"You've got to get off that couch. It's not healthy."

Imms slides off the couch and onto the floor, where he sits with his back against the couch. B snorts. "Smart-ass."

Imms doesn't look at him. "Write about it in your report."

"You're not helping yourself, or anybody, by acting like this."

To B's consternation, Imms buries his head in his arms. His shoulders shake.

B tilts his head, torn between irritation and a desire to comfort. A helplessness washes over him, brutal in its heaviness. He heads for the bedroom.

Imms stays on the couch and watches a special on the nature channel about ocean migrations. B can hear the gentle voice narrating the journey of thousands of cow-nosed stingrays from the Gulf of Mexico to New England. Imms must fall asleep, because he never comes to bed, and B doesn't go out to get him.

In early March, NRCSE appoints a redheaded woman named Scofield to meet with B and discuss Imms's future on Earth.

"We understand that with your schedule, it must be awfully hard to look after Imms," Scofield says. "We'd like to perhaps work out an arrangement where Imms would live part-time with a series of handlers."

"I thought the goal was to make him more independent, not less," B says.

"The long-term goal will be to set Imms up in a place of his own, then observe what choices he makes when living free of human influence."

"Free of human influence? Where's he gonna live, Walden Pond?"

"Relatively free," Scofield amends. "We want to know, what will he eat? What will he do for fun? That sort of thing."

"He makes those decisions right now."

"We think Imms could use a little variety in his interactions with humans. He's become very comfortable with the small social circle you've created for him—"

"His family."

"Why not make Imms part of multiple families? Let him experience *more*."

"He's not some pet that needs to be socialized," B says irritably. "He's not NRCSE's goddamn *project*."

"You can't deny how useful these observations would be."

"Useful for what? For when we colonize the Silver Planet and enslave the Silvers?"

Scofield smiles. "I don't think we need to go that far, Captain. Studying Imms has helped us shed light on what it means to be human. Dr. Hwong's analysis of Imms's unique brain, heart, and lung structures has enormous implications for the medical community."

"You want to observe him living a human life? Let him live like a human. Let him have a family. Give him the freedom to go where he chooses. Get rid of the guards. Let people meet him. I'll help him through that."

"What about safety?"

"Whose safety?"

"His. Yours. The public's. You have no idea what could happen. You haven't known him long enough to know what he's capable of."

"Capable of? You mean like, violence?" B asks.

"Partly."

B laughs.

Scofield's cheerfulness has subsided. "He attacked an investigator."

"That *investigator* came into our home and confronted Imms. Anything Imms did that day was done in self-defense."

"Well, regardless of why Imms tried to wound the man, he proved he's capable of violence. We understand the necessity of protecting both Imms and those around him."

"He saved me. Are you forgetting that? He saved my fucking life."

"I am aware."

B would like to shout, but he knows another outburst would be unwise. He leans back in his chair. "This is about the investigation, isn't it? The fire?"

"This is about what's best for Imms. Which may not be you, Captain."

B's surprised by how much the words sting. And by how familiar they are. He's thought them before. Still, the idea that NRCSE is a better option for Imms than B is ludicrous. "Keeping Imms at NRCSE is to refuse to acknowledge his essential humanity. It makes him a prisoner, an experiment. An animal."

"You make it sound as though we'd keep him in a cell in the bowels of this building. We're talking about houses, Captain. Other homes. Other families. Imms is struggling, Captain. His handlers here have noticed a marked change in his demeanor."

B doesn't answer.

"There are also some who believe the best option for Imms is to go home aboard the *Breakthrough II*."

"What?" This is the first B has heard of it.

"We haven't talked to Imms about it yet, but it is a possibility."

B is too numb to be angry. When he speaks, it's just a soft, "No."

"No?"

"He can make his own damn choices, and he's chosen to stay with me." The words sound like a little kid's saying them. His well-worn bravado has fear showing through its holes. He wishes someone else would decide what he does next. Tell him to run or stay put. Or relax, it's not the end of the world.

Scofield sighs and rubs the bridge of her nose. "We'd like to talk to Imms, Captain. Privately."

B tells Imms about his conversation with Scofield.

"No," Imms says, so loudly B winces. "No, B. Please."

"She just wants to discuss it with you."

"I want you there."

"She wants to talk to you privately. She thinks I'll influence your decision."

"Don't let them keep me there," Imms begs.

"You'll talk with Scofield for an hour or so, then I'll take you home."

"Shit," Imms whispers. "Shit, shit, shit."

"It's just to talk."

Imms takes a deep breath. "I want to stay here. Please let me stay here."

"You'll stay with me," B says firmly. "We just have to jump through the hoops so they'll leave us alone." He thinks about the bag under his bed. Then he thinks about the *Breakthrough II*. "And Imms . . . if you don't want to stay here . . ."

"Why wouldn't I?" Imms sounds hard, human.

"Listen to me."

"What's wrong, B? Are you mad? Did I do something? I'll be happier. I'll get off the couch. Just please let me stay."

"Shut up. You didn't do anything." B wraps his arms around Imms, pulls his head onto his chest. He can't explain anything to Imms when Imms is like this. "If you fight NRCSE, they're going to think I turned you against them. Listen to what they have to say. Pretend to think about it. But tell them you want to stay."

"You want to get rid of me." Naked accusation is in Imms's voice.

"Roach," B says softly. He hears Imms's breath catch, then feels the body against his relax slightly. "You don't have to do anything you don't want to do. Just like with the doctor."

Imms mutters something into B's shirt.

"What's that?"

"I had to. Let the doctor do what he wanted."

"What do you mean?"

"He said if I didn't, he'd make sure NRCSE took me away from you."

"When did he say that?" B asks over the pounding in his ears.

"Once when you were out of the room."

B's hand on Imms's back clenches into a fist. He feels Imms tense. "Why didn't you tell me?"

The fucking bastard doctor. That whole organization of fucking bastards. They *know* Imms has human thoughts and feelings, and they use that to exploit him. And Imms, so quick to put himself in danger for B. Why always for B? Imms braved the ship, Joele, to see him—twice. And now Imms has obeyed the instructions of a man he hates and fears to stay with B. That's twisted. B truly is a barrier to Imms's independence, to his happiness. Any fantasy of running off with Imms is a joke. Fuck, what if Scofield's right?

He pushes Imms away. "So why tell me now? You obviously decided you could handle the situation. You let him cut you open and stick that thing on your heart, and expose your body to all kinds of germs. What's the point in saying this now?"

Imms huddles against the back of the couch. "I don't get to do what I want." His voice is slow and sharp, like a needle pushed through skin. "I do what lets me stay." His eyes glitter. The jagged irises tremble, as though they might split open.

"When did you stop trusting me?" B stands. "That's what I want to know."

"You can't always protect me. You can't always rescue me. I know that."

"I could damn well have tried."

"You could try right now! You could try now."

The urge to strike is gone so fast it might not have been there at all. B stands there, all his power, all his energy gone. He doesn't want to hit Imms. He doesn't want to touch him at all. He feels strangely peaceful. If he keeps Imms outside of him, refuses to let him in, he will be alone, and he can finally get some rest. He just has to find a way to make that person on the couch into a shell. Like he was on the Silver Planet. Something to cut into.

B goes to the bedroom. He spends a lot of time there now that Imms and his cloud of darkness have taken up residence on the couch. If Scofield is right, and B isn't what's best for Imms, then maybe Imms should meet new people. Spend less time here. Maybe one day live on his own.

Except that won't happen, B knows. Imms will end up at the NRCSE facility, in a lab. The NRCSuckers aren't evil. But they are like B and his team when they first encountered the Silvers—their awe was temporary. They now see Imms as an opportunity, a project. The NRCSuckers may bond with Imms on a superficial level, but they will not love him. They will not protect him.

If Imms leaves B, he has to go back to the Silver Planet. But if Imms goes home, what kind of life is waiting for him there? Forgotten by his clan, he'll have nothing to do but wander around in the darkness, tending goddamn flowers.

He's more than that. B has always liked him because he's *more*.

B glances at his laptop, closed on the bedside table. Writing his reports on Imms for NRCSE is getting harder and harder. Last week, B caught Imms in front of the hall mirror, talking to his reflection in the Silver language. His tone was vicious, and he seemed to be searching for words at times. Once, Imms uttered a single word, a hard, sharp word that cracked across the room, and then he traced one side of his face with his finger.

"What are you doing?" B finally asked, stepping into the room.

Imms looked startled, then guilty, then so sad that B felt his own heart catch. He came to B and put his head on B's shoulder, wrapping his arms around him. Imms didn't answer any questions B asked, only pressed himself closer to B as though B were the ground on the Silver Planet, as though he wanted to sink into him. Then his hands went to B's shirt. He looked as if he were unraveling the garment, rather than unbuttoning it. He put his hands on B's bare chest, feeling the skin. Then he knelt and undid B's fly.

I can hardly write a report about that. He remembers how he let himself be distracted. How he didn't pursue the matter of the mirror.

B thinks of all he has done so far to avoid any mention in his reports of his relationship with Imms. The psychologist continues to ask if Imms has experienced feelings of attraction toward humans.

"No," B tells her. *"No,"* Imms tells her. B wonders now if he should have come clean from the beginning. It might have put a stop to all this business of sending Imms to live with someone else, if NRCSE only knew that B's bond with Imms goes beyond rescuer and rescued.

He thinks of Christmas Eve, the two of them in the bath. *"I wonder if I can stay underwater as long as I used to,"* Imms said. *"Want to time me?"* Without waiting, he plunged under the silver water. B felt Imms's body brush against his legs. He tried to spook himself with different scenarios. He was in the ocean, and the thing bumping his leg was a shark. Or a dead body bound in seaweed, about to surface beside him. Danger lurked beneath the surface of the water, and B had no choice but to drift and wait to be pulled under.

But no, he finally decided. The real danger is that this is how they live now. Imms below the surface, B just above.

B can't love below the surface.

He does, though. He goes deeper and deeper into dark ground where he can't breathe. With Imms there too, it doesn't seem so bad. It's what he's clinging to aboveground that hurts. Love, however sharp and fierce it gets, isn't so painful. But the house, the carpet, his job, his family—this all jabs him when he goes to make a decision. How is he supposed to be anyone but the man he's always been, trapped and at odds with his universe? If he's not trapped, he has nothing to push against, nothing to excuse his inaction.

Imms gives him something to fight for, a possibility of freedom, an excuse to exclude himself from a society he's never felt welcome in. NRCSE's got a planetary integration specialist working to make Imms a part of Earth. But B fell in love with the stranger, the outcast forgotten by his clan. Together they've woven a story. B wants them as they were, on bright earth under a black sky, the only two hearts on the planet that didn't hide from each other.

He takes the bag out from under the bed and rips everything out of it—the flashlight, the cans of soup, the spare clothes. It really does look pathetic, all strewn on the floor.

He hears Imms's words again. *"You want to get rid of me."*

Matty used to manipulate him that way. *"You hate me,"* he'd pout if B got the least bit angry.

B rolls a can of soup across the carpet and feels disappointed when it veers instead of hitting the wall.

"*I don't hate you,*" B would say, consciously placing his voice in a gentler register. B used to love his role of reassurer. Now he is older and doesn't have the energy. He has seen too much. He wants people to take responsibility for themselves.

He climbs into bed without taking his shoes off. He falls asleep and is surprised to wake and find Imms asleep beside him, one hand on B's chest. B looks at the hand, sees that the cuticles around the nails are chewed bloody. He picks up Imms's hand as carefully as possible. Imms doesn't stir. He touches the tiny stinging spots with his thumb. He kisses each knuckle. He gets up to fix lunch.

chapter
THIRTY-FOUR

Imms goes to see Scofield. The psychologist is there too, along with two other NRCSuckers. Imms listens politely to everything they say. He tells them very politely that he'd like to stay with B.

They tell him to think it over, and they'll be in contact when they get some potential handlers lined up. Then Imms can come and meet them.

He could tell them now about the fire. Then he won't get any new handlers—the NRCSuckers will take him to jail, and that will be that. B can stop worrying, stop feeling guilty. But when he opens his mouth, the words won't come out.

The psychologist asks him questions, and he tries to give the right answers. She asks which he likes better, the tip or the eraser of a pencil. She tells him there's a runaway trolley on a railway line, and five humans trapped on the main track. Imms can, if he chooses, pull a switch that will divert the car to a siding, thereby saving the lives of the five humans. However, a Silver is standing on the siding, and the Silver will be killed if Imms pulls the switch. What does he do? This doesn't make any sense to Imms. He is the only Silver on Earth. How can another Silver be on the siding? And what is a siding? The psychologist says the situation is hypothetical.

He hasn't had any Italian lessons for a while. And hardly any swimming. It's mostly just meetings with the psychologist, and sometimes trips to see Dr. Hwong.

B drives him home. He doesn't ask how the meeting went, so Imms doesn't tell him. Imms goes to sleep on the couch and wakes up when the phone rings.

"I told Don to stay the fuck away from me," Bridique announces by way of greeting. She sounds like she's been crying.

Imms doesn't answer.

"He was getting really clingy. I don't know what he thought. That we were in love or some bullshit. Anyway, he thinks there's something going on between you and me. That's what he said. Fucking cockwad." She waits. "Hello? You there?"

"Yeah," Imms says.

"So I'm a fucking idiot, right, for ever getting involved with him. But I just wanted to warn you, he's no fan of yours right now."

Imms is silent.

"What's wrong with you? Can a girl get a little support?"

"Why'd you have to do that?"

"What? Speak the fuck up."

"Why'd you have to do that?" Imms repeats. "Get him pissed at me?"

"Fuck you, too. Did you take an asshole pill today or something? Call me when you're ready to be a friend." She hangs up.

Imms curls tighter. So tight his organs might burst like pimples. He doesn't get pimples. Humans get pimples. Silvers are ugly enough without them. He practices the Silver word for *ugly*. He had to modify a couple of other words. The word for *unfortunate*, and the word for *appearance*, because Silvers have no word that means *ugly*. He likes to look in the mirror and speak to himself in his old tongue. He likes to bring human feelings to a language that never allowed for anger or hate.

Lady jumps onto the couch beside him, but he pushes her off. If she gets too close, she might get ugly too. She might stop listening to commands unless they're in the Silver language, because Imms used to talk to her in that language until B stopped him.

B has gone to work. B said things would be different. Better. But they are not.

The phone rings. It's Brid again.

"I forgot today was your meeting with the NRCSE assholes. So I guess I'm the cockwad. How'd it go? You tell them where to stick it?"

Imms drops the phone.

It stays light out a little longer each evening. B goes to bed a little later.

Sometimes after B goes to sleep, Imms lies outside in the backyard, pretending he's on the Silver Planet. He is glad B never asks what happened to the book he gave Imms for Christmas, because then Imms would have to tell him he dropped it behind Mary and Bridique's radiator in the basement with the spiders and dust, where his hands can't reach. It started hurting too much to look at it.

Imms is taking another pottery class at the Potter's Wheel. He's getting good, though he breaks most of what he makes—brings home vases and pots and ashtrays while B is at work and drops them on the kitchen floor, then cleans up the mess before B returns. He thinks B knows because sometimes B rubs the sole of his shoe on the kitchen floor, and clay dust crackles beneath.

He practices going into the ground. In the yard, when B's not home. For a long time, he can't. Then one day, he slips, just a little bit, beneath the surface. Part of him knows he shouldn't be satisfied with this. But he's so desperate for any sign he's still who he was that he doesn't mind that he can't go deeper.

"Walk the dog," B says one evening. Imms is lying on the couch, picking out shapes in the textured plaster of the ceiling.

"You walk her," Imms mutters.

B strides over to the couch and grabs Imms by the arm, pulling him up. For an instant, Imms is frightened and thrilled—finally, something will happen—but B looks into his eyes and eases his grip. Takes a deep breath and says, quietly, "Walk her, please. She misses you."

Imms wonders what is in his eyes that even B won't fight.

"Were you ever going to tell me?" B asks, dropping some papers on the coffee table in front of Imms. Grena's book of cryptowords. Imms eyes it. "Grena won't answer my calls. She's never in her office when I'm there. But she'll send you fucking coded messages." He slaps his hand on top of the book. He wants Imms to jump, but Imms doesn't. "Why does she think you'll need her?"

"I don't know."

"Christ." B rakes his hand through his hair. "What did she tell you? Did she tell you they want to send you home?"

"No," Imms lies.

"She thought we shouldn't bring you here. You know that? She tried to talk me out of it."

Imms doesn't answer.

"Is that what you think too? That I shouldn't have dragged you here?"

"It was my choice."

"No, it wasn't. What were you gonna say to us? To me? What fucking choice did you have? You didn't have a clue what you were getting into."

Imms stares at the floor. He can barely count the loops in the carpet. His brain feels unanchored, like his heart. Drifting around his skull.

B paces. "Whatever we were, whatever we had when we were on your planet, it's gone here, isn't it? And now you want to leave."

"Fuck you," Imms says. Not faking anger—feeling it. His body wants to move farther and more quickly than he can in this house, and maybe if he lights a fire in B, they'll both go somewhere. Somewhere no one else can touch them.

"Then where is it? *What* is it?"

Imms shakes his head. If he opens his mouth, he will throw up or cry. "You stopped wanting me," he shouts finally.

"*I* stopped wa— I gave up everything for you! What kind of a life do you think this is for me, feeding you, exercising you, training you like a goddamn dog?"

Lady barks at the raised voice.

"Worrying about you when I have to work late, wondering if NRCSE's gonna snatch you away, feeling like I can't go anywhere without—"

"I never asked you to do any of that."

"There's not a saint in history who could deal with all you *need*."

"I don't need anything! You're the one who won't let me take care of myself. It's humans who need and need. I was okay. I was fine until you got there."

"You're right. We do need. I needed some kind of connection on that godforsaken planet. I needed *something* to remind me I was alive. But now . . . we're holding something up that wants to sink. Let's let it sink." His voice softens. He sounds urgent now, pleading. "You can still live here, with me. We just won't be—"

"Stop," Imms shouts. He shouts it again and again, and the word acts as a barrier, keeping B from approaching him, touching him. Finally B retreats.

Hours later, Imms is alone in the house. B has gone somewhere; he didn't say where. Imms flips the pages of *Tin Star and Thunder Sam*. He has given up trying to concentrate on the words. It's is not the same story when it's not in Grena's voice.

He wants to see Grena sitting on the bright earth with the black sky all around her, wants to see her lips move, wants to hear the words for the first time and not know what they mean. He wants to feel light slipping through the dark shell around his mind, touching raw, ready space, making him aware of just how much he doesn't know.

He thinks a part of him has always understood Earth, anger, humans, space, pain, and love. He just needed the right pieces to touch one another.

He closes the book. He can only think of one way to stop B's guilt, to unfold his darkness and expose it to light. One way to stop being a criminal and a liar. To make people understand that Vir was a good person, not a murderer.

Imms has to tell the truth.

He has to tell Earth that the fire was his fault. Not Vir's.

Not B's. Not even Joele's.

If he does this, he might go to jail. Or to NRCSE for good. He certainly won't be allowed to stay with B.

It's very important to tell the truth, Imms, Sandy said. *Do you understand that? If you don't, bad things can happen.*

Bad things have happened to Imms because he is a liar. Because he pretended to be human.

He knows now what he is and knows he doesn't deserve B, or Mary, or Brid. Even if B claims he wants to keep Imms safe by lying about the fire, Imms knows B would be relieved if the world knew the truth.

This is his chance to rescue B. Rescuing someone doesn't just mean pulling them off a burning ship or busting them out of an outlaw prison. B hurts, and Imms can stop it.

"You need to tell the truth, even if you didn't tell it before. Even if you think it will get you or someone else in trouble."

"Okay," he whispers.

It's not easy, though. Every time he thinks about what he has to do, he seems to break apart. Tears come. He feels more human than ever.

But finally Imms goes to the bedroom and opens B's laptop.

chapter
THIRTY-FIVE

NRCSE is going to burn Vir's journals. Maybe not burn them. B doesn't know exactly what they'll do. But Vir's words will disappear, and her reputation will stay intact. The *Byzantine* fire will be cataloged as an accident. B and Grena will keep their medals. Imms will remain a hero.

B is more than ready to move on. To snap the past in half and toss it aside. But it leaps back at him, inexhaustible.

The pages he copied from Vir's journals were from her early months on the Silver Planet. The months she spent happy. He puts the copies in an envelope and drives to a small yellow house in a neighborhood on the edge of town. He double-checks the house number, is relieved the garage is closed, the lights off. He wouldn't actually be able to have a conversation with Vir's parents. But he was curious enough about where they lived to deliver the envelope in person rather than mailing it. He wonders if this is the house where Vir grew up. If she played in this small, patchy yard. If she pretended her sandbox was another planet.

He wonders how her parents grieved for her. If they still do. B has never really grieved for anyone. Grief is not the raw, tender mess people think it is. Grief happens when the wound is already scabbed over. You can point to someone's grief like a tattoo on their ankle and ask, *"Did it hurt?"* They say, *"For a little bit."* It is the cicada shell of the real feeling—which is not a feeling at all, but an absence of feeling so great that no matter how you reach, you're always touching nothing. Grief is not the true, dripping heartmeat of what it means to *lose*.

He walks up to the front porch and puts the envelope in Vir's parents' mailbox. Then he drives. He thinks he might be going home to apologize to Imms, but he ends up at his mother's house. She lets him in and doesn't ask how he is. She leads him into the kitchen, sits him at the table, and gives him a glass of water.

She hugs him, and it's too hard, almost painful, but also too short. She asks him to tell her everything, and he does—or most of it. From the moment he met Imms to the moment he shut the door this morning.

"And the world's still turning," Mary says when he's done.

His mother's brisk, easy confidence is still there. It drove him crazy as a kid, but it made him brave even when he was sure he couldn't be.

"I've lied to everyone."

Mary taps his shoulder and goes for the cheap wine on top of the fridge. She pours them each a glass. "Nothing that can't be fixed."

"What do I do?"

"First," Mary says, "call Imms."

"I can't talk to him."

"Why not?"

"I can't help him."

His mother doesn't ask what he means. "Tell him what matters."

"What's that?"

"That you love him."

"How do I know I do?"

"Of course you do. Love is all of it. The moments you can't stand him. The moments you think you'd be better off alone."

B rubs his temples. "Why are you alone? If you know so much about it."

Mary doesn't flinch. "You can love him even if you're not always together. But say the words, because he needs to hear them. Because that's a starting point."

"And after that?"

Mary stands. "I'm going to make lunch. You get him over here, and we'll have a meal. We're not going one step farther on empty stomachs."

B takes out his phone and calls the house. It rings and rings.

Mary hums in the kitchen. And B waits.

Imms sits on the bus with his hat pulled down and his scarf up over his nose. He remembers the building is near the Rose Sanctuary, because Brid pointed it out on their first drive to Rose. When he sees the familiar logo, he pulls the cord to request a stop. He realizes when he steps off the bus that he probably could have waited, gotten closer to the building. But he doesn't mind walking.

The lights are bright inside. The floor is reflective tile. His eyes try to find dark space, but there is none. He goes to the desk.

"Can I help you?" the young man asks. His smile falls as he looks at Imms.

"I need to see Elise Fischer."

"Elise. Um, do you have an appointment?"

A woman in heels clacks over, mouth hanging open. "Is that . . .?" she asks the man, as though Imms is not there.

"He wants to see Elise."

"Well, I'll *go get her*," the woman says as though she can't believe the man is stupid enough to still be sitting there. She glances at Imms, flashes him a quick smile.

She clacks back about ten minutes later, followed by a short, pretty blonde woman Imms immediately recognizes, though she looks smaller in person. Imms wonders why that is when TV is just a tiny, flat box, and the real world is enormous. She walks up to Imms and offers her hand.

"Elise Fischer."

"I'm Imms."

"Imms. A pleasure. It's quite a surprise to see you here. Where's your handler?"

"He's not here."

"You're alone?" Elise seems curious but not frightened.

"Yes."

"Well, come on back to my dressing room and sit down."

Elise's dressing room has a plant. Imms likes plants, and this one wants water. He tells Elise this, and she laughs. "I'm afraid I don't have a green thumb, Imms." She sits at her table. Imms tries not to look at the large mirror in front of them. "So. I'm dying to know why you're here."

B used that phrase once: *"I'm dying to know . . ."* All Imms heard was *"I'm dying,"* and the rush of fear was so great that it took several minutes for his heart to move again, to stop hiding.

"I want to go on the news," he says, "and talk about being on Earth."

For the first time, Elise looks a little nervous. "Does anybody know about this?"

He shakes his head. "It's my choice."

She nods. "It absolutely is." Elise reaches for the phone on the table and presses a button. "Jonathan? Tell Meryl we're scrapping the goat lawn-mowing thing. I'm going to interview the Silver at one."

"Got it," voice from the phone says.

"You look tired," Elise says to Imms. "Can I get you coffee? Tea?"

"Water?" Imms asks.

She pulls a bottle from a small refrigerator under the table and hands it to him. He drinks half, gives the rest to the plant. "Will the captain be worried?" she asks. "Does he know you're here?"

"He's at work."

Jonathan brings in some papers. He and Elise whisper for a minute. Jonathan leaves, and Elise slides the papers toward Imms. "If we're going to do this, I have to make sure I have your consent to be interviewed and recorded. Read these over . . . Can you read?"

Imms nods.

"Okay. Read, then sign. If you have any questions, just ask."

Imms barely glances at the forms. It doesn't matter what they say. He signs.

"I have to know before we start if any topics are off-limits," Elise says. "Things you don't want me to ask you about."

"No," Imms says. "You can ask me about fucking if you want. Bridique does."

Elise gets a strange look on her face. Then she laughs. "I won't ask you about that. We're network."

Imms doesn't know what that means, but he laughs too.

At twelve thirty, Jonathan takes Imms to another room to pick out a suit. Imms dresses, then someone guides him to a mirror and puts powder on his face. It makes him look like paste. Like mashed potatoes.

Soon he is sitting in a chair across from Elise, bright lights shining all around. He has a microphone clipped to his suit jacket. Somebody says, "Rolling."

Elise speaks to one of the cameras. "Good afternoon, I'm Elise Fischer with Channel 5 News. I'm in the studio today with a visitor from another *planet*." When she says the word *planet*, Imms thinks suddenly of the whole universe, bits of everything floating in nothing. How strange it is that when this interview is on TV, many humans will see it, but right now Elise is talking to nobody.

"You've all heard about Imms, a member of an alien race called the Silvers," Elise continues. "Imms was brought to Earth by the two surviving members of last year's Silver Planet mission, and has been living under strict government supervision for the last nine months. Now he's come to us with the request that he be allowed to tell his story. So Imms, let's start at the beginning." She sits back a little. "Tell us how you first encountered humans."

The first few questions are easy, and as Imms answers them, he feels the ache in his scars fade. He feels more like himself. Not the self he's been lately, but the self he was when he first arrived on Earth. He forgets about the cameras, about Elise. He remembers Grena, and learning English, and *Tin Star and Thunder Sam*. He leaves out Joele, but he says that he was hurt and B found him. He likes remembering this, even though it means remembering pain and losing blood. He likes to imagine B digging him out of the ground, even though he wasn't awake for it.

He slowly forgets the B who stormed out of the house this morning and remembers only the B who loved him.

"You said Silvers can't feel anger," Elise says. "But you can?"

"I think so," Imms says. "I learned to. I was angry when I came here today."

"And why was that?"

"B doesn't want to be in love with me anymore."

Elise blinks twice. Her lips are parted. "I think a lot of our viewers are probably surprised to learn that your relationship with the captain is, or was, romantic in nature. We were given the impression that he is your—your caretaker."

Imms nods. "I tried to take care of him too."

Elise's expression is soft, wondering. She is not performing for the camera anymore. "This may be a difficult question for you to answer, but do you think your motivation in coming here today was revenge?"

"I don't know."

"Because the captain told you he didn't want to be with you anymore?"

"I was mad," Imms says. "I'm not anymore." Imms suddenly feels cold, despite the heat from the lights. "Don't tell him. Don't tell him I was mad."

Elise hands him a glass of water, and he drinks. "Let's go back to the issue of emotion, Imms, because I'm curious. When did you begin to experience anger? Do you remember?"

"The fire." He pauses. "I didn't rescue B." The words aren't as hard to say as he'd imagined. He's wanted to say them for a long time. "He rescued me. The fire was my fault."

Lines appear between Elise Fischer's eyebrows and across her forehead. "What do you mean?"

Imms undoes the first few buttons of his shirt. Elise looks nervous again. He shows her his scars. "I was in the lab. On the table. And she was burning me."

"Who was?"

"Joele. I wasn't supposed to go near the ship. But I did and she found me, and she made a small fire. She burned me, and I knocked the fire to the floor. It got on her clothes. I escaped from the table, but I couldn't help her. I tried. Then I slept—I mean, passed out. And B saved me."

"Okay." Elise says it like she's reassuring him. Or herself. "That's not the story we've been told."

Imms shakes his head. "B said I'd be safe here if humans thought I was a hero. But now B feels guilty all the time because we lied. I went to the lab when I wasn't supposed to. I made the fire grow. I killed Joele, and Vir, and Gumm."

Imms doesn't remember if he answered her original question or not, so he adds, "I think the burning is what made me angry. At first."

Elise gives him another bottle of water for the road. She thanks him and shakes his hand again. She says, quietly so that no one else can hear, "I'm truly sorry."

He doesn't want to wait for the bus, so he walks past the building, keeps going until he reaches the Rose Sanctuary.

The guard at the entrance is the same one who was there when Imms first visited. Josh. "Hey," he says, grinning. "Silver man."

"Is Bridique here?"

chapter
THIRTY-SIX

They lie on Bridique's bed. The room smells grown-up, elegant.

"You're a caveman," Bridique says. "Swinging your club at rival cavemen. Painting stick deer on the wall. Creating fire."

"You're an angel," Imms says. "Soaring around heaven. Playing a—what's it called?"

"Trumpet?"

"With strings."

"A harp."

"Harp. And you play the best of all the angels. But you want to play rock 'n' roll, and all they want to play is heaven music."

Brid laughs. "That would be me."

"How do you win this game?" Imms asks.

"You don't. It's wishful thinking. No winners."

Imms looks at the rough plaster of the ceiling. "How about I'm a superhero? And when B tries to kill me, I turn invisible, or run through walls."

"He's not going to kill you."

"I shouldn't've told the news we were in love."

"I'm glad you did," Brid says.

Imms isn't sure what she means. "Now people know the fire was my fault. Will I have to live at NRCSE, do you think? Or just jail?"

Brid shakes her head. "The fire was Joele's fault. Plain and simple."

"But I—"

"Can it. Whether Channel 5 airs it or not, you did a brave thing. And you won't go to jail."

"But I lied."

"B lied."

"He did it to protect me."

"Partly. And partly to protect himself. I love my brother, but he is selfish, selfish."

"He's a good captain."

"And sometimes he's an idiot dickwad who tries to swing across Shit Creek and ends up neck-deep."

"What do you mean?"

She looks at Imms and puts the back of her hand on his cheek. "He lied, Imms. He's gonna be in trouble."

"Brid!" Imms sits up.

"Easy," Brid says.

"They can't do anything to him. He didn't mean to do anything wrong."

"I know. I know. And there's a chance this will all get settled in a small windowless room with a briefcase full of cash, and not in court. If Channel 5 doesn't air your interview—"

"How do we stop them from airing it?"

"We can't do much. Except wait."

"Will he go to jail?"

"B's done a lot for NRCSE. They might not be so quick to throw him to the wolves."

"He didn't want anyone to be blamed for the fire. He just wanted it to seem like an accident. But then Vir—"

"I know," Brid says. "Damn him. Damn him *really*."

"Why?"

"He shouldn't have fucking lied, that's why."

Imms hadn't thought he could get any stupider, but he has outdone himself. He knew B didn't want anyone to find out that they lied about the fire, but he thought that if he just explained the whole story and took the blame himself, people would leave B alone. They'd understand why B lied.

Instead, he's gotten B neck-deep.

Imms moves closer to Brid. "I told Elise she could ask me about fucking. Since you always do."

Brid turns her head toward him. "You did not tell Elise Fischer, Channel 5 News, that she could ask you about fucking."

"I did."

Brid yelps with laughter. "Why wasn't I there?" She rolls over and tucks her face against Imms's side. She rubs her nose against his ribs. "I don't understand fucking. I thought I did. I always thought I knew how to do it without feeling anything. That must've been nice, on your planet. No feelings to get in the way."

"We have feelings."

"But it's simpler, right?"

"Maybe," Imms says.

Mary comes home, and she's brought dinner. Chinese food. Nobody talks much, and that's okay with Imms because it gives him time to think. About what he's done, and what he needs to do. Mary tries to call B. No answer. Imms paces the house. He worries about Lady, who hasn't been walked for a long time. Bridique says she'll do it. Imms wants to come, but Mary asks him to stay and help with the dishes. He does a bad job on purpose. He doesn't really dry them. He waits to see if Mary will get mad.

She touches his arm. He jumps. She shuts off the water and keeps her hand on him, guiding him into the living room. "The dishes aren't done," he says.

"They can wait."

She opens a cupboard under the TV and takes out two large books with light-blue leather covers, which she sets on the coffee table. She sits on the couch and waits until Imms sits beside her before she opens the first book. "I thought you might like to see these."

The book is full of pictures in thin plastic. Words are written underneath the pictures in neat cursive hand. Imms focuses on the first photo. It shows a baby standing in white shorts and a red shirt, with pale hair that stands straight up like grass.

"That's my son," Mary says. "Eighteen months old."

Imms doesn't recognize the word under the picture, and he asks Mary what it means.

"His name," Mary says.

Imms folds the name and puts it away for safekeeping.

He knows he'll never use it. Imms had to stop being Roach, but B is always B.

Imms spends the next hour turning the pages of the blue books, looking at pictures of B, watching him grow up. B leaves his mother's arms and crawls across a brown carpet. He cries with displeasure in a frilly red outfit with a matching hat. He walks with Mary holding his arms. He stands with both hands shoved down his diaper, eyes squeezed shut, an enormous smile on his face. He blows out six candles on a cake shaped like a space shuttle. He rides a stick horse through a mud puddle. He tries to feed lettuce to a cat named Alice. He pulls Bridique in a wagon and hugs her in front of a Ferris wheel; she has long hair and is missing a front tooth.

He graduates from high school and towers over Mary. He stops smiling in pictures, except in one where he's kayaking with a boy who has dark, curly hair.

Soon he is always sitting, bent over desks, not looking at the camera. He rarely appears in pictures with Bridique, who is featured in her own set of photos, first with a group of three other girls, then with several different boys. B holds a certificate from NRCSE. He builds a snowman that wears suspenders, and Imms can see the smile underneath the scarf that covers most of B's face, because it reaches up and catches his eyes.

B kisses the boy from the kayak in front of Mary's house. He sleeps on the couch with a hand on his stomach.

His name—his real name—is under many of the photos, the name of a man who existed for years without knowing Imms. Mary's wrinkles deepen and Bridique's hair gets shorter. B and the kayak boy grow tan and brawny and move into the house where Imms lives now with B. They stand in the cluttered kitchen, B wearing an apron with a naked man's muscled torso painted on it, and the dark-haired man wearing an apron with a bikini-clad woman's body on it.

Imms doesn't feel sad, but he doesn't feel happy either. He feels quiet, like he could sit for a long time with these books and they would start to breathe. Then Imms and the books could match their breathing and forget the rest of the world.

"I love him." Imms doesn't even mean to say it out loud.

Mary closes her eyes, as though this causes her the same slow flood of pain as her arthritis. "I know."

"I *can* love him," Imms says. "I've always been able to."

"Of course you can." Mary says. "And you do. I never doubted that."

"I—" Imms has to stop because his throat is suddenly thick. He thinks he must look like a snake that's swallowed an egg. He makes himself say the words in his head before he says them out loud. "I didn't save him."

He doesn't know if Mary understands what he means. The news has said for so long that Imms saved B. That a Silver risked its life for a human. And it's a lie. If Channel 5 airs the interview, everyone will know.

Mary stares at Imms until his eyes meet hers, until she has his full attention. "I think you did."

They're silent after that. Imms flips through the pictures until Bridique gets back with Lady. Lady jumps out of Brid's arms and runs to Imms. She gets on Imms's lap and Imms lies back on the couch, holding her close.

"Is B home?" Imms asks. From the corner of his eye, he sees Bridique and Mary look at each other.

"No," Brid says.

Imms lets Lady lick traces of dinner off his mouth.

"'He's in six kinds of trouble,'" Imms says. It's a quote from *Tin Star and Thunder Sam*, and Imms wishes B were here to hate it.

"I like seeing you two here," Mary says softly. Imms and Lady both look at her. "You belong here. This—" She pats one of the photo albums. "You have it too. All right, Imms? A family."

Brid sits on the edge of the couch next to him. "Whatever happens, we'll help you." She bumps him. "We'll hide you if we have to."

Imms shakes his head. "I'm not hiding anymore."

Silvers go into the ground and into lakes. They avoid danger. They run from humans. They are fast, good at vanishing, at closing their eyes, at pretending there is no danger. Creatures on Earth fight for what they want. B told him that a long time ago.

Imms is not getting onboard the *Breakthrough II*, or going to live at NRCSE, or meeting different handlers. He is going to stay right here, like he promised B he would. And if anyone tries to hurt B, Imms will protect him—even if he has to take blood.

chapter
THIRTY-SEVEN

Only one house on Mary and Brid's street has daffodils. Imms wonders if the neighbors are jealous. This isn't something he would have wondered a few months ago. Jealousy wasn't something he thought about. But he is different now.

The new handler points out something on the other side of the street, but Imms has to watch Mary and Bridique's house go by. The new handler has said Imms can still see Mary and Bridique on occasion. But not yet. She says first he should spend some time away from them, meeting new people.

He has lived with the new handler for a week and refuses to remember her name. She is nice enough—long brown ponytail, rimless glasses. She lives with her husband and two sons, who are sixteen and fourteen. The sixteen-year-old doesn't like video games. The fourteen-year-old isn't good at them. They both like science. They invited Imms to look at their basement lab, but Imms refused, and the new handler wrote down that he refused. She was nice about it, though.

He doesn't want to know her name because he will be leaving soon. He hasn't been able to leave yet because the new handler watches him all the time and has an even bigger entourage on her property than B had.

"Do you need anything from the store?" she asks.

"No," he replies. She makes him fix all his own meals.

As a result, he gets away with not eating much. Just a lot of apples. And pears. He loves pears more than apples now.

They drive home. The boys are doing homework at the table. It is only four o'clock. Imms knows from Dave and his friends that doing homework any time other than five minutes before it's due is for nerds. Still, he asks if they need help with math, and the older boy asks him the square root of two hundred and fifty-six. Imms answers instantly.

"Stop," the new handler says. "They need to do the work themselves." It is always his fault, never the boys', when they ask him something and he answers. The other day, the fourteen-year-old asked him what a BJ was, and Imms told him. The new handler documented the incident angrily.

The new handler's phone buzzes. She fishes it out of her pocket and checks who's calling. She sighs and answers. "Hello?"

"Put Imms on," Bridique's voice says loudly on the other end.

"This isn't a good time," the handler says, glancing at Imms.

"It's a plenty good time, it's a goddamn emergency."

"What is it?"

"Put him the hell on!"

The new handler hands the phone to Imms.

"Hello," he says.

"Thank God. What a lousy bitch. Can she hear me?"

"I think so. I could hear you." Imms glances at the new handler, who is pretending to sort mail.

"Go into another room. I don't want her to hear this."

Imms retreats into the den. "Okay."

"Okay. I went to Grena's."

"And?"

"Let me make sure I've got this right. I wrote it all down, but backwards, in case anyone finds it. I'm kidding. You go to NRCSE as scheduled on Monday morning. Nine o'clock?"

"Right."

"At nine forty-five, there's going to be a diversion."

"A diversion?"

"You'll see. Once you're out of the natatorium, Grena will meet you and take you to the underground lair where they're keeping my brother."

B's not in jail exactly. He is being held at NRCSE in one of the rooms that used to be barracks in the military base. In that hallway Imms passed through when the NRCSuckers took him to be interviewed. Brid said it's more like a crappy hotel room than a prison. *"Think house arrest in an Econo Lodge,"* she'd told him.

For three hours each day, B has access to one of the fitness fields. *"It's the field closest to the river,"* Brid said. *"So he's got a nice view through the chain link."*

NRCSE is working with federal investigators and lawyers to try to settle things as quietly as possible. B has pleaded guilty to the cover-up, and this means B might be able to strike a deal with the government.

"Okay," Imms says.

"That's as far as we got," Brid says. "How you actually bust into his room without getting caught is a kink we're still trying to work out. We're assuming his room is monitored. Grena says she has an idea for how you might slip in, though."

"I'll figure it out," Imms says.

"Okay. But the NRCSuckers will only be distracted by controlled chaos for so long. Once they realize you're gone, B's room'll be one of the first places they'll look."

"I have to try."

He tries not to feel guilty for lying to Brid. He told her he needs to see B, to talk to him. He asked her if she could get hold of Grena using the address from the book of cryptowords.

It's true. He does need to see B. But he has no intention of letting B stay at NRCSE, and no intention of going back to the new handler.

"Grena didn't lie," Brid says. "She admitted her role in the cover-up to the investigators. But they need her for this new mission, so she'll get off easy. My oh-so-uncooperative brother won't be so lucky."

"Is it bad?"

"Well, they haven't thrown him in prison or hooked electrodes to his balls, and they allow him more than one phone call. I think he'll come out of this in one piece." She doesn't sound sure.

"Brid—"

"Monday at nine forty-five. Tell the bitch I had to ask you what shoes to wear with gaucho pants."

She hangs up.

At nine forty-five on Monday, Imms is at the swimming pool, ready to dive in, when Dave Welbert enters the natatorium, wearing a white coat. He hurries over to Violet Cranbrim and the other NRCSuckers. Imms is surprised to see Dave there, and even more surprised to see him dressed like a doctor, but he's fairly certain he should keep his mouth shut.

"Hey," Dave says to Violet. "Sorry to interrupt. I'm with Biomed. Dr. Hwong's been monitoring Imms's heart's trajectory this morning, and noticed something—" Dave lowers his voice, but still stage-whispers "—off. Probably nothing to worry about, but Dr. Hwong wants to check him out right away. I'm supposed to bring him to the medical center."

One of the NRCSuckers glances at the badge clipped to Dave's coat. Violet calls to Imms, who leaves the edge of the pool where the blue water laps his toes. Violet smiles at him. She is still kind to him, even after finding out he loves B. Some of the NRCSuckers, though they remain indifferent and professional within his hearing, don't like him anymore. Devin, who drives the jeep, said once if NRCSE had any sense, they'd put Imms down. He didn't know Imms was listening. Or maybe he did.

"Get dressed," Violet says. "Dr. Hwong needs to see you."

Imms glances at Dave, who offers him a very small nod. Imms goes to the changing area and puts on his clothes. He hopes he doesn't really have to see Dr. Hwong. He searches for his heart and finds it near his left hip, glowing faintly. He slips his shoes on and goes back to the pool. Dave motions for Imms to follow him and leads him out of the pool and down the corridor toward the medical center.

"What do you think?" Dave whispers as they walk. He pinches the white coat. "Not bad, huh?"

"How did you—"

"Grena. Nicked the coat and the badge off an intern."

"Are we really going to the doctor's?"

"Nope. But Biomed's on the way to the old military barracks. Grena's gonna meet us in just a minute."

They round a corner, following the arrow on a sign for the medical center. Suddenly Dave pulls Imms into a small alcove with a door marked No Admittance. "We wait here."

After a moment, they hear someone coming down the hall. Imms feels a flash of fear. What if it's not Grena?

But it is. She wears a black suit and still looks thin. She thanks Dave and directs him toward a side door close to the visitor parking lot. She and Imms face each other.

"I can lead you to his room," she says. "That's all. I don't know the code to get in."

He nods. "Just show me where he is."

They go through the No Admittance door and cross a wide, cluttered room with a cracked concrete floor. The room looks like it's full of junk. He tells Grena so. "NRCSE's storage closet," she confirms. At the back of the room is another door, and it takes them into a hall that is white, just like NRCSE's other corridors, but somehow softer, less headache inducing. It has thin, coarse carpet in a blue diamond pattern, and the lights on the ceiling are smaller and gentler than the long fluorescent tubes in most of the building. The doors are lined with rivets and painted a deep red, with numbered pads below their knobs like the pads by the *Byzantine's* doors.

Grena reaches out and tugs him to a stop. "He's in 142. That's just around the corner. There are surveillance cameras in the hall. I'd recommend . . ." She leads him to a door marked Staff Only and pushes it open. Inside are bottles of cleaning supplies, jugs of bleach and laundry detergent, and a large yellow bin on wheels containing a pile of white sheets. "The laundry cart. Housekeeping staff makes their rounds at eleven. You could hide under the sheets. You might be able to slip into his room that way. That's the best I could come up with."

"Who lives down here?" Imms asks.

"Some of the interns. Visiting researchers. Employees who spend so much time here it's pointless for them to go home. Criminals." She tries to grin.

Imms stares at the cart. He has been sneaky before. He got back into B's room on the *Byzantine* after B kicked him out. He went to Rose Sanctuary with Brid, and the entourage didn't even know he was gone.

"There'll be a camera in B's room," Grena says. "Motion sensitive. It might swing toward the door when housekeeping opens it. It'll record the main room. There won't be a camera in the bathroom, I'm fairly certain."

"Okay."

"B goes to one of the outdoor training fields three hours a day, for exercise and rec. I'm not sure what time."

Imms nods.

"Be careful. You don't have much time. Eventually someone's going to realize you're not at Biomed."

He looks at her and wishes he knew how to tell her what she means to him. In a way, he owes her a greater debt than B. "Thank you," he says.

She touches his shoulder, just like she did the day of the *Breakthrough II* meeting. "Good luck."

Then she's gone.

chapter
THIRTY-EIGHT

Imms waits in the laundry cart, in darkness, smelling sweat, humans, and bleach. Alone climbs into the cart with him and makes things colder. Alone opens its coat, and Imms doesn't need light to know what promises dangle from the lining like pelts, like ribbons and jewels and scalps.

Moments of connection, of truth. Of two souls tugging on the same bone. A trip to the park and Christmas morning and laughing because B can burp on cue. A long kiss and a short kiss. The scratch of beard bristles, the healing of torn skin. A small hollow inside someone. The willingness to climb into a secret place, to occupy it so that cold can't.

What price wouldn't Imms pay for those moments?

The door to the supply room opens, and someone comes in humming. The light goes on. Imms sees a man's hand grip the cart handle, then release it again. Something soft but heavy lands on Imms, a mesh bag full of stained and smelly rags. The man shoves the cart out of the Staff Only room and into the hall. If he thinks it's heavier than usual, he doesn't check to see why.

After a few feet, the cart stops. Imms hears a knock on one of the doors. No one answers, and Imms listens to the man press numbers on the keypad. The door clicks open, and the man goes inside. A moment later he returns, and a new snarl of dirty sheets and towels lands on Imms. Imms holds his breath.

He realizes he needs to be able to see where he is, so when the man goes into the next room, Imms makes himself a tunnel in the laundry pile through which he can just make out the room numbers on the doors. At room 139, a woman answers and hands some towels to the man.

"Present for ya," she says.

"And here I thought Christmas was over," the man says.

She can open the door herself, so she must not be a prisoner, Imms decides.

One forty. One forty-one. Imms still doesn't know how he's going to get inside B's room. The man always leaves the cart in the hall while he goes in to get the laundry. The cart rolls toward room 142.

Then it comes to Imms. All he needs to know are the code numbers. The man knocks on B's door. No answer. When the man leans down to press the keypad, Imms follows his fingers. Three-seven-one . . . The man shifts, blocking Imms's view as he punches the final number. The door opens, and B stands there holding a small bag of laundry.

B looks thinner and his beard is completely shaved. He offers the man the bag.

It's all Imms can do not to jump out of the cart and run to him.

"That's it?" the man asks.

"Wash my sheets every day, and I'll start to think I'm on vacation."

The man chuckles. "Doin' everyone else's. Might as well do yours. Sheets right out of the dryer—best smell in the world. Live a little."

"Maybe tomorrow."

The door is wide open. Behind B, Imms sees a large bed, a table with a lamp, and a desk with a stack of books on it. The stack looks precarious. Imms wishes he could straighten it.

The door closes, the bag lands on Imms, collapsing his tunnel, and the cart rolls on. Imms presses his face to the bag. Familiar smells, B's smells. The towels belong to this place, but Imms recognizes the clothes. He has seen them in their bedroom hamper, on B, hanging up in the laundry room, on the floor beside the bed. What was the last number? Imms tries to remember the man's finger, to guess where it was heading before the man moved and Imms couldn't see.

The bottom row of numbers. Seven, eight, or nine. Or was it the zero, in the lowest corner? Three more doors. At the fourth, the man goes inside the room, and Imms hears him talking to somebody. The two of them are laughing, and the door is only partway open. He's probably not going to get a better chance than this. He extracts himself from the laundry pile as quickly as possible. The cart creaks and wobbles as he climbs out, but the man is still laughing with the occupant of room 146, and he doesn't notice.

Imms races back to 142. He remembers the camera at the end of the hall too late. It is perched in a corner, looking right at him. He sticks up his middle finger, because this is what Bridique would want him to do. Then he takes off one shoe and punches three-seven-one-nine. Nothing. He tries three-seven-one-eight. The door clicks. He pushes it open.

Immediately he throws his shoe at the stack of books on the desk. The books topple.

B, who is sitting at the desk, shouts in surprise. Imms sees the camera in the corner of the room swivel toward the book wreck. Imms enters the room and slips through the door to his left, into the bathroom. "Stay there," Imms calls to B.

Silence. B has stopped moving. Imms hears the camera swivel again.

Imms leans his head against the bathroom wall. He is uneven, one shoe on, one off. "Just stay there a few minutes and pick up the books. Pretend like everything's normal. Then come in here."

He hears B collecting the books, placing them back on the desk. He waits, his heart so bright and active he wants to reach inside himself and grab it, shake it, tell it to settle down. After a few minutes, he hears B stand. He listens to B's footsteps come closer. The bathroom door opens, and B steps inside, closing the door behind him.

Imms can't remember the word *hello* or his plan or even how he got here. He catches his own reflection in the mirror over the sink, his colorless, injured-looking skin and the golden-brown back of B's head. B doesn't say anything, and for the first time Imms considers how furious B must be at Imms for landing him here.

Imms opens his mouth, but before he can speak, B's arms are so tight around him Imms isn't sure whether he's being crushed or held. He decides it's the latter and wrenches his arms out from under B's, squeezing back.

"How the hell?" B whispers.

"The laundry cart. The camera outside saw me, but I don't care."

"I don't believe this."

"I came to rescue you."

"Huh?" B's grip slackens.

"I'm going to get you out of here."

B releases Imms. "All right, pardner. There are a couple of problems with that."

"Shut up," Imms says. "I'm going to save you, but when I do, things are going to be different. Do you understand? We can't go home."

"You're never gonna get me out of here." B gestures to the door. "The guards—"

"Grena said you were allowed outside, in the field closest to the river."

"Grena?"

"She helped me." B doesn't answer. "We need to get out there. Then we go into the ground."

B laughs and shakes his head. Imms's hands fall away.

"You think I'm kidding?"

"I can't go into the ground. Are you crazy?"

"You almost did, on my planet. You would have. You were just afraid."

"I wasn't—"

"You were. But you can't be afraid now, because I'm going to protect you." Imms watches B's eyes, willing him to understand. "We'll go into the ground, deep, and we'll go under the fence. Then into the river."

"This is sounding worse by the minute," B grumbles.

"Once we're in the river, I'll keep you up. I can stay underwater forever, and I can swim in the current."

B's not laughing anymore.

"We're going to run," Imms says. "You understand?"

"I can't. I've tried."

"No." Imms shakes his head. "You haven't really." B stares at Imms a moment, then slowly nods.

"We're gonna go somewhere they can't find us."

"And after that?" B asks.

"I don't know."

B snorts. Whatever hold Imms had on him a moment ago breaks.

"You didn't ask, 'And after that?' when you brought me here," Imms points out. "You just did it."

"I was wrong," B says.

"You weren't." It's important B knows this. He wasn't wrong. Imms has gone deeper than any Silver has before. He feels the beauty in that, but also a sorrow that could never have been his without B.

He waits for B's answer, but it doesn't come. He can't believe someone didn't see him on the camera out in the hall. He expects guards to burst in at any moment.

"You know how much more trouble I'll be in if this doesn't work?" B asks. "If I stay here, there's a chance I could make a deal. If we get caught, we're both fried."

"So let's not get caught."

B thinks too much. Silvers know what is *right now*. What is dangerous *right now*, what is beautiful *right now*.

They can love without *and after that?*

But Imms doesn't push. B has to decide on his own.

"When I'm ready to go out, I buzz them on the intercom," B says finally. "They put in the code that unlocks the door at the back of my room. A long, narrow run leads to the fitness field. The run doesn't have a camera, but a couple are on the field. If I stay in the run too long, the guard on duty yells at me to get onto the field. If I don't, someone comes around the corner to check on me." He offers a hint of a smile. "It's at least fifty yards from there to the fence around the field."

"We'll go into the ground there. How long can you hold your breath?"

"Not long. A couple minutes."

"Okay."

"*Okay?* How long will we be underground?"

"A couple minutes."

"You sure?"

Imms nods.

"You don't look sure."

"I'm pretty sure."

"Imms—"

"Please, B. I can do this. Let me do this."

Imms waits, holding his breath. After all this, B can't say no.

"I'll buzz them. Slip out while the camera's following me. Then stay along the left-hand wall. The camera's blind there."

Imms grins. "All right, pardner."

B reaches out and touches Imms's face. Leans in and kisses him.

Then he flushes the toilet and leaves the bathroom. A moment later, Imms darts out and moves along the wall, very slowly. B hits a button on the box by the bed. "Going for a run," he reports to the box.

"Okay," a voice crackles back.

Imms hears the door along the back wall click. B opens it and motions Imms to follow. B has retrieved Imms's shoe. Imms thinks B wants to give it back to him, but B throws it into the center of the room, and the camera swivels to follow the vibrations. Imms kicks off his other shoe and follows B outside into the narrow, fenced run. B walks quickly toward the end of the run. "Through that gate," he whispers. "That's the field. And once you're in the field, the fence is fifty yards to your right. Shit." He stops. "We can't do this."

"Lie down."

Imms is about to pull B to the ground with him when a door opens behind them, and Violet Cranbrim emerges through the back door of one of the rooms neighboring B's. She freezes when she sees them. It seems to take her a moment to realize what's going on. She doesn't speak, just stares at Imms. He begs her without words to please, please stay quiet. She turns and goes back into the room. To tell the NRCSuckers?

Imms lies down in the grass next to the gate, drawing B with him. He pulls B close, wraps both arms around him. "Deep breath," he says.

Imms feels B breathe in. He wills all other thoughts out of his head and sinks. For a second, he fears B won't follow him, that B will resist. But then the body he is holding yields and comes into the earth with him.

Dark earth, not bright. Muddy, damp, thick. Hard to move in. Imms doesn't let himself panic. He moves through the ground, slowly at first—inch by inch. Then more quickly. His body swims along the contours of the earth. Dirt rains on them, in their eyes and ears. When this happens, B tenses, and Imms has a harder time moving him. He wishes he could tell B to relax. He tries to say it with his body. It almost works.

B chokes. He must have opened his mouth. The sound is horrible, somehow both muffled and amplified underground. Imms tries to tunnel faster, but he is losing energy. If he's not careful, they'll both be trapped here. B's body twists, and Imms navigates a patch of roots that looks like those close-up videos of the inside of the human body— blood vessels dangling like cave formations, cells clustered in plasma, the walls of organs looming like shadows.

B is still now. Imms can no longer feel him breathing. He is about to surface, fence or no fence, when he sees the glistening points of chain link diamonds in the dark-earth ceiling above him. He drags B under the fence. And up.

They emerge into sudden sunlight through a rush of dirt and stones. B's eyes are closed, his face streaked with dirt. He isn't breathing. Imms hears shouts from the other side of the fence— distant, but coming closer. Imms drags B a few feet, then stoops and lifts him. B is heavy, but the weight is not too much for Imms. He runs toward the river.

He stops partway and sets B on the ground. B is breathing, Imms realizes, but faintly. Imms lifts him again and carries him to the river. They arrive at the wide part just in front of the dam. Imms gets into the water, then pulls B after him. B's body makes a splash and starts to sink, but Imms pulls him up and swims, holding B's body close against his own in the chilly water.

B coughs dirt. His eyes open, "We made it," he murmurs.

"Can you hold on to me? That way I can swim faster, and you can stay above the surface."

B grips Imms's shoulders, and Imms ducks under the water, careful not to go too deep. Imms swims until he feels the water start to pick up, the current urging him forward. He has no time to hesitate at the dark entrance to the deep, swift part of the river. The current shoves them headlong through warnings, into danger, toward escape. Suddenly Imms doesn't need to swim. All he has to focus on is helping B stay above the water. That, and avoiding rocks. The latter is more difficult than he anticipated.

He doesn't know how long they travel downriver, but eventually the water grows shallow and is full of stones. Imms pulls B to the bank, lifts him out, and drapes him on the ground. He doesn't recognize where they are, but this place is quiet and surrounded by trees. Imms sees a house in the distance, but it is mostly cloaked in brush, and the windows are dark.

Imms lies down next to B. Jostles B's arm. "Hey."

B doesn't reply. Imms swallows, trying not to let fear crawl between them. He remembers the day Lons shut off, how he begged Lons to stay with him and Lons left anyway. He can't let himself think about B gone.

B's chest rises and falls restlessly, the way water does in lakes just before waves form. The movement is promising, as though B is gathering momentum. Eventually his chest will break from the rest of his body, become white-capped and slide toward shore. Imms puts his head on B's ribs and kisses his soaked shirt.

Finally, B opens his eyes. He stares at the sky, then turns his head toward Imms.

"You did it." His voice is rough, strained.

Imms is too wrecked by wonder to even smile.

B settles back down and is silent a long time. Imms counts fifty-seven breaths before B speaks again. "I messed up. I wanted to tell you that. I'm sorry."

"Turn over."

B resists only for a moment. Imms rolls him onto his side and rubs his back. Thick, ropy muscles Imms has loved since his fingers first discovered them. "I'm tired," B says.

"Sleep," Imms whispers. "I'm right here."

"How long?"

"Sleep," Imms repeats.

Finally, B does. His breathing deepens. His body relaxes. Imms stays awake as the sun dips in the sky, turning things comfortably gold. A helicopter passes overhead, and Imms wants to pull B into the ground with him, but doesn't. The helicopter is too far away to see them. They'll have to get up soon, though.

And after that? The question keeps entering Imms's mind, and he chases it away. *And after that?*

He knows no ending. No riding off into the sunset. They are in this continuing story, a story in which he grows, loves, hurts, and is. He remembers B on Christmas, trying to follow his drifting heart with their joined hands. The truth hides, it shifts. But it is always somewhere inside him. Sometimes it shines so brightly, it can't be missed. Maybe now that humans know the truth is out there, they will demand it.

He leaves B and walks to the water. The sun is almost down. The river is slow here, but as Imms walks, he sees it pick up again. He doesn't want to get too far from B, so he turns back. When he can see B again, he sits on the riverbank and dips a toe into the water, flinching at the cold. They'll use the river as long as they can. See where it takes them.

This is B's dream—escape, freedom. A point from which they can go any direction but back. But B can't do it by himself, because B has no experience with Alone. He'll need a guide through a world emptied of any obligations beyond survival and love.

They'll both miss Mary and Bridique. But B is in those books of photos. And Imms is somewhere—out of sight, but part of that family. Mary, Bridique, Grena, Dave, Cena . . . they'll be waiting, when one day it's safe for B and Imms to come home.

But right now, it's time for a journey.

Imms will swim underwater with B on his back. He'll interrupt fish and break clouds of algae. He'll dodge sharp rocks. He'll be a cow-nosed stingray migrating. They'll go as far as they can.

Silver children stay underwater for eight years. Nobody knows what happens to them during that time. Some of them never resurface. The ones who do don't remember. Once, long ago, Imms went into the water. He closed his eyes. He breathed only when necessary. He didn't mind the cold.

This journey will be different. He will not be alone. He will keep his eyes open as much as he can. To see the color, the life. The danger.

Dear Reader,

Thank you for reading J.A. Rock's *The Silvers*!

We know your time is precious and you have many, many entertainment options, so it means a lot that you've chosen to spend your time reading. We really hope you enjoyed it.

We'd be honored if you'd consider posting a review—good or bad—on sites like **Amazon, Barnes & Noble, Kobo, Goodreads, Twitter, Facebook, Tumblr,** and your blog or website. We'd also be honored if you told your friends and family about this book. Word of mouth is a book's lifeblood!

For more information on upcoming releases, author interviews, blog tours, contests, giveaways, and more, please sign up for our weekly, spam-free newsletter and visit us around the web:

Newsletter: tinyurl.com/RiptideSignup
Twitter: twitter.com/RiptideBooks
Facebook: facebook.com/RiptidePublishing
Goodreads: tinyurl.com/RiptideOnGoodreads
Tumblr: riptidepublishing.tumblr.com

Thank you so much for Reading the Rainbow!

AnglerFishPress.com

ACKNOWLEDGMENTS

Thank you to Del and to Jerry Wheeler. And to my mom. I was nervous about sharing my first novel with her, especially since it involved man/alien sex. She let me read the whole thing aloud to her while she was quilting, and when I was done, she told me I wasn't allowed to abandon it in my Documents folder forever. She's the reason it eventually went out into the world, and probably one of the big reasons I continued writing novels after that.

also by
J.A. ROCK

The Subs Club Series
The Subs Club
Pain Slut
Manties in a Twist
24/7

Minotaur
By His Rules
Wacky Wednesday (Wacky Wednesday #1)
The Brat-tastic Jayk Parker (Wacky Wednesday #2)
Calling the Show
Take the Long Way Home
The Grand Ballast

Playing the Fool Series, with Lisa Henry
Two Gentlemen of Altona
The Merchant of Death
Tempest

With Lisa Henry
When All the World Sleeps
The Good Boy (The Boy #1)
The Naughty Boy (The Boy #1.5)
The Boy Who Belonged (The Boy #2)
Mark Cooper Versus America (Prescott College #1)
Brandon Mills Versus the V-Card (Prescott College #2)
Another Man's Treasure

about the AUTHOR

J.A. Rock has worked as a dog groomer, knife seller, haunted house zombie, standardized patient, census taker, state fair quilt hanger, and, for one less-than-magical evening, a server—and would much rather be writing about those jobs than doing them. J.A. lives in Chicago but still sees West Virginia behind Illinois's back.

Website: www.jarockauthor.com
Blog: jarockauthor.blogspot.com
Twitter: twitter.com/jarockauthor
Facebook: facebook.com/ja.rock.39